D1464594

Robert Musil

The absolute uncommitted sceptic of German letters, Musil was born in Klagenfurt, Austria in 1880. He left his military academy to qualify as an engineer and later studied philosophy and psychology. After distinguished service as an officer in the First World War, he worked as a civil servant and later a critic until he settled on making his living as a writer. Inflation devastated his small private fortune and a society was formed to offer him financial support, but he left Austria for Switzerland at the time of the Anschluss. From the 1920s to the end of his life, Musil laboured on his unfinished novel *The Man Without Qualities*. His plays and short stories were published between the wars. The last years of his life were lived out in poverty that probably contributed to his death in Geneva in 1942.

PICADOR *Classics*

Photograph of Robert Musil courtesy of the Austrian Institute

ROBERT MUSIL

Tonka and other stories

Translated from the German by
EITHNE WILKINS
and ERNST KAISER

published by Pan Books
in association with
Secker & Warburg

First published 1965 by Secker & Warburg Ltd
This Picador Classics edition published 1988 by
Pan Books Ltd, Cavaye Place, London SW10 9PG
9 8 7 6 5 4 3 2
Translation © Secker & Warburg 1965
ISBN 0 330 30190 X
Printed and bound in Great Britain by
Anchor Press Ltd, Tiptree, Essex

This book is sold subject to the condition that it
shall not, by way of trade or otherwise, be lent,
re-sold, hired out, or otherwise circulated without
the publisher's prior consent in any form of
binding or cover other than that in which it is
published and without a similar condition
including this condition being imposed on the
subsequent purchaser

CONTENTS

TRANSLATORS' NOTE

THE FIRST two of these stories, in the original entitled *Die Vollendung der Liebe* and *Die Versuchung der stillen Veronika*, were published in 1911 (Georg Müller, Munich and Leipzig) under the general title *Vereinigungen* (*Unions*).

The last three were published in 1924 (Ernst Rowohlt Verlag, Berlin) in a volume entitled *Drei Frauen* (*Three Women*). *Tonka* had already been published in a periodical, *Der neue Roman*, 1921–22. *Grigia* had appeared as an illustrated book in 1923 (Müller & Co., Potsdam). In the same year *Die Portugiesin* was published in a limited, hand-printed edition (Rowohlt Verlag, Berlin).

Unions, which Musil described as 'hermeneutic' writing that should be 'kept under glass', seems to have been his own favourite among his works, judging from the fact that in notes for novels he frequently attributed its authorship to his hero. The passage on page 70 of *Veronica*, beginning "Yet what he meant", will be recognised by readers of *The Man without Qualities* as almost identical with that quoted in Book I, Chapter 98, by Arnheim—who admires the elusive unnamed author because acquaintance with his work is a status-symbol.

Both stories have their genesis in a commission, received shortly after the publication of *Törless* in 1906, to write a story for a literary periodical. Musil's account of what happened is rather obscure and contradictory. He did write a story, *The Enchanted House*, which was published in 1908, in *Hyperion*, edited by Franz Blei and Carl Sternheim. The

Veronica story is an elaboration of this. Whether or no *The Perfecting of a Love*, which uses some of the same material, also derives directly from the short earlier story, we do not know. At that time Musil was much occupied with the subject of jealousy, by which he meant not merely sexual jealousy, 'but one's uncertainty about the value, or even the real nature, of one's self and of the person nearest to oneself'. He set out to do a mere literary exercise, 'somewhat in the Maupassant manner', light and 'cynical'. As he said much later, the reader might well be baffled by the discrepancy between that intention and the result. Further, he had intended tossing off one little story in a week or ten days, but found himself working at these two stories for two and a half 'desperate' years, 'practically day and night'. Nervously exhausted, he completed *The Perfecting* at five past three in the afternoon of the 18th November, 1910, in Rome. That a creative work should have such a history is, as he was the first to point out, symptomatic either of a private obsession or of something that has more than private significance.

The story *Grigia* was worked up from memories of various episodes during Musil's active service as an Austrian officer on the Italian front in 1915. Many passages are only slightly adapted from entries in the notebooks he kept during that period.

Tonka is likewise autobiographical in inspiration. It is based on an early love-affair that he originally intended exploiting in a novel about himself, the servant-girl, and the two friends who ultimately became Walter and Clarisse in *The Man without Qualities*.

The Lady from Portugal is the only piece of his writing that has a non-contemporary setting. Alternative titles that he considered were "Tapestry" and "The Kitten from the World Beyond".

The Perfecting of a Love and *The Temptation of Quiet Veronica* were published by Marguerite Caetani in *Botteghe Oscure*, XVIII (autumn 1956) and XXV (autumn 1960) respectively. Both these translations have now been considerably revised.

The first translation of *Tonka* appeared in 1953, in an anthology of *Modern Writing*, edited by William Phillips and Philip Rahv (Avon Publishers, New York). The present version is entirely new.

Grigia and *The Lady from Portugal* are here published for the first time in English.

UNIONS

The Perfecting of a Love

"You really can't come?"

"Quite impossible, you know. I must try to get this job finished now as fast as I can."

"But Lilli would be so pleased. . . ."

"I know. Oh, I know. But it simply can't be done."

"And I don't like the idea of travelling without you, not a bit . . ." his wife said as she poured out tea; and she glanced across to where he sat, in the corner of the room, in the bright chintz-covered armchair, smoking a cigarette. It was evening. Outside, looking out upon the street, the dark green shutters were part of a long row of dark green shutters and in no way distinct from the rest. Like a pair of dark eyelids, lowered in indifference, they concealed the glitter of this room, where from a satin-silver teapot the tea now flowed, striking the bottom of each cup with a faint tinkle and then remaining poised in mid-air, straw-coloured, a translucent, twisted column of weightless topaz. . . . In the slightly concave planes of the teapot there lay reflections, green and grey, with here and there a gleam of blue or yellow, a pool of colours that had run together and now lay quite still. But the woman's arm stood out from the teapot, and the gaze with which she looked across at her husband formed an angle with the line of the arm, a rigid pattern in the air.

Yes, there was an angle: that was evident. But there was something else, something almost physical, that only these two people within it could feel, to whom this angle was as taut as a steel strut, holding them fast in their places and yet uniting them, making of them—for all the space between—

an almost tangible unity. This invisible support rested on the solar plexus, and there they could feel the pressure of it; yet even while it made them sit stiffly upright in their chairs, with faces immobile and eyes unswerving, there, at the point where it conjoined with them, there was a tender stir of animation, something volatile, as though their hearts were fluttering together and merging like two swarms of tiny butterflies.

On this thin, scarcely real, and yet so perceptible sensation the whole room hung as on a faintly trembling axis, and this in its turn rested on the two people in the room. The objects all around held their breath, the light on the walls froze into golden lace . . . everything was a silence and a waiting and was there because of them. Time, which runs through the world like an endless tinsel thread, seemed to pass through the centre of this room and through the centre of these people and suddenly to pause and petrify, stiff and still and glittering . . . and the objects in the room drew a little closer together. It was that standstill and then that faint settling which occurs when planes all at once assume order and crystal forms: a crystal, forming here round these two people, the centre of it corresponding to their centre—two people gazing at each other through this holding of the breath and this ensphering, this converging upon them, of everything, and gazing at each other as through thousands of mirroring planes, seeing each other as for the first time. . . .

The woman put the teapot down and her hand dropped to the table. As though exhausted by the weight of their happiness, each sank back into the cushions; and while they were still holding each other fast with their eyes, they smiled, as though lost, both feeling the need to speak—and yet not about themselves. So they talked again about the sick man, that mentally sick man, G., in a book they had been reading. Both spoke of a certain passage, and a problem it raised, as if this were what they had just been thinking of; but in fact they were merely resuming a discussion that had strangely fascinated them for days past—as though it were hiding its face and, while seemingly concerned with the book, were actually gazing elsewhere. And indeed after a while their thoughts imperceptibly returned, by way of this unconscious pretext, to a preoccupation with themselves.

"How does a man like that see himself, I wonder?" the woman said. And, sunk in her thoughts, she went on almost to herself: "He corrupts children, he lures young women into debauching themselves, and then he stands smiling and staring in fascination at the little scrap of eroticism that faintly flickers in him like summer lightning. Do you think he realises he's doing wrong?"

"It's hard to say. Perhaps he does—perhaps not," the man answered. "Perhaps one simply can't raise that sort of question about such feelings."

"What *I* think," the woman said—and it was now apparent that she was really speaking not of a random character in a book but of something specific that was beginning to loom up, for her, behind the character—"what I think is that he believes his actions are good."

For a while their thoughts ran on silently side by side, and emerged then in words that were again at a remove; and yet it still was as though they were holding hands in silence and as though everything had been said long ago. ". . . He does his victims harm. He hurts them. He must *know* he's demoralising them, confusing their erotic urge, stirring it up so that it'll never again have a single aim, a point of rest. And yet it's as though one could see him smiling, too—his face quite soft and pale, quite melancholy and yet resolute, and full of tenderness—a smile that hovers tenderly over himself and his victim, as a rainy day hovers over the land—heaven sends it, there's no comprehending why—and in his mournfulness, in the feelings that accompany the destruction he wreaks, there lies all the excuse he needs. . . . Isn't every mind solitary, lonely?"

"Yes indeed, isn't every mind solitary?"

These two people, now silent again, were joined in thinking of that third person, that unknown, that one out of so many third persons, as if they were walking through a landscape together: trees, meadows, sky, and all at once the impossibility of knowing why here it is all blue and over there the clouds are gathering. They felt all these *third persons* surrounding them, enveloping them like that huge sphere which encloses us and sometimes turns an alien, glassy eye upon us, making us shiver when the flight of a bird cuts an inexplicably lurching streak across it. In this twilit room there was all at once a cold, vast solitude, bright as noon.

Then (and it was like the faintest note drawn from a violin) one of them said: "He's like a house with locked doors. All he has done is within him, like a gentle music perhaps—but who can hear it? It might turn everything into soft melancholy."

And the other replied: "Perhaps he has walked through himself again and again, with outstretched, groping hands, trying to find a door, and in the end he stands still, and all he can do is put his face close to the impenetrable windowpanes, and see the beloved victims from a long way off, and smile. . . ."

That was all they said, but in their blissfully communing silence there was a resonance that rose higher and higher. 'And there's only this smile, overtaking them and floating above them, and binding their last hideous, twitching gestures into a thin-stemmed posy as they bleed to death. . . . And it lingers tenderly, wondering if they can feel what it has done, and lets the posy fall, and then the mystery of its solitude bears it upwards on vibrant wings, it soars resolutely —an alien beast entering into the marvel-crowded emptiness of space.'

It was on this solitude that they felt the mystery of their

union rested. There was an obscure sense of the world around them, which made them cling to each other; there was a dreamlike sense of chill on all sides except the one where they leaned against each other, disburdening themselves, uniting like two wonderfully well-fitting halves, which, being conjoined, undergoing reduction of their outer limits, in the act of fusion inwardly expand into a larger unity. They were sometimes unhappy because they could not share everything down to the very last and least thing.

"Do you remember," the woman suddenly said, "a few nights ago, when you held me in your arms——? Did you realise there was something between us then? Something had occurred to me at that moment, nothing of the slightest importance, but it was not *you*, and I was suddenly desperate that there could be anything other than you. And I couldn't tell you about it, and then I couldn't help smiling at the thought of how you didn't know and believed yourself very close to me, and later I stopped wanting to tell you and became angry with you for not feeling it yourself, and your caresses could no longer reach me. And I couldn't bring myself to ask you to let me be, for it wasn't anything *real*, I was really close to you, and all the same it was there like a vague shadow, it was as if I could be far from you and could exist without you. Do you know that feeling—how some-times everything is suddenly there twice over, one sees all the things around one, complete and distinct as one has known them all along, and then once again, pale, twilit, and aghast, as if they were already being regarded, stealthily and with an alien gaze, by someone else? I wanted to take you and wrench you back into myself—and then again to push you away and fling myself on the ground because it could happen at all. . . ."

"Was that the time when——?"

"Yes, that was the time when, in your arms, I suddenly began to weep. You thought it was from excess of longing to enter deeper into your feelings with my own. Don't be angry with me—I simply had to tell you. I don't know why. It was all just fancy, but it hurt so much, and I think that was why I couldn't help thinking of that man G. You do understand——?"

The man in the armchair stubbed out his cigarette and stood up. His gaze interlocked with hers, both of them swaying as with the tension there is in the bodies of two tightrope-acrobats close together on the rope.

Then, instead of speaking, they drew up the shutters and looked out into the street. It seemed to them they were listening to a crackling of tensions within themselves, to something suddenly stirring into life and then becoming dormant again. They knew they could not live without each other, and that only together, like an ingenious structure of supports and counter-supports, could they carry the burden they had chosen. When they thought of each other, it all struck them as almost painfully morbid, so delicate and daring and incomprehensible did their relationship seem in its sensitiveness to the slightest instability within.

After a while, when the sight of the alien world outside had restored their sense of security, they felt tired and wanted only to fall asleep side by side. They felt nothing but each other, and yet there was—though by now quite small, disappearing into darkness—another feeling too: an opening out as to all four quarters of the sky.

The next morning Claudine set out for the little town where her thirteen-year-old daughter Lilli was at boarding-school.

The child had been born in the time of her first marriage, but the father was an American dentist to whom Claudine had gone, being plagued by toothache during a holiday in the country. She had been vainly waiting to be joined by a lover, whose arrival had been delayed beyond the limits of

her patience, and in a queer state of intoxication, com-
pounded of frustration, pain, ether, and the dentist's round
white face, which she had seen hovering over hers day after
day, it had happened. Her conscience never troubled her
on account of this episode, nor indeed on account of any
other such that had occurred in that first, wasted part of her
life. When some weeks later she had to go for more treatment,
she went accompanied by her maid, and with that the affair
was over; her memory of it was merely of a strange cloud of
sensations that had for a while bewildered and agitated her,
as if a cloak had been suddenly flung over her head and then
had slid swiftly to the floor.

There was something strange about all her actions and
experiences at that period. She could not always bring them
to such a quick and sober end as on that one occasion:
indeed, at times she seemed to be entirely under the domination of one man or the other, for each of whom she was
capable of doing everything demanded of her, to the point
of complete self-abnegation and lack of any will of her own.
Yet she was never left with any sense of having had intense
or important experiences. She performed and suffered acts
of a passion so violent as to amount to humiliation, but never
lost the awareness that whatever she did, fundamentally it
did not touch her and essentially had nothing to do with her.
These excesses committed by an unhappy, ordinary, pro-
miscuous woman were like a brook rushing along, always
away from her, and her only feeling was of sitting quietly
on its bank, lost in thought.

It was an awareness of some ultimate integrity deep within
her, never clearly defined, yet always present, that brought
about this final reserve and assurance that she possessed
even in her headlong abandonment of herself to others.
Behind all the intricacies of her actual experiences there was
a current of something undiscovered, and although she
had never yet grasped this hidden quintessence of her life,

perhaps even believing that she would never be capable of penetrating to it, nevertheless, whatever happened, it gave her a sense of liberty such as a guest may have in a strange house, knowing he will be there only on that one occasion and therefore resigning himself, nonchalantly and with a trace of boredom, to whatever comes his way while he is there.

And then all she had done and suffered sank into oblivion when she met the man who was now her husband. There and then she entered into a tranquillity and seclusion in which whatever had gone before no longer mattered. All that mattered was what would come of it now, and the past seemed to have existed only so that they might experience each other the more intensely—or else it was simply forgotten. An overpowering sensation of growth rose about her like drifts of blossom, and only a long way off did there linger a sense of anguish endured, a background from which everything detached itself as in the warmth frost-stiffened limbs slowly and drowsily stir into movement.

There was, perhaps, one feeling that ran, a thin, wan, and scarcely perceptible thread, from her former into her present life. And her having to think of that former life again precisely today might have been chance or might have been because she was travelling to see her child. Whatever its cause, it had emerged only at the railway station, when—among all those many people, and oppressed and disquieted by them—she had suddenly been touched by a sensation that, even as it drifted by, only half recognised, already vanishing, conjured up, obscurely and distantly and yet with almost corporeal verisimilitude, that almost forgotten period of her life.

Claudine's husband had had no time to see her off at the station, and she was alone, waiting for the train, with the crowd pushing and jostling and, like a great ponderous wave of slop-water, slowly shoving her this way and that. Upon the pallid, early morning faces that were all around her emotions seemed to float through this dark precinct like spawn on dim pools of stagnant water. It nauseated her. She felt an urge to brush out of her way, with a negligent gesture, all that was here drifting and shoving; but—whether what horrified her was the physical dominance of what surrounded her or only this murky, monotonous, indifferent light under a gigantic roof of dirty glass and a tangle of iron girders—while she passed, with apparent calm and composure, through the crowd, she felt the compulsion she was under, and she suffered intensely as from a humiliation. In vain she sought refuge within herself; it was as though she had slowly and meanderingly lost herself in this throng— her eyes strayed, she was no longer fully aware of her own existence. and when she strained to remember, a thin soft headache hung like a cloud before her thoughts, and her thoughts leaned into it, trying to reach her yesterday. But all that she seized of it was a feeling as if she were secretly carrying something precious and delicate. And she knew she must not betray this to others, because they would not understand and because she was weaker and could not defend herself and was afraid. Slender, shrinking into herself, she walked among them, inwardly arrogant but starting and withdrawing whenever anyone came too near, and hiding behind an unassuming air. And at the same time, in secret delight, she felt the happiness of her life growing more beautiful as she yielded and abandoned herself to this faint, ravelled anxiety.

And that was how she recognised what it all amounted to. For this was what it had been like at that other period. What she suddenly felt was: *once, long ago* . . . as though for a long time she had been somewhere else, though never really far away. There was something twilit and uncertain in her, like deranged people's frightened concealment of their passions, and her actions tore loose from her in shreds and were borne

away in the memories of strangers. Nothing had ever im-
pregnated her with that fruitful germ of experience which
softly begins to swell a soul when those who think they have
stripped it of its petals turn away, satiated. . . . Yet all she
suffered shone as with the pallid glitter of a crown, and the
muted whispering anguish that was the background of her
life was shot with a tremulous gleam. At times then she felt
as if her sorrows were burning like little flames in her, and
something impelled her to go on kindling new ones. And,
doing so, she seemed to feel the pressure of a diadem cutting
into her brow, invisible and unreal as something spun of
dream-glass. And sometimes it was only a far-off, circling
chant inside her head. . . .

Claudine sat quite still while the train travelled through
the landscape, quietly shaking and rocking. The other people
in the carriage talked to each other, but she heard it only as a
distant buzz. And while she was thinking of her husband, and
her thoughts were enclosed in a soft, weary happiness as in
snow-filled air, for all the softness there was something that
kept her from moving, as when a convalescent, accustomed
to being within four walls, is about to take the first steps out
of doors—a happiness that keeps one transfixed and is
almost agonising. And behind that again there was still that
undefined, wavering chant which she could not quite catch,
remote, blurred, like a nursery-rhyme, like a pain, like herself. . . . In wide, rippling circles it drew her thoughts after
it, and she could not see into its face.

She leaned back and gazed out of the window. It fatigued
her to think about that any more. Her senses were alert and
achingly perceptive, but there was something behind the
senses that wanted to be quiet and expand and let the world
glide away over it. . . . Telegraph-poles slid slanting past.
The fields with their dark brown furrows standing out of the
snow rolled past and away. Bushes stood as though on their
heads, with hundreds of straddling little legs from which

there hung thousands of tiny bells of water, dripping, trickling, flashing and glittering. . . . There was something gay
and light about it all, a dilation as when walls open out—
something loosened and unburdened and full of tenderness.
And from her own body too the gentle weight was now lifted,
leaving in her ears a sensation as of melting snow, gradually
passing over into a ceaseless, light, loose tinkling. She felt as
if with her husband she were living in the world as in a foam-
ing sphere full of beads and bubbles and little feathery
rustling clouds. She closed her eyes and abandoned herself
to it.

But after a while she began to think again. The light,
regular swaying of the train, the loosening up, the liquescence
of nature there outside—it was as if some pressure had lifted;
and she suddenly realised that she was on her own. Involuntarily she glanced up. There was still that softly whirling
vortex in her senses; but it was like going up to a door that
had always been shut and suddenly finding it wide open.
Perhaps she had long felt the desire for this; perhaps without
her knowing it something had been oscillating in the love
between herself and her husband; but all she had known of
it was that ever and again it drew them more closely together. And now it had secretly burst open something within
her that had long been locked up. Slowly, as out of an almost
invisible but very deep wound, in an unceasing stream of
little drops, thoughts and feelings welled up, steadily widen-
ing the gap.

There are, in the relationship to those one loves, a great
many problems that become buried under the edifice of the
shared life before they can be fully worked out; and later the
sheer weight of things as they have actually turned out leaves
one no strength even to imagine it all differently. Then somewhere on the way there will stand some queer sign-post, there
will be some face, a hovering fragrance, an untrodden path
petering out amid grass and stones, and the traveller knows

he should turn and take the other road, but everything urges him forward; and all that impedes his steps is something like cobwebs, dreams, a rustling branch—and he is quietly paralysed by some thought that has never quite taken shape. Recently it had sometimes happened, perhaps increasingly, that there was this looking back, a more intense leaning into the past. Claudine's constancy revolted against it, for this constancy was not repose but a setting free of forces, a mutual lending of support, an equilibrium arising out of unceasing movement forwards. It was a running hand-in-hand. Then, in the midst of it, there would come this temptation to stand still, to stand there all alone and look around. At such times she would feel her passion as something tyrannical and compulsive, threatening to sweep her away; and even when the temptation was overcome and she felt remorseful and was once again seized with awareness of how beautiful her love was, that awareness was rigid and ponderous as a narcotic state, and she apprehended, with delight and dismay, how each of her movements was laced into it, tall and bulky and stiff as though encased in gold brocade. And yet somewhere there was still a lure, something that lay quiet and pale as March sunlight, the shadows upon earth aching with spring.

Even in her happiness Claudine was occasionally assailed by a sense of how it was all merely a fact, almost accidental; and she sometimes wondered whether there must not be some other kind of life in store for her, different and remote. This was perhaps only the shape of a thought, an outer shell, which had remained with her from earlier times, and not a real thought with any intention behind it—only a sensation such as might once have gone with the real thought, an empty, unresisting motion, all a craning and a peering, which, withdrawing always and never fulfilled, had long lost its content and was like the entrance to a dark tunnel in her dreams.

But perhaps it was some other, solitary happiness, much

more wonderful than everything else—something loose, limber, and obscurely sensitive at a point in their relationship where in other people's love there is nothing but a solid substructure, bony and inanimate. There was a faint unrest in her, an almost morbid yearning for extreme tension, the premonition of an ultimate climax. And sometimes it was as though she were destined to suffer some unimaginable sorrow in love.

Now and then when she was listening to music this premonition touched her soul secretly, somewhere a long way out. . . . She would feel a start of terror, suddenly aware of her soul's existence in the realm of the undefined. But every year, as winter passed away, there came a time when she felt nearer to those outermost frontiers than at other times. During those naked, strengthless days, suspended between life and death, she felt a melancholy that could not be that of ordinary craving for love; it was almost a longing to turn away from this great love that she possessed, as though faintly glimmering ahead of her there were the road of an ultimate destiny, leading her no longer to her beloved but away from him, defenceless, out into the soft, dry, withered expanses of some agonising desert. And she realised that this came from a distant place where their love was no longer solely between the two of them, but was something with pallid roots insecurely clutching at the world.

When they walked together, their shadows had only the faintest tinge of colour and dangled loosely at their heels as though incapable of binding their footsteps to the ground they walked on; and the ring of hard earth under their feet was so curt and clipped, and the bare bushes so stared into the sky, that in those hours a-shudder with enormous visibility it was as if all at once all things, the mute and docile objects of this world, had weirdly disengaged themselves from them. And as the light began to fail, they themselves grew tall, towering like adventurers, like strangers, like unreal beings, spellbound by the fading echo of their own existence, knowing themselves to be full of shards of something incomprehensible to which there was nowhere any response and which was rejected by all things, so that only a broken gleam of it fell into the world, forlornly and irrelevantly flickering here and there, now in an object, now in a vanishing thought.

Then she could imagine belonging to another man, and it seemed not like betrayal but like some ultimate marriage, in a realm where they had no real being, where they existed only as music might, a music heard by no one, echoing back from nowhere. For then she felt her own existence merely as a line that she herself incised, gratingly, just to hear herself in the bewildering silence; it was simply something leading from one moment to the next, something in which she became, inexorably and irrelevantly, identical with whatever it was she did—and yet always remained something she could never achieve. And while it suddenly seemed to her as though perhaps they loved each other as yet only with all the loudness of a refusal to hear a faint, frantically intense and anguished call, she had a foreboding of the deeper complications and vast intricacies that came about in the intervals, in the silences, in the moments of awakening out of that uproar into the shoreless world of facts, awakening to stand, with nothing but a feeling, among mindless and mechanical happenings; and it was with the pain of their tall and lonely separateness, standing side by side—something against which all else was no more than an anaesthetising and shutting off and lulling of oneself to sleep with sheer noise—that she loved him when she thought of doing him the final, the mortal injury.

Even weeks after such an experience her love still had this colouring; then that would gradually fade. But often, when she felt the proximity of another man, it would return, though fainter. It sufficed that there should be someone there

—a man of no real concern to her, saying something of no real concern to her—and she would feel herself being gazed at as from that other realm, with a look of amazement that held the question: 'Why are you still here?' She never felt any desire for such outsiders; it was painful to her to think of them; indeed it disgusted her. But all at once there would be that intangible wavering of the stillness around her; and then she would not know whether she was rising or sinking. . . .

Claudine looked out of the window. Out there it was all just the same as before. But—whether as a result of her thoughts or for some other reason—now it was overlaid by a stale, unyielding resistance, as if she were looking through a film of something milky and repugnant. That restless, volatile, thousand-legged gaiety had become unendurably tense; it was all a prancing and trickling, all feverishly excited and mocking, with something in it of pygmy footsteps, far too lively and yet, for her, dull and dead. Here, there, it flung itself upwards, an empty clatter, a grinding past of tremendous friction.

It was physically painful to gaze out into all that stir, for which she no longer had any feeling. All that life, which only a short while ago had been one with her emotions, was still there outside, overbearing and rigid; but as soon as she tried to draw it to her, the things crumbled away and fell to pieces under her gaze. What came about was an ugliness that twisted and turned in her eyes, as though her soul were leaning outwards there, leaning far out, taut, stretching after something, groping into emptiness.

And all at once it occurred to her that she too—just like all that was around her—spent her life passively, a captive in her own being, committed to one place, to a particular city, to one house in that city, one habitation and one sense of herself, year after year within that tiny area; and with that it seemed as though, if she were to stop and linger for one single moment, her happiness might rush past her and away, like this rumbling, roaring mass rushing through the countryside, rushing away from everything.

This, it seemed to her, was no mere random thought. On the contrary, there was in it an element of that unbounded, uprearing blankness in which her feelings groped vainly for any support. She was impalpably assailed by something like what comes upon a climber on the rock-face: an utterly cold, still moment when she could hear herself as an unintelligible small sound on that huge surface and then, in the abrupt silence, realised the faintness of her own existence, creeping along, and how great, in contrast, and how full of dreadful forgotten sounds, was the stony brow of the void.

And while she was shrinking from this like a delicate skin, feeling in her very fingertips the voiceless fear of thinking about herself, and while her sensations clung to her like granules and her emotions trickled away like sand, she again heard that peculiar sound: a mere point it seemed, like a bird hovering high in the empty air.

She was overwhelmed by a sense of destiny. It lay in her having set out on this journey, in the way nature was withdrawing before her, in her having been so scared and huddled and timid even at the very beginning of the journey —scared of herself, of others, and of her happiness. And all at once her past seemed the imperfect expression of something that was yet to come.

She continued to gaze anxiously out of the window. But gradually, under the pressure of the huge strangeness out there, her mind began to be ashamed of all its protestation and struggle, and it seemed to pause. And now it was becoming imbued with that very subtle, final, passive strength which lies in weakness, and it grew thinner and slighter than a child, softer than a sheet of faded silk. And it was only now with a mildly looming delight that she experienced this ultimate human ecstasy in being a stranger in the world, in seeming to take leave of it, a sense of being unable to penetrate into the world, of finding, among all her decisions, none that was meant for herself; and, being forced by them to the very edge of life, she felt the moment before the plunge into the blind vastness of empty space.

She began obscurely to yearn for her past, wasted and exploited as it had been by people who were strangers to her —yearning for it as for the pale, weak wakefulness there was in the depths of illness, when in the house the sounds moved from one room to another and she no longer belonged anywhere, but, relieved of the pressure of her own personality, continued to lead another life, floating somewhere else.

Outside, the landscape stormed soundlessly by. In her thoughts people grew very tall and loud and confident, and she huddled into herself, escaping from that, until there was nothing left of her but her nullity, her imponderability, a drifting somewhere towards something. And gradually the train began to travel very quietly, with long, gently rocking movements, through country that still lay under deep snow, and the sky came lower and lower until it seemed only a few paces ahead, trailing along the ground in grey, dark curtains of slowly drifting flakes. Inside the train twilight gathered, yellowish, and the outlines of her fellow-passengers were only vaguely visible: they swayed to and fro, slowly and spectrally. She was no longer aware of what she was thinking, and pleasure in being alone with strange experiences now took a quiet hold of her: it was like the play of very faint, scarcely tangible inquietudes and of great shadowy stirrings of the soul, groping for them. She tried to remember her husband, but all she could find of her almost vanished love was a weird notion as of a room where the windows had long been kept shut. She made an effort to get rid of this, but it yielded only a very little and remained lurking nearby. And the world was as pleasantly cool as a bed in which one stays behind alone. . . .

Then she felt as if she were about to be faced with a

decision, and she did not know why she felt this, and she was neither glad nor resentful; all she felt was that she did not want either to act or to prevent action. And her thoughts slowly wandered into the snow outside, without a backward glance, always deeper and deeper into the snow, as when one is too tired to turn back and so walks on and on.

Towards the end of the journey the man opposite said: "An idyll, an enchanted island, a lovely woman at the centre of a fairy-tale all white *dessous* and lace . . ." and he made a gesture towards the landscape. 'How silly,' Claudine thought, but she could not think of anything to say.

It was like someone knocking at the door and a big dark face floating behind pale window-panes. She did not know who this person was; she did not care who he was. All she felt was that here was someone wanting something. And now something was beginning to take on shape and become real.

As when a faint wind rises among clouds, ordering them in a row, and slowly passes away, so she felt the motion of this materialising reality stirring the still, soft cloudiness of her feelings—insubstantial, passing through her, passing her by. . . . And, as with many sensitive people, what attracted her in the unintelligible passage of events was all there was in it that did not pertain to herself, to the spirit: what she loved was the helplessness and shame and anguish of her spirit— it was like striking something weaker than oneself, a child, a woman, and then wanting to be the garment wrapped about its pain, in the darkness, alone.

So they arrived, late in the afternoon, the train almost empty. One by one people had trickled away out of the compartments; station after station had sifted them out from among the other travellers. And now they were swept swiftly together, for there were only three sledges available for the hour's trip from the station to the township, and these had to be shared. Before Claudine knew where she was, she found herself seated with four other people in one of these small conveyances. From in front there came the unfamiliar smell of the horses steaming in the cold, and ripples of scattered light from the lanterns. But at times, too, darkness came flooding right up to the sledge, and away over it, and then she realised they were travelling between two ranks of tall trees, as though along a dark corridor that grew ever narrower the closer they came to their goal.

Because of the cold she sat with her back to the horses. Opposite her was that man—big, bulky, encased in his fur coat. He blocked the way along which her thoughts strove to travel back home. Suddenly, as though a door had slammed, every glance of hers encountered his dark figure there before her. She was aware of glancing at him several times in order to make sure what he looked like, as though that were all that mattered now and everything else were long settled. She was excited to find that he remained entirely vague: he might have been anyone; he was no more than a sombre bulk of alien being. And sometimes this seemed to be drawing nearer to her, like a moving forest with its mass of tree-trunks. And it was like a weight upon her.

Meanwhile, talk spread like a net among the people in the little sledge. He joined in, making remarks of the tritely well-turned kind that many people make, with a pinch of that spice which is like a sharp, confident aura enveloping a man in a woman's presence. In these moments of male dominance, so much a matter of course, she became uneasy and embarrassed and ashamed at not having effectively rebuffed his earlier insinuating advances to her. And yet when she, in her turn, could not avoid speaking, she felt it came to her all too easily, and she had an awareness of herself as of a feeble, ineffective waving with the stump of an amputated arm.

Then indeed she observed how helplessly she was being flung this way and that, at each curve in the road being touched now on the arms, now at the knees, sometimes with the whole upper part of her body leaning against some other person's body; and remotely, by some analogy, she experienced it as if this small sledge were a darkened room and these people were seated around her, hot and urgent, and she were timidly a prey to shameless acts that she endured, smiling, as if not noticing anything, her eyes focused straight ahead.

All this was like feeling an irksome dream in half-sleep, always remaining slightly conscious of its unreality, always marvelling at feeling it so strongly. Then a moment came when that man leaned out, looked up at the sky, and said: "We're going to be snowed up."

With a start her thoughts leapt into complete wakefulness. She glanced around: the people were exchanging cheerful, harmless pleasantries, as those do who at the end of a long journey through darkness get their first glimpse of light and of tiny figures in the distance. And all at once she had a strangely indifferent, sober sense of reality. But she noticed with astonishment that something nevertheless touched her, moved her intensely. It frightened her a little, for it was a pallid, almost unnatural lucidity, in which nothing could sink into the vagueness of reverie and through which no thought moved and within which nevertheless people now and then became jagged and huge as hills, as if suddenly gliding through an invisible fog where all that was real expanded, taking on a gigantic, shadowy, second outline. Then she felt something that was almost humility and dread of them; yet she never quite lost the awareness that this weakness was only a peculiar faculty: it was as if the frontiers of her being had extended, invisibly and sensitively, and everything came into faint collision with them, setting up tremors. And for the first time she was truly startled by this queer day, the solitariness of which, like a passage leading underground, had gradually sunk with her into the confused whisperings of multitudinous inner twilight and now suddenly, in a distant region, ascended into the midst of inexorably actual events, leaving her alone in a vast, unfamiliar, unwanted reality.

Furtively she looked across at the stranger. He was striking a match: for an instant his beard was lit up, and one eye. And even this trivial act seemed remarkable; she felt the solidity of it, felt how naturally one thing linked with the next and was merely there, insensate and calm and yet like a simple and tremendous power, stone interlocked with stone. She reflected that he was certainly quite an ordinary person. And at that she had again a faint, elusive, intangible sense of her own existence; she felt herself floating in the dark before him, dissolved and tattered, like pale, frothing foam, and felt an odd stimulus in answering him agreeably. And even while speaking she watched herself and what she was doing, helpless, unmoved in spirit, and yet with an enjoyment that was divided between pleasure and torment, which made her feel as though she were crouching in the innermost depths of some great and ever expanding exhaustion.

It struck her that this was the way it had sometimes begun in the past. At the thought of such a recurrence her mind reeled with voluptuous, enervated horror as of some still nameless sin. She wondered whether he had noticed her looking at him, and her body filled with a faint, almost docile sensuality—a dark hiding-place for the stealthy urges of the soul within. But the stranger sat there in the darkness, big and calm, merely smiling sometimes—or perhaps even that only seemed so to her.

So they travelled on into the falling night, at close quarters, facing each other. And gradually her thoughts were again invaded by that softly forward-thrusting unrest. She tried telling herself that all this was nothing but delusions, arising out of the confused inner stillness of this sudden lonely journey amid strangers, and then again she would think it was the wind wrapping her with its stiff, searing cold, petrifying her, robbing her of her will; and then at other times it oddly seemed to her as if her husband were very near to her and all this sensual weakness were some ineffable aspect of their great love. And once—when she had just glanced across at the stranger again and was conscious of this shadowy abandonment of her will, all her firmness and inviolability gone—suddenly there was a radiance high and bright over her past, as over an indescribable, strangely ordered panorama. It was a queer premonition, as if all that seemed long past and gone were still alive. But in the next moment it was no more than a fading streak of intuition in the darkness and all that remained was something faintly reverberating within her, rather as if it had been the never-before-glimpsed landscape of her love, filled with colossal forms and a quiet rushing sound, confused and alien, already beyond her grasp. And she felt herself lingeringly and softly enveloped in her own being, which was full of strange, not yet comprehensible resolutions whose origin was in that other realm.

She could not help thinking of the days to come, isolated from the rest of her days, lying ahead of her like an *enfilade* of remote rooms, each one opening into the next. And all this time she heard the beat of the horses' hooves, bearing her—helplessly flung into the meaningless actuality of this situation, these close quarters here in the sledge—nearer to all that was to come. With hasty, nervous laughter she joined in a commonplace conversation; but within her everything was vast and ramified, and she was helpless before the incomprehensibility of all things as under a huge cloak of silence.

In the night she woke up: it was as though little bells had been jingling. She knew at once it was snowing. She looked towards the window; there it was in the air outside, soft, and heavy as a wall. Barefoot, she tiptoed to the window. It was all a matter of an instant. Darkly she sensed that she put her naked feet to the ground like an animal. Then, with her face close to the glass, she stared numbly out into the dense trellis-work of the snowflakes. She did all this as one may, starting up from sleep, with a consciousness so narrowly confined that it is like a little uninhabited island emerging from the sea. It was as if she were standing a long way off from herself. And all at once she remembered, and remembered even the emphasis with which he had said it: 'We're going to be snowed up.'

She tried to collect herself. Turning round, she saw how small and cramped the room was. And there was something strange in this smallness, as of being caged, of being beaten.

She lit a candle and held it high, moving its light over the things. Slowly the sleep began to ebb from them, but they were still as though they had not yet quite found their way back into themselves. Wardrobe, chest of drawers, and bed, there they were, and yet there was somehow either too much or too little, a mere shadowy nothing, a harsh whispering shadow of nothingness. Blank and sunken they stood in the bleak half-light from the flickering candle, and over table and walls there lay an endless feeling of dust, and of walking, walking barefoot through an infinity of dust. Outside the room there was a narrow passage with a wooden floor and whitewashed walls; at the top of the stairs, she knew, there was a dim lamp hanging in a wire ring, casting five pale, swaying circles on the ceiling, and beyond that the light trickled away on the chalky walls, like marks left by the fumbling of greasy hands. Five pale, inanely swaying circles were like five sentries guarding a strangely excited emptiness. . . . All around were people she did not know, all asleep. She felt a wave of sudden unreal heat and she almost began to scream, faintly, the way cats sometimes scream in fear and desire, as she stood there, wide awake in the night, while soundlessly the last shadow of her actions, strange even to herself, slipped back behind the walls of her inner being and these grew smooth again. And suddenly she thought: 'Supposing he came now . . . and just did what I know he wants to. . . .'

She was more startled than she realised. Something rolled away over her like a glowing ball. For minutes there was only this wild panic and behind it the constriction of the room, a soundless strait, tense as a cracked whip. She tried to form a mental image of the man. But she failed; all she could feel was the warily prowling, beast-like tread of her own thoughts. Only now and then she caught a partial glimpse of him as he was in reality—his beard, one eye lit up. . . . And she was sickened. She could never again belong to a stranger. And precisely there, precisely coincident with this abhorrence of all other men that rose in her body, with its mysterious yearning only for the one, she felt—as though on some other, deeper plane—a leaning over, a vertigo, and had a sense of all human insecurity. And with it went something like dread of herself, something that was perhaps also an intangible, irrational, groping desire that the stranger should really come. Fear swept through her like the biting cold that comes as though driven by the current of some destructive lustful urge.

Somewhere a clock began placidly talking to itself. Footsteps passed under her window and faded away. Quiet voices. . . . The room was chilly; the warmth of sleep slipped away from her skin, and vaguely, unresistingly, she swayed to and fro with it in the dark as in a cloud of faintness. The things around her made her feel ashamed, hard and straight as they were—once again disengaged, once again entirely themselves, blankly staring at nothing, while she was confusedly conscious of standing there, waiting for a stranger. And yet she realised obscurely that it was not the stranger who tempted her, but simply this standing and waiting, a fine-toothed, savage, abandoned ecstasy in being herself, in being alive, awake here among these lifeless objects—ecstasy that had opened like a wound. And while she felt her heart beating, like some frenzied wild creature trapped within her breast, her body in its quiet swaying drew itself up, like a great exotic, nodding flower that suddenly shudders with the infinitely expanding rapture of mysterious union as it closes round its captive. And softly, far off, she could hear the beloved's heart wandering unquiet, restless, homeless, chiming through the stillness like the lilt of some wind-blown, remote music, flickering as starlight; and she was moved by the haunting loneliness of those chords that were in quest of her, moved as by some vast diapason resounding far beyond the limits of the human soul.

Now it seemed to her that something was about to reach fulfilment and, standing there, she lost all count of time. Minutes . . . hours . . . time lay motionless around her, fed by invisible springs, a shoreless lake, without beginning or end. Only once, at some moment she was but vaguely aware of, something slid darkly across the outermost reaches of her mind: a thought, a notion. . . . And as it passed, she recognised it as the memory of dreams long lost, of dreams belonging to her former life, in which she thought herself enslaved by enemies and was compelled to perform humiliating acts; but even as she recognised it, it began to diminish and disappear. One last time it rose out of the hazy distance, phantom-clear, sharply outlined against the background like the rigging of a ship, masts and tackle . . . and she remembered how she had always been defenceless, remembered her own shrieks waking her from sleep, and how she had struggled in dull despair until her strength gave out and her senses reeled—all the shapeless, boundless misery of that earlier life. . . . Then it was gone. In the stillness that closed in round her again there was only a radiance, a last receding wave, a lull, as though something unutterable had happened. And then from there beyond—just as once, behind her dreams, this terrible helplessness of hers had lived another, second life, remote, intangible, imaginary—suddenly she was overtaken by a sense of promise, a glimmer of longing, and knew a surrender such as she had never known before, a naked, bare self-awareness that the irrevocability of her fate had stripped of anything personal and which, while driving her towards ever deeper frenzies of exhaustion, yet weirdly bemused her, as though it were, far within her, the stray tender particle of a love in quest of its own perfection—a love for which there are still no words in the language of day, that language with its heavy upright gait on solid ground.

She did not know whether it had been only a short time ago, just before waking, that she dreamt that dream once more. For years she had not dreamt it, had not even thought of it, and now all at once this dream and the time to which it belonged seemed to be quite close, hovering just behind her. It was like turning round and suddenly staring into a face. How strange it was!—as if here in this lonely room her life were turning back upon itself like tangled traces going round and round in an enormous plain.

Behind her back there shone the little light that she had lit; her face was in darkness. Gradually she lost the feeling of her own shape, and her outlines seemed to become the limits of some monstrous cavity in this darkness, in this lingering moment that enveloped her. She began to feel as if she were not really here at all, as if merely something of herself had long ago set out and had been travelling ever since through space and through the years, and were now wakening here, alone and lost, at an infinite remove from that real self which she was, she herself standing still some- where in the sunken realm of her old dream. Somewhere . . . a place she lived in . . . people . . . a dreadful maze of fear. . . . The blood shot into her face, her lips grew soft, and she realised: it *was* going to happen all over again . . . another of them. . . . And the feeling of her loosened hair, her open arms, was different and as of long ago, as if all she had done then were an act of unfaithfulness here and now. And as in dismay she clung to the wish to keep herself for her beloved—her raised, imploring hands now slowly tiring—there came the thought:

'We were unfaithful to each other before we knew each other. . . .'

It was the mere gleam of a thought, hardly more than a tremor—an exquisite and lovely bitterness, just as in the wind that rises from the sea there is sometimes a whiff of keener freshness, an intenser presence that lingers fleetingly and then drifts away—almost the thought: 'we loved each other before we knew each other'. And it was as if the infinite tension of their love all at once expanded far beyond the present into that earlier unfaithfulness from which it had first come to them, as though deriving from some older form of its eternal existence between them.

She sank down and for a long time, as though stunned, was aware of nothing except of sitting on a hard chair at a bare table. Her thoughts strayed to the talk they had had before her journey, about the man G., that figure in a novel—the veiled words and the words never uttered. And then she realised that through a chink in the window there came the moist, mild air of the snow-laden night, faintly caressing her bare shoulders. And remotely, mournfully, as a wind blows over rain-darkened fields, she began to think it would be a delight like quiet rain, like a sky over-arching a landscape, to be unfaithful—a mysterious, last, deathly delight.

With the morning there came a queer atmosphere of the past, pervading everything.

Claudine intended going to the school. She had woken early and it had been like rising out of heavy, clear water. She remembered nothing of all that had stirred her during the night. She moved the looking-glass to the window and began to put her hair up. It was still dark in the room. But while she was doing her hair, straining her eyes to see herself in the small, tarnished glass, she was overcome by a feeling that, somehow, here was a peasant girl beautifying herself for her Sunday outing. She felt quite strongly that it was all for the benefit of the schoolmasters who would see her, or perhaps for the stranger. She could not rid herself of this senseless notion. It did not spring from her inner being, but it clung to everything she did: all her movements took on something of oafishly sensual affectation, at once straddling and mincing, and slowly, disgustingly, irresistibly, it seeped from the surface down into the depths. For a while she paused to rest her arms. All this was really quite silly and could not prevent what was bound to happen. But while the fancy remained— merely swinging to and fro, with an intangible suggestion of things forbidden and things desired and undesired, all part of another chain of events that was mistier and less corporeal than that of real decisions, yet remotely accompanying all she did—and while her fingers slid through her soft hair, the sleeves of her wrap slipping up her bare arms, it seemed to her again that at some point in time—once? always?—it had all been like this before. And it struck her as odd that now when she was awake, here in the emptiness of the morning, her arms were moving up and down as though subject not to her own will but to some other, alien, indifferent power. And then slowly the mood of the past night began to reassert itself, and memories rose almost to the surface of her mind, only to sink away again. A tension lay between her and those half-remembered experiences, like a quivering curtain.

Outside the windows day was breaking, bright and uneasy. Looking out into the monotonous, blank light, Claudine felt a stirring like the voluntary loosening of her fingers' grasp, a slow, alluring sensation of gliding down among silvery shining bubbles and motionless fishes, strange and goggle-eyed. The day began.

She took a sheet of paper and wrote a few words to her husband: 'It's all so odd. It'll only be for a few days, but I feel as if I were somewhere high above myself, involved in something I don't understand. Tell me, what is our love? What is it? I need help, I need to hear you! I know it is like a tower, but what I feel is only the trembling of something rising into the air, slim and tall. . . .'

When she went to the post-office to post the letter, she was told that communications had broken down.

She walked to the edge of the little town. There the plain stretched away into the distance, a wide, white sea all around. Sometimes a crow flew through this whiteness; here and there a bush stood out, black and stiff. Only some small, dark dots strewn along the far skyline were a sign that over there, too, there was human life.

Turning back, she walked through the streets, restlessly, for perhaps an hour. She went through all the sidestreets, after a while finding herself covering the same ground, only in the other direction, and turned aside again, crossing squares where she had the feeling of how she had walked there just a few minutes earlier. Everywhere there was the same white play of reflections from the empty plain, a feverish flicker sliding through this little town that was cut off from all reality. Before the houses there lay high banks of snow. The air was clear and dry. It was still snowing a little, but the flakes were falling thinly—flat, almost shrivelled, glittering little scales—as if it might stop soon. Here and there, from above the shut doors of the houses, windows looked down into the street with a bright blue glassy gaze, and the ground underfoot rang like glass too. Sometimes a piece of hard, frozen snow crashed down through a gully, tearing a jagged hole in the stillness. And suddenly the wall of a house would glow in rosy light, or in delicate canary-yellow. . . . Then all Claudine did seemed oddly heightened, more intensely alive; and in the hushed silence all things visible seemed to light one another up, as it were echoing one another in a larger visibility. And then it would all withdraw into itself again and in meaningless streets the houses were like little groups of mushrooms in the woods, or like a thicket of wind-bent shrubs on a wide plain, while she still felt a dizziness and an immensity beyond. There was in her some kind of fire, some burning, bitter fluid, and while she walked and mused, she seemed to herself a huge, mysterious vessel that was being carried through the streets— a thin-walled, flaming vessel.

She tore up the letter and went to the school, where she spent the time till midday in discussion with the masters.

The rooms there were quiet. When, from where she sat, she looked through the sombre, heavy vault out into the open, everything seemed remote and muted, veiled in grey, snowy light. Then the men with her seemed too corporeal, oppressively ponderous, like great weights pressing down on hard, sharp ground. Her discussions with them were of the most matter-of-fact kind, but at moments even that seemed almost like abandonment. She wondered at this, for she did not like these men at all. There was not one among them who was in the slightest attractive to her; they all repelled her by their manners, which revealed their lowly origins. Yet she sensed the masculinity, the other sex, in them with an acuteness never experienced before, or at least not for many years. She realised that this was caused by the expression of their faces, which the half-light enhanced by the dull commonness in them that was incomprehensibly trans-formed by their very ugliness, by a whiff of rutting-time, of enormous, clumsy, troglodyte beasts, that hung about them like an aura. She recognised again, here too, that old feeling of defencelessness which had overcome her time and again since she had been alone. A peculiar submissiveness crept into all she did and said, into every detail, every turn of the conversation. It was there in the attentiveness with which she felt compelled to listen, even in the very fact that she was there, sitting in a chair, talking.

Claudine grew restive. She had lingered much too long, and the atmosphere and the half-darkness of the rooms closed in on her, suffocating and bewildering her. For the first time she was struck by the idea that all that had prevented her from sliding back into her former life was the fact that she had never before been away from her husband, on her own.

What she felt now was no longer vague, roving, inscrutable: it was now associated with real people. Yet it was not these men she was afraid of, but her own reactions. While their talk surrounded her, something stirred within her, shook her mysteriously—not one distinct emotion, but the very foundation of all emotions—as it may happen when one walks through other people's homes, places that fill one with distaste, and gradually, insidiously, one begins to think how these other people can live and be happy there, until there comes a moment when it all takes hold of one, as if one were one of those people, and one wants to jump free, but, transfixed, feels on all sides how the world revolves, solidly, quietly, round this centre too.

In the grey gloom here these black, bearded men became giant shapes inside twilit bubbles, alien worlds, and she wondered what it would feel like to be enclosed in such a world. Her thoughts seemed to sink deep into soft, swampy ground; and then there was only a voice, roughened by smoking, and words, muffled in a haze of cigarette-smoke, that constantly brushed against her face, and after that another voice, high and tinny, and she tried to imagine this second voice breaking and deepening in sexual excitement. Then again clumsy gestures caught her attention, drawing her feelings after them in weird convolutions. There was one ludicrous Olympian whom she tried to regard as would a woman who took him seriously. Something strange that had nothing to do with her own life rose up before her, casting its shadow on her, too close, too big, like a shaggy animal that gave off an overpowering smell. She felt for a moment as if all she wanted were a whip to lash it with, and then, suddenly checked, but without really understanding, she caught the play of expressions intimately known of old in a face that somehow resembled her own.

Then she thought secretly: 'People like us might even be able to live with men like these. . . .' And in this thought there lay a queerly tormenting fascination, an expanding titillation of the brain; and there was something like a thin pane of glass before it, against which her thoughts pressed painfully to stare through it into a vague murkiness. She enjoyed looking into these men's eyes meanwhile with a limpid, innocent gaze. Then she tried to picture her husband, estranged and as though seen from that murky region beyond. She succeeded in thinking of him quite calmly: he remained a wonderful, an incomparable person, but something imponderable, something that reason could not grasp, had left him, and he seemed somehow faded and not so close to her as before. Sometimes, when an illness reaches its last critical stage, one's experiences have that cool, detached lucidity. How odd that once it had been possible really to experience these things with which she was now toying, that there had been a time when, undisturbed by any questionings, she would undoubtedly have felt about him just as she had been trying to feel about him now! All at once everything seemed very strange.

One moves, day in, day out, among the same people: one walks through the same countryside, through the same town, the same house; and his landscape, these people, go along with one, always, every day, at every step, in every thought, unresistantly. Then one day, with a faint jolt, they stop: and there they stand, incomprehensibly stark and still, aloof, in some alien, stubborn atmosphere. And when one turns to look back at oneself, there is a stranger standing there with them. And so one has a past. 'But what is it?' Claudine asked herself. And there was no seeing what could have made the difference.

There was nothing simpler than the answer that it was oneself that had become different. But she began to feel a peculiar resistance to granting that possibility. And perhaps one does experience all that is great and fateful in the pattern of one's life only in some oddly reversed state of mind? While at one moment she could not understand the ease with which she felt a stranger to a past that once had been as close to her as her own body, and at the next moment could not understand how anything could ever have been different from the way it was now, something else occurred to her: now and then it happens that one sees something in the distance, an unfamiliar thing, and walks towards it, and at a certain point it enters into the circle of one's own life; but the place where one was before is now strangely empty. Or one has only to reflect: yesterday I did this, did that. . . . A moment always comes that is like an abyss, and, left behind at its brink, there stands a sick person whom one does not know and who is gradually fading from sight. Only one does not often think of it. And in a flash of illumination she saw her whole life dominated by this inexplicable, unremitting betrayal that one commits in every instant, by cutting loose from oneself without knowing why and nevertheless sensing in it an ultimate, inexhaustible tenderness far removed from conscious thought, a tenderness through which one is more intimately linked with oneself than with any of one's actions. And while this is going on, for everyone else one remains always one and the same person.

And while these feelings were still shining clearly in her, their very depths revealed, it seemed to her as if the certainty that bore her outer life along, making it revolve round her, had all at once ceased to work. Her life began to fan out into a multitude of possibilities, unfolding, one behind the other, like stage-scenery of many different lives; and, in a pallid, empty, unquiet area between, the schoolmasters loomed up, obscure, floating shapes, and sank as though in search of something, gazing at her, until, heavily, they fell into place again. She felt a quaint and melancholy pleasure in being the strange lady, sitting here before them with an unapproachable smile, entrenched behind her physical appearance, while within herself she was merely a haphazard being, separated from them only by a deciduous husk, the fabric of chance and actuality. And while talk issued from her lips, fast and meaningless, soulless, facile, unwinding like thread from a spool, she was slowly becoming bewildered by the thought that if the atmosphere peculiar to any of these men were to close around her, all she would do then would be just as truly herself as if any given 'reality' were something without significance, merely something that comes spouting up through an indifferent crack in the surface of things, while far below, out of one's own reach, one's solitary self floats along in a stream of unborn realities whose otherworldly, gentle music no one else can hear. All her security, all her anxious clinging to the one beloved, now suddenly appeared arbitrary, irrelevant, and merely superficial, compared with her apprehension—almost beyond the grasp of mind—of the utterly other communion of their beings at that depth of solitude, in boundless, final, immutable inwardness.

And there was the lure when now she-suddenly remembered the stranger. She realised that, since he desired her, all that was here still a mere toying with possibilities would, with him, become reality.

Something in her shuddered, something warned her. Sodomy, she thought. That is what it would amount to. But behind that there lay her love's ordeal: 'So that in the realm of reality you shall feel it is I . . . I . . . here under this beast! The unimaginable thing! So that, over there, you can never again believe in me, *me* solidly and simply. So that I shall become a mirage beyond your grasp, a fading glimmer as soon as you let go of me. Only a mirage, which means you will know: I am only something within you and by virtue of your own existence, as long as you hold me fast, and am something different—anything—when you let go of me, my beloved, with whom I am so strangely united. . . .'

She was overtaken by the quiet, fickle sadness of the adventurer, that mournfulness attaching to things one does not for their own sake but for the sake of having done them. She felt that somewhere the stranger was now standing, waiting for her. Her shrunken field of vision was already dense with his breathing, and the air close to her seemed filled with the smell of him. Growing uneasy, she prepared to take her leave. She knew that her way was leading her straight to him, and the thought of the moment when it would have happened was like a cold hand gripping her body. It was as if something had taken hold of her and were dragging her towards a door. And she knew this door would slam behind her, and she struggled, and yet she was already craning forward, all her senses reaching out ahead.

When she encountered the man again he was no longer someone she was just beginning to know: the whole thing had become imminent. She realised that in the meantime he had been thinking about her too and had laid his plans.

She heard him say: "I have reconciled myself to the thought that you reject me. But never again will any man venerate you as unselfishly as I do."

Claudine did not answer. His words had come slowly, emphatically; they did not affect her, but she could imagine what it would be like if they did.

After a while she said: "Did you know?—we *are* snowed up!"

Everything seemed as if she had experienced it once before; her words seemed to drag in the groove of words she had surely spoken once before. She paid no heed to her actions as such; what interested her was simply the distinction between what she was doing now and something identical in the past—the arbitrariness of it, this sense of something very intimate and yet accidental that went with the experience. And she had a vast, immobile awareness of her own existence with past and present rippling over it, ever recurrent, in little waves.

After a while he said abruptly: "I can feel there is something in you that hesitates. I know that hesitation. Every woman is faced with it at some point in her life. You respect your husband, you certainly don't wish to hurt him, and so you put up a barrier. But actually, you know, you ought to shake all that off, for a while at any rate, and let the great storm sweep over you."

Again Claudine remained silent. He was bound to misinterpret her silence, and that gave her an odd sense of relish. And in her silence she realised more profoundly that there was something in her that could not express itself through any action, that could not be harmed by any action, that could not defend itself because it lay below the realm of words: something that, in order to be understood, had to be loved as it loved itself, something that she shared with no one but her husband. That was the inward communion; and what she was about to abandon to this stranger, for him to ravage, was only the surface of her being.

So they strolled along, talking. But her feelings were bending over the brink, and there was dizziness in her, and it made her feel ever more deeply the marvellously incomprehensible nature of belonging to her only beloved. At moments it seemed to her that she was beginning to adapt herself to the man at her side, even though outwardly she might appear unchanged; and then sometimes it was as if repartee, phrases, and gestures from her earlier life were coming back to her, things that she had thought herself grown out of long ago. "The lady has a wit," he said.

When he spoke thus, walking at her side, she observed how his words went out into an utter void, which they gradually populated—first with the houses they were walking past—only these houses were a little different now, askew as one sees them mirrored in window-panes; and then there was the street too, and after a while herself, also a little changed and distorted, though still recognisable. She felt the force, the elemental vitality, emanating from this otherwise unremarkable man—causing a scarcely perceptible displacement of the surrounding world, a shifting and bending of things, flattening them out. It disconcerted her to see her own image too within that mirrorlike sliding world; it was as if she had only to yield a little more and she would be entirely that image.

Then there was a moment when he exclaimed: "Believe me, it's all a matter of habit. If, let's say, at seventeen or eighteen, you had met some other man and married him, today you would find it just as difficult to imagine yourself the wife of the man whom, as it happens, you *have* married."

They came to where the church was. Tall and solitary they stood there in the wide square, and, looking at her companion, Claudine saw his gestures projecting out of him into the emptiness round about. For a moment she felt as if thousand of crystals bound together to form her body were bristling and writhing; a scattered, splintered, restlessly flickering light rose within her, and the man on whom it fell all at once looked quite different in the glitter of it: his outlines shifted closer to her, twitching, jerking like her own heart, and she felt each of his movements inside her, passing through her body. She wanted to cry out, reminding herself who he was; but this feeling was only an insubstantial chaotic gleam floating strangely somewhere within her, as though it had nothing to do with her.

And then everything seemed to disappear in a vortex of misty light. She glanced about her: there were the houses,

as before, standing straight and silent around the square. In
the tower the clock began to strike. Round and metallic the
chimes came bowling through the dream-holes, scattering as
they fell, and skimming away over the roofs. Claudine
imagined them rolling on over the countryside, far away,
resounding. . . . And all at once, in awe, she felt: voices go
through the world, many-towered and massive, clangorous
as brazen cities—something that is beyond reason, an
independent, incomprehensible world of feeling, combining
as it were arbitrarily and at random with the everyday world
of reason and then again vanishing into stillness—something
that is like those vast abysmal wings of darkness that sometimes move softly across a blank and rigid sky.

It was as if something were standing all around her and
gazing at her. She felt the excitement in the man beside her,
a surging and billowing, a lashing out, lonely and sombre,
in an expanse of futility. And gradually it began to seem to
her that what this man desired of her, this act ostensibly so
great and important, was something entirely impersonal; it
amounted to no more than being gazed at like this, with a
gaze all stupor and vacuity—just as dots in space, combined
into a random pattern, gaze at each other inertly. It made
her shrink, compressing her until it seemed that she herself
was no more than such a dot. And this gave her a peculiar
sense of her own existence: it was remote from normal
rationality and self-awareness and yet left her intrinsically
unchanged. All at once she ceased to feel how repellently
commonplace was the way this man's mind worked. And
she felt as if she were standing somewhere in open country,
and around her the sounds in the air and the clouds in the
sky stood quite still, etched into the surface of this fleeting
instant. And she herself was no different from them, a vapour
merely, an echoing . . . and it seemed to her she could understand the way the animals loved, and the clouds, and the
sounds in the air.

She felt the man's eyes searching for hers, and all at once she was frightened and longed for the solid certainty of her own existence. She felt her clothes clinging to her, a husk enclosing the very last of the tenderness she knew to have been her own, and beneath that she felt her blood pulsing, and she could almost smell its quivering pungency. And all she had was this body that she was now to surrender, and this utterly other, spiritual feeling, this yearning beyond all reality—a sense of the soul that was now a sense of the body—ultimate bliss. And she did not know whether now her love was taking the final, most daring step of all, or was already fading and her senses were curiously, inquisitively, opening all their windows. . . .

Later, that evening, in the dining-room, she felt lonely.

A woman spoke to her across the table: "I saw your little girl waiting for you this afternoon. What a charming child! She must be a great joy to you."

Claudine had not been to the school again and she had nothing to say to this. She felt as if only some insensitive part of herself were present here among these people—her hair or nails, or a body that was all of horn. Then she did make some non-committal reply, and even while she spoke it seemed that her words became entangled in something, caught in something that was like a sack or a net. Her own words seemed alien among the alien words of others, like fishes struggling and jerking among the moist, cold bodies of other fishes, in the incoherent mesh of opinions.

She was overcome by disgust. Once again she felt that what mattered was not what she could say about herself, what she could explain in words, but that all justification lay elsewhere—in a smile, in a way of falling silent, in listening to oneself within. Suddenly she felt an ineffable longing for that one and only man who was as solitary as she and whom nobody here would understand either—for him who had nothing but that soft tenderness filled with floating pictures, a tenderness that like the veils of fever absorbed the hard thrust of material things, leaving all outer happenings behind in vast, dim flatness, while within everything remained secure in the eternal, mysterious balance of self-awareness.

But whereas at other times, in similar moods, a room crowded like this would be a solid, heavy, hot mass revolving round her, enveloping her, here and now it was different and there was at times some furtive standstill, a dislocation of the things—a sideboard, a table, that then jumped into place again—an atmosphere of sullen rejection. Discord grew between her and these familiar objects; there was something uncertain, wavering, about them. All of a sudden there was again that ugliness which she had experienced on the journey, not a plain, straightforward ugliness, but something that made her perceptions, when they reached out like a hand for solid things, go right through them and come out the other side. Gaps opened up, as if—since that ultimate certainty within her had dreamily begun to contemplate itself—something in the order of things, at other times impalpably embedded in her, had worked loose, and where there had been a coherent chain of impressions, a world of harmony, now everything was rent and riven, the surrounding world turned into mere unceasing uproar.

Gradually it made her feel as someone might who walks at the edge of the sea. One cannot make any impression on this roaring that tears away every thought and every act down to the bare bones of the very instant. And gradually there comes uneasiness, an increasing sense of overflowing one's limits, of losing one's identity and pouring away: an urge to shout, a yearning for incredible, enormous gestures, a soaring flash of will, action without end—action with the sole purpose of making one's own existence real. There was a ravening, devouring, annihilating force in this sense of dissolution, and every second of it was wild, irresponsible solitude, cut off from everything, staring at the world in oblivious stupor. And it wrenched gestures and words from her, which seemed to rush past her, coming from somewhere else, and which yet were part of herself. And there before her sat that stranger, that man, and could not fail to notice how this was drawing her body closer to him, like a vessel containing all her longing and desire, all the deepest love she knew. Then she no longer saw anything but his beard going up and down as he talked, monotonously, lulling her to sleep, going up and down like the beard of some horrible he-goat that sat there muttering, slowly munching wisps of words.

She felt very sorry for herself. Everything turned into a rocking sing-song of grief at the thought that all this could really happen.

He said: "I can tell—you are one of those women whose destiny it is to be swept away by a storm. Oh yes, you have your pride—and so you try to deny it. But believe me, a man who understands women is not deceived."

It was as if she were sinking, irresistibly, back into her past. But when she gazed around her, as she sank through aeons of the soul's life, which were like layer upon layer of deep water, what struck her was the random nature of her surroundings: not the fact that everything looked the way it did, but that this appearance persisted, adhering to things as if it were part of them, perversely holding on to them as with claws. It was like an expression that has remained on a face long after the emotion has gone. And oddly—as though a link had snapped in the silently unwinding chain of events and swivelled out of its true position, jutting out of its dimension—all the people and all the things grew rigid in the attitude of that chance moment, combining, squarely and solidly, to form another, abnormal order. Only she herself went sliding on, her swaying senses outspread among these faces and things—sliding downwards—away.

The whole complex pattern of her emotions, interwoven

with the years of her life, was momentarily visible in the distance behind all this, isolated, dreary, and almost of no account. She thought: 'One digs a line in the ground, any unbroken line by which to keep one's bearings among the silent, towering things that tilt in all directions. That is our life. It's like talking on and on and deceiving oneself into believing that every word relates to the word before and demands the next, because one dreads to think how, if the thread broke, if words failed, one would sway and stagger and be swallowed up by the silence. But that's only weakness, only fear of the horribly gaping contingency of all one does. . . .'

"It's a matter of destiny," he went on. "There are men whose destiny it is to bring unrest with them wherever they go, and it's no good barricading oneself in—there's no defence against it."

But she scarcely heard what this stranger said. Her thoughts were moving in queer, aloof, contradictory ways. She wanted to free herself with one single phrase, with one wild gesture, to take refuge at her beloved's feet: there was still time. But something restrained her, made her shrink from the mere thought of such screaming, panic-stricken flight. She did not want to turn from the great river's bank for fear of being swept away, to hug her life to herself for fear of losing it, to sing merely for fear of falling into bewildered silence. She rejected that. She groped for hesitant, meditative words. She did not want to shriek, as all the others did for fear of the silence around them. Nor did she want to sing. What she longed for was a whispering, a falling silent . . . nothingness, the void. . . .

And then there came a slow, soundless edging forward, a bending over the brink. "Don't you love the theatre, the illusion of the stage?" she heard him say. "What I value in art is the subtlety of the right ending, which consoles us for the humdrum of everyday life. Life is disappointing, so often depriving us of the effect on which the curtain should fall. If we were to leave it at that, wouldn't it mean accepting the bleak matter-of-factness of things?"

And suddenly she heard it quite distinctly, very close to her. Somewhere there was still that other hand, that faint warmth reaching out for her, a conscious flash: You. . . . And she let go of herself, borne up by an inner certainty that even now for each other they were all that counted, that they belonged together, wordless, incredulous, a fabric light and slight as the sweetness of death, an arabesque belonging to a style not yet evolved, each of them a note resounding meaningfully only in the other's soul and ceasing to exist when that soul no longer listened.

Her companion straightened up and looked at her. And then she realised she was here with him, and how far from her was that other man, her beloved. What was he thinking now? Whatever it was, she would never know. And she herself? Hidden in the darkness of her body there was a swaying, aimless urge. At this moment she felt her body— that sheltering home and hedge around its own feelings—as a vague and formless obstacle. She recognised its independent existence and how its feelings and urges shut her in, closer than anything else—recognised in it the inevitable act of betrayal separating her from her beloved. And in a darkening of her senses such as she had never known before, she felt as if, suddenly, in some uncanny innermost depth, her ultimate fidelity, which she still preserved in her body, were turning into its opposite.

Perhaps all she wished now was to yield this body to her beloved, but the profound spiritual uncertainty with which it trembled somehow turned that impulse into desire for this stranger here with her. She faced the possibility that, even while she was being ravaged in her body, this body might still give her the sense of being herself, and she shuddered, as at a darkness, a void, into which she was being locked, at the body's autonomy and its mysterious power to disregard all decisions of the mind. And a blissful bitterness tempted her to disown, to abandon this body, to feel it in its sensual forlornness dragged down by a stranger and as though slashed open with knives, filled to the brim with the helpless twitchings of horror, violence, and disgust—and yet to feel queerly, and as in ultimate truthfulness and constancy, its presence round this nothingness, this wavering, shapeless omnipresence, this certainty of sickness that was the soul—feeling it in spite of everything as in a dream the edges of a wound are felt, striving in endlessly renewed, agonising endeavour to close, each torn part vainly searching for the other.

As a light rises behind a delicate network of veins, out of the expectant darkness of the years the mortal nostalgia of her love rose up among her thoughts, gradually enveiling her. And then all at once, from a long way off, from some radiant expanse, and as though she had only now understood the implication of the stranger's words, she heard herself say: "I don't know whether he could bear it. . . ."

It was the first time she had spoken of her husband. She was startled: it did not seem part of this reality. But she instantly saw the meaning in the words she had just uttered, and their inevitable consequence.

Seizing upon this, her companion said: "Do you mean to say you love him?"

She did not miss the absurdity of the assurance with which he flung this at her. Trembling but determined, she said: "No, no, I don't love him at all."

When she was upstairs again, in her room, she wondered how she could have uttered such a lie; but she relished the masked, enigmatic fascination of it. She thought of her husband. Now and then in her mind's eye she caught a glimpse of him—it was like standing in the street, looking through a window at someone moving about in a brightly lit room. Only then did she really grasp what she was doing.

He seemed beautiful in that light and she wanted to be there with him, for then she too would partake of the radiance about him.

But she shrank back into her lie again, and once more it was like being outside in the street in darkness. She shivered with cold; it was anguish merely to be alive—anguish to look at things, to breathe. The feeling that bound her to her husband was like a globe of warm light into which she could easily slip back. There she was safe; there the things could not thrust at her like the sharp prows of ships looming up out of the night; there everything was softly padded and the things were warded off. And yet she rejected that.

She remembered that she had lied once before. Not in her earlier life, for then the lie had been simply part of herself. But once in this second life of hers she had told a lie, even though what she had actually said was true enough— that she had been out for a walk, in the evening, for two hours. She suddenly realised that that was the first time she had told a lie. Just as she had sat among the people downstairs tonight, so at that time she had walked about in the streets, forlorn, restless as a stray dog, and had gazed into the windows of the houses. And somewhere somebody opened his front door, letting a woman in, smugly satisfied with his own affability, his gestures, the style of his welcome. And somewhere else a man walked arm in arm with his wife, going out for the evening, filled with dignity from head to toe, smug in the security of wedlock. And everywhere, as in a broad river that placidly shelters multifarious life, there were small whirling eddies, each revolving on its own centre, gazing inwards, blind and windowless, closed to the indifferent world. And within, in everyone, there was the same feeling of being held in balance by one's own echo in a narrow space that catches every word and keeps it ringing until the next is uttered, so that one does not hear the insufferable interval, the chasm between the impact of one action and the next, the chasm between two sounds, where one drops away from the sense of one's own identity, plunging into the silence between two words, which might just as well be the silence between the words of somebody utterly different.

And then she had been assailed by the secret thought: 'Somewhere among all these people there is someone—not the right one, someone else—but still, one could have adjusted oneself even to him, and then one would never have known anything of the person that one is today. For every feeling exists only in the long chain of other feelings, each supporting the next; and all that matters is that one instant of life should link up with the next without any lacuna, and there are hundreds of different ways in which it can do so.' And for the first time since the beginning of her love the thought had flashed through her mind: 'It is all chance—by some chance something becomes reality, and then one holds on to it, that's all.'

For the first time she had felt her being, down to its very foundations, as something indeterminate, had apprehended this ultimate faceless experience of herself in love as something that destroyed the very root, the absoluteness, of existence and would always have made her into a person that she called herself and who was nevertheless not different from everyone else. And it was as if she must let go, let herself sink back into the drift of things, into the realm of unfulfilled possibilities, the no-man's-land. And she hurried through the mournful, empty streets, glancing in through windows as she passed, wanting no other company than the clatter of her heels on the cobbles—reduced to that last sign of physical existence, hearing nothing but her own footsteps echoing now in front of her and now behind her.

At that time all she had been able to grasp was the dissolution, the ceaselessly shifting background of shadowy unrealised feelings that frustrated any power by which one might have held on to another human being—that, and the devalued, undemonstrable, and incomprehensible nature of her own life. She had almost wept with confusion and fatigue, entering that realm of utter isolation.

But now, in this moment when it all came back to her, it carried her right to the end of whatever possibilities of real love, real union, there were in this transparently thin, glimmeringly vulnerable world of illusion—of illusions without which life could not be maintained: all the dream-dark straits of existing solely by virtue of another human being, all the island solitude of never daring to wake, this insubstantiality of love that was like a gliding between two mirrors behind which nothingness lay. And here in this room, hidden behind her false confession as behind a mask, and waiting for the adventure that she would experience as though she were someone else, she knew the wonderful, dangerous intensification of feeling that came with lying and cheating in love. She felt herself stealthily slipping out of her own being, out into some territory beyond anyone else's reach, the forbidden territory, the dissolution of absolute solitude—entering, for the sake of greater truthfulness, into the void that sometimes gapes for an instant behind all ideals.

And then suddenly she heard a furtive tread, a creaking first of the stairs and then of the floorboards outside her door, a faint creaking under the weight of someone who had stopped there.

Her eyes turned towards the door. How strange that there outside, behind those thin panels, there was another human being, standing motionless. . . . And on each side of this indifferent, this accidental door tension rose high as behind a dam.

She had already undressed. Her clothes lay on the chair by the bed, where she had just flung them, and from them the vague scent of what had been next to her body rose and mingled with the air of this room that was let one day to this person, the next day to another. She glanced round the room. She noticed a brass lock hanging loose, on a chest of drawers. Her gaze lingered on a small threadbare rug, worn thin by many footsteps, at the side of her bed. Suddenly she could not help thinking of all the bare feet that had stepped on this rug, permeating it with their smell, and how this smell was given off again and entered into other people's being, a familiar, protective smell, somehow associated with childhood and home. It was an odd, flickering, double impression, now alien and abhorrent, now fascinating, as if the self-love of all those strangers were a current flowing into her and all that was left of her own identity were a passive awareness of it.

And all the while that man was there, standing on the other side of her door, his presence known to her only through the faint, hardly detectable sounds that he could not help making.

Then she was seized by a wild urge to throw herself down on this rug and kiss the repulsive traces of all those feet, exciting herself with their smell like a bitch on heat. But this was no longer sexual desire; it was something crying within her like a small child, howling like a high wind.

Suddenly she knelt down on the rug. The stiff flowers of the pattern loomed larger, spreading and intertwining senselessly before her eyes, and over them she saw her own heavy thighs, a mature woman's thighs, hideously arched and without meaning, yet tense with an incomprehensible gravity. And her hands lay there before her on the floor, two five-limbed animals staring at each other.

All at once she remembered the lamp in the passage there outside and the horribly silent moving circles it cast upon the ceiling, and the walls, the bare walls, remembered the emptiness out there and then again the man who was standing there, faintly creaking sometimes as a tree creaks in its bark, his urgent blood in his head like the thicket of the leaves. And here she was on her hands and knees, only a door between her and him. And still she felt the full sweetness of her ripe body, felt it with that imperishable remnant of the soul that stands quietly, unmoved, beside the ravaged body even when it is broken open and disfigured by the infliction of devastating injuries—that stands beside it, in grave and constant awareness and yet averted from it, as beside the body of a stricken beast.

Then she heard the man outside walking cautiously away. And even through the turmoil in her rapt senses she realised: all this was betrayal itself, greater and weightier than the mere lie.

Slowly she began to rise on her knees, spellbound by the baffling thought that by now it might all have really happened, and she trembled like someone who has escaped from danger by mere chance, not by any effort of his own. She tried to picture it. She saw her body lying underneath that stranger's body, saw it with a lucidity that branches out into every smallest detail, like spilt water seeping into every cranny. She felt her own pallor and heard the shameful words of abandonment and saw above her the man's eyes, holding her down, hovering over her, like the outspread wings of a bird of prey. And all the time she was thinking: '*This* is betrayal!' And now she pictured herself at home again after all this and how he would say: 'I can't feel you from inside. . . .' And she had no answer but a helpless smile, a smile that tried to say: 'Believe me, it was not meant against us. . . .'

And yet there was one knee still pressed against the floor —a senseless, alien thing—and she felt her very existence in it, inaccessible, with all the forlorn, defenceless frailty there is in the ultimate human potentialities that no word can hold fast and no return can ever weave into the pattern of life as it once has been.

She was empty of thought. She did not know if she was doing wrong. Everything turned into strange and lonely grief—and the grief itself was like another room around her, enclosing a gentle darkness, a diffuse, floating room, softly rising in the air. And then gradually she perceived a strong, clear, indifferent light shining from above. In it she saw everything she did, her own gestures of surrender, and the abandonment of her innermost being, torn out of her in ecstasy, all that in its enormity seemed so real and yet was mere appearance. . . . There it lay, crumpled, small, and cold, all its relevance lost, far, far below her. . . .

And after a long time it seemed to her as if a cautious hand were again trying the door, and she knew he was there outside, listening intently. A whirling dizziness took hold of her, almost forcing her to creep to the door on all fours and draw back the bolt.

But she remained crouching on the floor in the middle of the room. Once again something held her back—a sense of her own sordidness, the atmosphere of the past. Like a single, violent thrust cutting her sinews, there was the thought that perhaps it was all nothing but a relapse into her past. She raised her hands above her head. 'Oh my beloved, help me, help me!' she cried out in her thoughts, and felt the cry was true. And yet it was only a soft, caressing thought: 'We moved towards each other, mysteriously drawn through space, through all the years . . . and now, by sad and hurtful ways, I enter into you.'

And then there was stillness, a great expanse: strength that had been painfully dammed up now pouring in through the breaches in the walls. Like a quiet, mirroring pool of water her life lay there before her, past and future united in the present moment. There are things one can never do— one does not know why. Perhaps those are the most import- ant things? Indeed one knows they are the most important things. And one knows: a deadly languor lies upon life, one feels the stiffness and numbness of it as in frozen fingers. And sometimes again it loosens its hold, dissolves like snow and ice on meadows—one marvels, one is a sombre brightness expanding far, far away. But life, one's own hard and bony life, one's irrevocable life, resumes its callous grip—somewhere the links close—one does nothing at all.

Suddenly she rose to her feet, and the thought that now she *must* do this drove her soundlessly forward. Her hands drew the bolt back. There was no sound. The door did not move. And then she opened the door and looked out into the passage: there was no one there. In the dim light from the lamp the bare walls stared at each other through empty space. He had gone without her hearing it.

She went to bed, her mind full of self-reproaches. And, already on the borders of sleep, she thought: 'I am hurting you.' But at the same time she had the strange feeling: 'It is you who do whatever I am doing.' And sinking towards oblivion she knew: 'We are casting away everything that can be cast away, to hold on to each other all the more tightly, to wrap around us closely what no one can touch.' Then for an instant, thrown up into wakefulness, she thought: 'This man will triumph over us. But what is triumph?'

Sinking back into sleep, her thoughts slid down along that question into the depths and her bad conscience accompanied her like a last caress. A vast egoism, deepening and darkening the world, rose over her as over someone dying. Behind closed eyes she saw bushes and clouds and birds, and she became quite small among them, and yet it all seemed to be there only for her sake. And then there was the moment of closing up, of shutting out everything alien; and on the threshold of dream there was perfection, a great and pure love mantling her in a trembling light, dissolution of all apparent contradictions.

The visitor did not return. She slept undisturbed, her door unlatched—quiet as a tree on a meadow.

With the next morning a mild, mysterious day began.

She woke as though behind bright curtains keeping out all the reality of the light outside. She went for a walk; and he accompanied her. Her mind swayed with an intoxicaton that came from the blueness of the air and the whiteness of the snow. They walked to the edge of the little town, and there the white plain before them lay radiant and festive.

They stood by a fence and looked at a small path behind it. A peasant woman was throwing corn to her hens. A patch of lichen shone yellow in the wintry light.

"Do you think——?" Claudine asked, gazing back through the street and up into the pale blue air; but she did not finish her sentence. After a while she said: "Look at that wreath—I wonder how long it's been hanging there. Does the air feel it? Is it alive?" That was all she said and she did not even know why she said that. He smiled.

She stood beside him, and it was as if everything were engraved in metal, still trembling from the pressure of the engraver's burin. And while she felt him looking at her, observing her, something within her fell into shape and lay wide and brilliant as fields lie one next to the other under the eyes of a circling bird.

'This life, now bright blue, now dark—somewhere a small bright patch of yellow—what is the meaning of it? This voice calling to the hens, this faint patter of the strewn grains of corn, and then all at once something that strikes across it all like the tolling of a bell on the hour—what does it say, and to whom? This thing without a name, eating its way down into the depths and only sometimes shooting up through the narrow slit of seconds and flashing through some passer-by and at other times lying as though dead—what can it mean?' She looked around with quiet eyes and felt all the things about her without thinking of them, felt them as one feels the touch of hands laid on one's forehead when there is nothing more to say.

And after that she listened merely with a smile. It was

obvious that he felt he was carefully drawing his net tighter round her, and she let him have his way. While he talked to her she felt no more than one feels when walking between houses, hearing people talk indoors. The pattern of her thoughts was sometimes invaded by another current, which drew her thoughts along with it, now this way, now that; and she would follow of her own free will—then for a short time, half emerging from shadowy depths, would almost return to herself, and once again would follow the current, would sink. Softly and silently the entangling flow of it took her captive.

And in between she felt this man's love of himself as intensely as if it were a feeling of her own. His tenderness towards himself infected her with a faint sensual excitement. It was like entering a realm where everything was hushed, and silent decisions prevailed, decisions not of one's own making. She knew herself hard pressed and knew herself to be giving way, but it no longer mattered. Something far within her was like a bird upon a branch, singing. . . .

She ate a light supper and went to bed early. There was a deadness in things now; she no longer felt any erotic excitement. Yet after a short sleep she woke, thinking: 'He's downstairs, waiting.' She groped for her clothes and dressed, simply got up and dressed—without feeling, without thought, with only a remote awareness of doing wrong; and then perhaps, at the very last moment, there was a sense of being exposed and defenceless. And so she went downstairs.

The room was deserted. The tables and chairs were tense and still, looming indistinctly in the silence of the night. In one corner, there he sat.

She said something, without quite knowing what— perhaps: "I was feeling so alone there upstairs. . . ." And she knew just how he was bound to misinterpret it. After a while he took her hand. She rose, hesitated, and then ran out of the room. She knew this was behaving like any silly little woman, and there was a thrill in that. On the stairs she heard footsteps behind her. The stairs creaked. Her thoughts were suddenly very remote and abstract, but her body was trembling like an animal hunted down, deep in the forest.

Then, sitting in her room, he said: "You are in love with me, aren't you? I grant you, I'm no artist or philosopher, I'm just human—but a whole man, yes, I think I may say, a whole man."

"What is a *whole man*?" she asked.

"What a queer question!" he exclaimed, chafing.

"No, that's not what I mean," she said. "I'm thinking how odd it is that one can be fond of someone just because one is fond of him—fond of his eyes, his tongue—not his words, but the sound of them. . . ."

He kissed her and said: "So that is how you love me?"

Claudine found the strength to answer: "No, what I love is being with you—the fact, the mere chance, of being with you. One might equally well be among the Eskimos, wearing trousers made of skins, and have drooping breasts. And be delighted with it all. Can't there, after all, be other kinds of *whole* people?"

But he said: "You're mistaken. You are in love with me. Only you can't face it yet. And just that is the sign of true passion."

Involuntarily something in her shrank when she realised how he was assuming possession of her.

But he murmured: "No, don't say anything."

Claudine was silent. But while they were undressing, she began to talk—again out-of-place, aimless, even senseless talk, merely like a disconsolate movement of her hands, an urge to stroke and smooth away, a sort of by-play. . . . "It's like slipping through a narrow pass—suddenly everything's changed. Animals, people, flowers, oneself—it's all quite different. You wonder: if I'd always lived here, how would

I think about this, how would I feel about that? Isn't it odd that there's only a line—only one line one has to cross? I should like to kiss you and then jump back across that line and look from over there. And then jump back to you, time and again. And each time, crossing the frontier, surely I'd feel it more and more distinctly. I should grow paler all the time, people would die—no, not die, shrink, shrivel up. . . . And so would the trees and animals. And in the end there'd be nothing left but faint, faint smoke . . . and then only a tune . . . floating through the air . . . over a void. . . ."

And all at once she said: "Go away. Please. . . . It sickens me."

But he only smiled.

"Please go away," she said.

And then she felt in horror how, in spite of everything, her body was swelling up with lust. Yet at the back of her mind there was a shadowy memory of something she had once experienced on a day in spring: a state that was like giving herself to everyone and yet belonging only to the one beloved. . . .

And from a long way off—as children say of God: He is great—she saw and knew the image of her love.

The Temptation of Quiet Veronica

Somewhere there are two voices. Perhaps they merely lie mute on the pages of a diary, now side by side, now intertwining, according as the pages come: the woman's a dark deep voice that is from the first instant rounded, self-collected, and yet enclosed by the mellow, expansive, ever expanding voice of the man, and the man's voice with many ramifications, like a thing unfinished, the sound of it revealing all that the speaker has had no time to conceal. Or perhaps not even that. Or perhaps after all there is, somewhere in the world, a point towards which these two voices—scarcely distinguishable as they are amid the dull confusion of everyday humdrum noises—dart like two rays of light, there at last to mingle. Perhaps one should feel the need to search for that point, which may be nearer than one thinks, though it betrays its nearness only in a stirring like that of a music not yet audible, but already imprinted, in heavy folds vaguely outlined in the still impenetrable curtain of things far off. If one found it, perhaps these scattered fragments here would once more assume their wholeness, would shed their malady and weakness, and stand erect and firm in the lucidity of day.

"Oh wheeling and revolving of things!" It was afterwards that he spoke to it as though it were a person: afterwards, in those days of fearful crisis when he was suspended between imagination—now drawn tight as a sheerest thread by some imperceptible certainty—and the accustomed reality of every day. It was in those days when he made a desperate last effort to drag the incomprehensible other thing into the realm of hither reality and then, in his exhaustion, surrendered, letting himself fall back into the simplicity of real life as though into a mound of warm and tumbled pillows. It was then that he spoke to it as though it were a person.

There was no hour in those days when he did not talk to himself; and he talked aloud because he was afraid. Something had sunk deep into him with all the unintelligible, irresistible force of a pain suddenly intensifying somewhere in the body and turning into a mass of inflamed tissue and assuming ever more tangible reality, until finally and unmistakably it is there as an illness and asserts its domination over the body, smiling the torturer's mild, ambiguous smile.

"Oh, wheeling and revolving of things!" Johannes cried out imploringly. "Oh, would that you were also outside of me!" And he would cry: "Would that you had a garment so that I could clutch the hem of it and hold you fast! Would that I might speak with you! That I might say: You are God. And I would keep a little pebble under my tongue when I spoke to you, to make it more real! Oh, that I could say: I commend myself to you, you will help me, you who watch all that I do. For do what I may, something of me lies utterly still, still as the centre of a turning wheel, and that is you."

But as it was he merely lay with his mouth in the dust, and his heart groped for this thing as a child might grope in yearning. And all he knew was that he needed it because he was a coward; that he knew. And yet it was something that happened as though to draw strength out of his weakness, a strength of which he had a premonition and which lured him on as nothing else had ever allured him except something—sometimes—in his youth: the mighty, still faceless head of some great force as yet only dimly apprehended, yet making a man feel that his shoulders might grow up into it from below and that he might wear it as his own head, his own face fusing with it, gazing out of it.

And once he had said to Veronica: "It is God." He was timid and pious then—that had been long ago; it had been his first attempt to give a shape to this indefinable thing of which they both felt the presence. In the dark house they glided past each other, upstairs and downstairs, always passing each other by. But when he had put it into those words, the words had lost their meaning and told nothing of what he meant.

Yet what he meant was, at that time, perhaps only something like those patterns one may see in stones, or in the cracks of a wall, in clouds, in swirling water: intimations of no one knows what, or where, or what its full reality may be. What he meant was perhaps only the indecipherable manifestation of something that is itself not yet there; perhaps it was like those rare expressions that will appear on a face to which they have no relevance, being relevant only to other faces suddenly surmised beyond the horizon of visible things—little tunes amid the sound of wind or water, feelings flickering through people. Indeed there were feelings in him that, when he groped for them with words, turned out to be something else: not yet feelings at all, but only as if something in him had extended beyond him, the tips of it already dipping into some liquescence—his fear, his stillness, his taciturnity—as things sometimes do extend on fever-bright spring days when their shadows creep out beyond them and lie as quietly, all flowing in one direction, as reflections lie in the mirror of a stream.

And what he often said to Veronica was this: it was not really fear or weakness that he felt, but something like the vague dread that may hover, like a rustling of leaves, about some experience that one does not yet know, has not even glimpsed; that it was the way one sometimes is quite sure, though without understanding why, that dread has the aura of a woman or that weakness will some time be a morning in a country house and the air outside filled with the trilling of birds. It was in this strange condition that he lived; and so it was that such vague patterns arose in his mind, defying definition.

Once, however, Veronica looked at him with her large, quietly unconsenting eyes—they were sitting alone in one of the big shadowy rooms—and asked:

"So there's something in you too, is there, that you can't feel or really understand, and you only call it God, thinking of it as outside yourself and as something real because you have thought it, as though it would then take you by the hand? And perhaps it is the thing you never want to call cowardliness or softness? Something imagined in human shape, capable of hiding you among the folds of its garment? And you use such words as 'God' for something that has direction but no substance, for something that is movement although there is nothing that moves, for visions that never emerge all the way into the light of real day—you use such words for it, do you, because the words in their dark robes come walking out of another world, with the assurance of strangers who come from some great realm where all is well ordered, and they walk like living people? Tell me, is it because they come like the living and because at any price you must feel that they are real?"

"They are things beyond the horizon of consciousness," he said thoughtfully, "things that can be seen gliding past, along the horizon of our consciousness—or rather, it is only a new horizon, tense with strangeness, inscrutable, no more than a possibility, a sudden intimation, and there is nothing on it yet."

And even in those days he spoke of these intimations as ideals. They were not a clouding of the mind, he said, or signs of a morbid condition; they were premonitions of some wholeness that it was still too soon to apprehend. And if it were only possible to fit them together in their right order, then suddenly, in a blaze of lightning, something would appear, reaching outwards from the most delicate ramifications of thought to the tops of the trees, and it would be there in one's slightest gesture like the wind taking hold of sails. And he jumped to his feet and flung out his arms in a movement of almost physical desire.

And after that she did not say anything for a long while. Then at last she replied: "There is something in me too. . . . You see: Demeter. . . ." She faltered and was silent. After that they talked of Demeter. It was for the first time.

At first Johannes could not understand why they should speak of him at all. She said that once she had been standing at a window, looking down into a poultry-yard, watching the rooster, simply watching and thinking of nothing at all. It was only after some time that Johannes realised she was speaking of the poultry-yard at their own home. Demeter came (she recounted) and stood beside her. And she began to realise that she had been thinking of something all that time, thinking it as it were in deep darkness, and now she began to know what it was. There was Demeter quite close, she said—"you do understand, don't you?"—it was in a sort of darkness that she had begun to know what it was all about—and his closeness to her at once helped her to know what it was and made her feel constrained. And after a while she knew it was the rooster she had been thinking about. Yet perhaps she had not been thinking at all, only watching, watching, and what she had been gazing at remained like an alien body, hard, within her, and no thinking about it would dissolve it. And it seemed to remind her vaguely of something else, but she could not discover what that other thing could be. And the longer Demeter stood there beside her, the more distinctly and strangely, frighteningly, did she feel the empty shape of that image within her.

And Veronica looked at Johannes as if to ask whether he understood.

"I saw it again and again," she said, "that unutterably indifferent way that animal slid down." And she was still seeing what she had seen then, seeing it happening so quite simply and yet beyond comprehension: that unutterably indifferent sliding downward at that sudden release from all excitement and that way he stood there for a while, as though stupefied, all sensation gone, as though far away in thought, somewhere in a stagnant, putrefying light. "Sometimes, on dead afternoons," she went on, "when I went for a walk with Aunt, there was a light like that on everything. I could feel it bodily, as though the very notion of that ghastly, nauseating light were radiating from my stomach."

There was a pause, and Veronica seemed to be groping for words.

But then she came back to the same thing. "Afterwards I could always see it coming from a long way off," she said, "a wave rolling on, catching him, flinging him up, and then letting him go again."

And once more there was silence.

At last her words tiptoed through the silence, as if they were trying to hide mysteriously in that big, sombre room, crouching down very close to Johannes' face. "And at a moment like that Demeter took hold of my head and pressed it down against his breast," she whispered. "He didn't say anything. He only pressed my head down, hard." And again there was that silence.

For Johannes it was as though in the obscurity a stealthy hand had touched him, and he trembled when Veronica went on talking.

"I don't know how to explain what happened to me at that moment. It suddenly came to me that Demeter must be like that rooster, living in some terrible enormous emptiness and suddenly leaping forth out of it."

Johannes felt her eyes on him. It tormented him that she should speak of Demeter, at the same time saying things that he dimly felt concerned himself. An incomprehensibly frightening suspicion rose in his mind: a suspicion that whatever was abstract in him, whatever it was that could not aim straight at God—like visions of the Self stretched taut over sleepless nights, visions that were all uncertainty and lack of purpose, like empty frames of feeling—was precisely what Veronica might be exhorting, exhorting him to act. And it seemed to him that as she went on talking her voice took on a note at once of cruelty and of pity and of lust; and he was defenceless against it.

"That time," she said, "I cried out: 'Johannes would never do such a thing!' But all Demeter said was: 'Johannes —bah!' And he put his hands in his pockets. And after that, when you came back to us for the first time—do you remember how Demeter challenged you? 'Veronica says you're a better man than I am,' he said, sneering at you. 'But you're just a coward!' And in those days you hadn't yet learned to take that sort of thing lying down, and you retorted: 'Go on then, prove it!' And he struck you in the face with his fist. And then—wasn't it so?—you wanted to hit back. But when you saw how threatening he looked, and felt the pain growing more intense, you were suddenly terribly afraid of him, oh, I know, it was an almost docile, friendly kind of fear, and all at once you smiled. Wasn't it so?—you didn't know why, but you smiled and smiled, and there was a twist in your face that I could feel in myself, a timid smile for his angry eyes, and yet with such a warm sweetness in it too, and a sureness that went seeping deeper into you until all at once the insult was levelled out and found its proper place in you. . . . And then later you told me you were going to become a priest. . . . So it was that I suddenly realised: It isn't Demeter, it's you who are the animal. . . ."

Johannes jumped to his feet. He could not understand.

"How can you say such a thing?" he exclaimed. "What is going on in your mind?"

But in her disappointment Veronica defended what she had said. "Why didn't you become a priest? In a priest there *is* something of an animal! There's that emptiness at the point where other people possess themselves. That meekness—their very clothes reek of it. That empty meekness like a sieve that things may heap up in for an instant—and then it runs empty! *That's* what one ought to make something of! I was so glad when I realised that. . . ."

Then he realised how unfitting the loudness of his expostulation had been, and he became very quiet. He was aware too that musing on what she had said was beginning to divert his attention from himself. And he grew hot and clammy with the effort of keeping his own imaginings distinct from hers, which seemed to merge with them somewhere as in a deep fog and which was nevertheless much more real, and constricted as a little room shared with another person.

. . . When they were both calmer, Veronica said: "It's the thing that I somehow haven't quite understood yet, the thing we both ought to search for together."

She opened the door and gazed down the stairs. Each of them felt that the other was looking to see if they were alone, and now the dark and empty house had become a great bell lowered upon them, enclosing them.

"I've tried to say it," Veronica went on, "but all I've said still isn't it at all. . . . I don't know what it is myself. But tell me, tell me what went on in you that time, tell me what that smiling sweet fear is like. . . . That time when Demeter struck you. It seemed to me then you were quite impersonal, stripped right down to something naked, warm, and soft."

But Johannes could not explain it. A multitude of possibilities flashed through his mind. It was as if he could hear someone talking in an adjoining room and gathered, from what he could catch of it, that the talk was about him. At one point he asked: "And so you talked to Demeter about it too?"

"But that was much later," Veronica said. She hesitated and then added: "Only once." And after a while she went on: "It was a few days ago. I don't know what made me do it."

Somewhere in Johannes there was a dull sensation like a far-off shock: this must be what jealousy was like.

It was only after a long time that he realised Veronica was speaking again. He heard her say: ". . . it was such an odd feeling, I understood her so well."

Mechanically he asked: "Her?"

"The peasant woman. Up on the hill."

"Oh, yes, I see. The peasant woman."

"The one the village lads talk about," Veronica went on. "Can you imagine it? She never had a lover again, only those two big dogs of hers. Of course it's perfectly horrible what they say, but just try to imagine it: those two huge beasts, sometimes standing up on their hind-legs, their teeth bared, insistent, masterful, as though you were just the same as they are—and somehow you are. You're terrified of them, with their hairiness, it's all terror except for a tiny point in you where you're still yourself. Yet you know—it needs no more than a single gesture and it'll all be gone in a flash, they'll be servile, they'll crouch, they'll just be animals again. So it's not just animals: this thing is yourself and a solitude, it's you and once again you and an empty, hairy room. It's not an animal's desire, but a desire coming from something else that I can't find any name for. And I don't know how it is that I can understand it so well."

Johannes said imploringly: "But all this is sin! Such talk is filthy."

But Veronica would not let it go at that. "You meant to

become a priest, didn't you? Why? I thought it was—
because then you wouldn't be a man for me. Listen—listen
to what I'm going to tell you. Demeter said to me, out of
the blue: '*That* one won't marry you, nor *that* one either.
You'll stay here for ever, growing old like Aunt. . . .' Oh
can't you understand that I began to be frightened? Isn't it
just the same for you? I'd never have thought of Aunt as a
person. For me she wasn't anything like a man or a woman.
And when Demeter said that I was suddenly frightened at
the thought that she was something I too might some day
become, and I felt something had to happen. And it suddenly
seemed to me that for a long time she didn't grow any older,
but then all at once she became very old and has stayed like
that ever since. And Demeter said: 'We can do as we please.
Even if we've no money, we're the oldest family in the
province. We live in our own way. Johannes didn't go into
the government service and I didn't go into the Army. He
didn't even become a priest. People look down on us a little
because we aren't rich, but we don't need money and we
don't need them either.' And perhaps it was because I was
still aghast at the thought of being like Aunt—what he had
said was almost uncanny, it had startled me obscurely, like
a door faintly sighing—it gave me a feeling, somehow, of this
house of ours. But you know how it is, you've always felt the
same way yourself—about the garden and the house . . .
oh, the garden. . . . Sometimes in the very height of summer
I would think it must be like this lying deep in snow, so
mournfully voluptuous and not as on solid ground at all, but
floating between heat and cold, and you want to leap up and
yet swoon away, as if dissolving, into some sweet oblivion.
If you think about the garden, don't you feel that blank
unremitting beauty? It must be the light . . . a paralysing
excess of light, light that leaves you dumb, that's senselessly
pleasant on your skin, and a moaning and scraping in the
bark of the trees, and an unceasing soft whirring among the

leaves. . . . Don't you feel that life, coming to a standstill here in this garden of ours, has a beauty that is somehow flat and endless, surrounding us on all sides like a sea, isolating us, and that we would sink and drown if ever we tried to set foot on it?"

Veronica had leapt to her feet and was standing face to face with Johannes. And the fingers of her hands, shimmering in some last forlorn gleam of light, seemed to be anxiously plucking the words out of darkness.

"And then I often feel, in this house of ours," she said, fumbling with the words, "the gloomy darkness of it, with the creaking stairs and whimpering windows, all the nooks and crannies and the towering cupboards, and sometimes, somewhere, at some high small window, there's light trickling through, as though slowly pouring from a tilted pail, and spreading on the floor. . . . And there's fear, as though someone were standing there with a lantern. And Demeter said: 'I am not a man of words. Johannes is the one who can talk. But you must believe me if I tell you that sometimes there's something in me that rears up senselessly, a sort of swaying as of a tall tree, a terrible inhuman sound, a battering, clattering, rub-a-dub as from those wooden rattles that children go round with at Easter. . . . I need only bow down to the ground and I feel myself an animal. . . . Sometimes I could almost bedaub my face. . . .'

"It seemed to me, then, that our house is a world where we're all alone, a dim world where everything's weird and askew as under water, and it seemed almost natural that I should yield to Demeter's desire. He said: 'No one will know of it but you and me, and since no one knows, it will scarcely be real at all, it has no relation to the real world, no means of getting out, into it. . . .'

"Johannes, you must not think that he meant anything to me. It was just that he opened up before me like a huge mouth bristling with teeth, preparing to devour me. As a man he remained as much a stranger to me as all other men. But in my imagination it was like being poured into him, a falling, falling over his lips, drop by drop, it was like being swallowed by an animal drinking, it was so utterly without feeling . . . numb. . . . Sometimes one would wish to experience something if only one could experience it merely as an act, as a thing in itself, with no one else involved. But suddenly I thought of you, and without having any clear intention I said no to Demeter. . . . There must be a way of doing that thing as you would do it, a good way. . . ."

"What are you talking of?" Johannes said thickly.

She said: "I have a vague notion of what people might be to each other. Aren't we all afraid of one another? Even you, sometimes when you talk, are as hard and solid as a stone flung at me. But what I mean is a way of dissolving and becoming wholly what each is for the other, so that nothing is left to stand outside, eavesdropping, estranged. . . . I don't know how to put it. What you sometimes call God is like the thing I mean. . . ."

And then she went on to say things that Johannes could not fathom.

"He whom you must surely mean is nowhere, because He is in everything. He is a vile fat woman who makes me kiss her breasts and at the same time He is myself, a person who sometimes, when she is alone, lies down flat on the floor before a cupboard and thinks such things. And perhaps you are like that too. Sometimes you are as impersonal and withdrawn as a candle in the darkness, which is itself nothing and only makes the darkness bigger and more tangible. Since that time when I saw you being so frightened it's as if now and then you dropped away out of my thoughts, as if there were nothing remaining but the fear, like a dark speck with a warm, soft rim round it. And, after all, the only thing that matters is that one should be like the act and not like the person enacting it. Each of us ought to be alone with what is going on, and then again we ought to be together, mutely united as the inside of four windowless walls that form a room where everything can really happen, and yet in such a way that what is in the one does not affect the other, but is as if it were happening only in one's thoughts. . . ."

But Johannes did not understand.

Then she suddenly began to change, like something sinking away from him, and even her features seemed to blur, growing smaller here and larger there. Although it seemed there was something else she might have said, it was as if she no longer felt herself to be the person who had just been speaking. And only hesitantly, as if down some long and unaccustomed road, her words then came: " . . . What do you think? . . . To me it seems no human being could be so impersonal. . . . Only an animal could. . . . Oh, help me! Why does it always make me think of an animal. . .?"

And Johannes tried to find some way of recalling her to herself. All at once he began to speak, for now he wanted to know more about it.

But she only shook her head.

From that time on Johannes realised how terrifyingly easy it would be to stretch out his hand for what he wanted and miss it by a hair's breadth. Sometimes a man does not recognise what it is he wants in the darkness, only knowing that he will fail to grasp it; and then he lives his life as in a locked room, alone with fear. At times Johannes was afraid, as though he might suddenly begin to whimper and run on all fours and sniff at Veronica's hair. Such impulses assailed him. But nothing happened. They passed each other by. They looked at each other. They spoke to each other about trifles, or sometimes spoke as though questingly. So it was day after day.

Yet once he suddenly felt this to be like an encounter in the midst of solitude, when a vague, haphazard proximity all at once arches like a solid vault. Veronica was coming down the stairs, and he was waiting at the foot: there they paused, each standing alone in the twilight. It was not that he wanted anything of her, it was merely as if the two of them, standing there separately, were no more than a delirious fantasy in a sick person's brain. So it was a sense of quite another necessity that made him say to her: "Come, let's go away together."

But of what she said in reply he understood only: ". . . no love . . . not marry . . . I can't go away and leave Aunt."

And once again he tried, saying: "Veronica, a human being—sometimes indeed a word, a sudden warmth, a breath of air—is like a pebble in an eddy, revealing the centre on which you turn. . . . If we set about it together, perhaps we might find it. . . ."

Yet her voice had an even deeper sensual undertone now than it had had that other time when she gave him the same answer: "Surely no human being can be so impersonal, only an animal . . . yes, perhaps if you were going to die. . . ." And then she said: "No." And at that he was once again overwhelmed by something that was not so much a resolve as a vision, something that had no bearing on reality but was self-contained, like music. And he said: "I am going away. Certainly—perhaps I shall die." But even while saying this he knew it was not what he had meant to say.

And there was no hour, during all that time, when he did not try to work it out, asking himself what she must really be like that there was such power in her. Sometimes he would say: "Veronica . . ." and feel the sweat that clung to her name, the humble and irrevocable submissiveness of being an attendant shadow and that moist and chilly resignation contenting itself with reality at second hand. And he could not help thinking of her name whenever he saw those two little curls that were so carefully stuck to her forehead as if they did not belong to her, or when he saw her smiling the way she sometimes did when they were sitting at table together and she was waiting on Aunt. And he could not help looking at her whenever Demeter spoke. But there was always some impediment, something that prevented him from being able to understand how a person like her could have become the central point of his passionate resolve. And when he thought about it all he found that even in his earliest memories there was something hovering about her like the faint acrid smoke of candles that have guttered out, an aura of things to be shunned—like the drawing-rooms of this house, motionless, asleep under dust-covers and behind drawn blinds. And only when he heard Demeter talking, saying things that were as ghastly, commonplace and colourless as that furniture which no one ever used, did he feel as if it were all like some vicious practice involving all three of them.

And for all this, whenever he thought of her in later days, he could not help hearing only one thing: how she had said 'no'. Three times she had said 'no', quite suddenly, and it made her an utter stranger to him. The first 'no' had been spoken softly, and yet it had been queerly as though detached from all that had gone before, floating through the house and away; and the second had been like the crack of a whip or like a panic-stricken clutching at something; and the third had been very quiet again, a sort of collapse, and almost like anguish in the awareness of inflicting pain.

And at times now, when he thought of her, it seemed to him she was beautiful: of a very complex beauty, the kind one may easily forget to admire and even fall back into regarding as ugliness. And whenever she appeared before him, looming up out of the darkness of the house, which closed again behind her and lay there strangely immobile; or whenever she glided past him with that extraordinary sensuality of hers which was a sort of authority, an aura like that of some mysterious illness—he could never help remem-

bering that she had told him he was an animal for her. This
was incomprehensible and how terrifying, much bigger and
more real than it had been in the past. And even when he
did not see her, he conjured up her image with piercing
clarity: her tall figure with the broad, rather flat breast; her
low straight brow and the dense, gloomy mass of hair high-
piled over those two irrelevant, gentle curls; her large,
voluptuous mouth; her bare arms shadowed with faint,
black down; and the way she bore her head bowed, as
though that fragile neck could not support the load of it
without bending, and the peculiar gentleness, at once
negligent and almost shameless, with which she thrust her
belly a little forward as she walked. But they hardly ever
spoke to each other any more.

Veronica had suddenly heard a bird call, and another
call in answer. And that was the end of it. With that little
chance happening—as it so often is with these things—there
was an end to what had been; and what began now had its
existence solely for her.

For then, cautiously, hastily, like the quick touch of a
soft, slightly hairy, pointed tongue, the fragrance of the tall
grass and the wild flowers came flitting past their faces. And
their last conversation, which had gone on and on, lingeringly, like something one has ceased to pay attention to and
yet goes on turning over between one's fingers, here broke off.
Veronica had felt a shock, and it was only afterwards that
she realised what a strange shock it had been, recognising it
by the flush in her face and by a memory that all at once
came back to her across an expanse of years: there it was,
all unforeseen, hot, and alive. True, a great many memories
had come back to her recently, and it seemed to her she
must have heard that bird-call even the previous night, and
in the night before that, and one night two weeks earlier.
And it seemed to her too that she had been tormented by

that touch before, she did not know when, perhaps in her sleep. Recently these weird memories had been coming to her time and again, falling into her mind in droplets, falling to left and to right of something, before it and behind it: they were like swarms of birds winging towards a roosting place, her whole childhood. But this time she knew with uncanny certainty: it was the right thing, the real thing, the thing itself. It was a memory that she all at once recognised, even across that expanse of years: there it was at last, in incoherent fragments, hot, and still alive.

In those days, so long ago, she had loved the hair of a big St. Bernard dog, especially the hair in front where the big chest-muscles rose like two hillocks over the curving bones, protruding at every step the dog took. The mass of that thick coat, and the intense golden-brown of it, over-whelmed her; it was like a treasure beyond counting and like some serene infinitude, so that whenever she tried to keep her eyes fixed on one spot her vision blurred. What she felt was no more or less than the strong, simple, inarticulate affection, the tender companionship that a fourteen-year-old girl will feel for a possession whether animate or inanimate; and yet at this point it was sometimes almost like being in a landscape. It was like walking—here were the woods and the meadow, and here the hill and the field, and in the order of it all each thing was no more than as a little stone simply and perfectly locking into a great pattern, though each, when looked at for its own sake, was seen to be terrifyingly com-plex and pulsating with repressed life, so marvellous that one had to pause in awe as before an animal crouching tense and still, about to spring.

But once, when she was lying beside her dog like that, it struck her: giants must be like this, with mountains and valleys and forests of hair on their chests, and songbirds among the trees in those hairy forests, and tiny lice on the songbirds, and . . . she could not follow the thought any further, but it might go on like that for ever, here too each thing fitting within the other, so tightly fitted into it that the only reason it stayed still, it seemed, was that it was under the pressure of such great and potent order. And secretly she thought: if the giants grew angry, all this would suddenly fly apart in all directions, screaming, overwhelming one, over-brimming like some terrifying cornucopia . . . and if it were to fall upon her, raging with love, it would be like thundering mountains and roaring trees, and tiny wind-blown hairs would grow on her body, crawling with tiny insects, and there would be a voice shrieking in ecstasy because of the ineffable wonder of it all, and her breath would be like a multitude of animals enveloping everything, engulfing the world.

And then, when she noticed that her own breathing made her small pointed breasts rise and fall in the same rhythm as the rising and falling of the shaggy chest beside her, suddenly she felt a sharp dismay and held her breath lest something happen, she did not know what. But when she could not maintain the effort any longer and had to let her breath continue to rise and fall that way, as though that other living creature were slowly drawing it out of her, breath after breath, she closed her eyes and returned to thinking of the giants: it was an uneasy procession of images behind her shut eyelids, but now much nearer to her, and warm as though low clouds were passing over her.

And when she opened her eyes again, much later, every-thing was just as it had been, only that the dog was now standing beside her, looking at her. And now she suddenly became aware of something protruding from under his meer-schaum-yellow coat, a pointed thing, red and crooked as though in voluptuous pain, and in the moment when she tried to get up she felt the warm, flickering caress of his tongue on her face. And then she had been so strangely paralysed, as though . . . as though she were an animal herself, and in spite of the ghastly fear that came upon her something in her cringed and was burning hot, as though now, at any moment . . . like the crying of birds and a fluttering of wings in a hedge, and then a quieting down, soft as the sound of feathers sliding upon feathers. . . .

That was how it had been, that time long ago, and this now was just the same strangely hot shock of fear, so that she recognised it for what it was. For hard though it is to know what a feeling is, this at least she could tell: now, after so many years, she had felt exactly the same fear as then.

And there stood Johannes, who was going away this very day. And here she stood. It was thirteen or fourteen years since all that had happened, and her breasts were no longer so pointed, so inquisitively red-beaked; they had dropped a little and were now faintly mournful, like two paper hats abandoned on a wide floor—for her chest had broadened and it was as though the very space surrounding her had grown away from her. But she was aware of this less from seeing it in the looking-glass—for it was a long time since, being naked, in her bath or changing her clothes, she had done anything but mechanically go through the necessary motions —than from a feeling. It seemed to her that formerly she had been able to lock herself tight in her clothes, armouring herself on every side, whereas now she merely covered herself with them. And when she thought about her sense of her bodily self, she realised that in earlier days she had had an awareness of herself emanating from within, a sense of being something like a round, tense drop of water; and now for a long time she had been like a small puddle, soft-edged, on the ground. So flattened, so slack and inelastic this feeling was that it would have amounted to no more than sluggishness and torpor had it not been for something else, something incomparably soft in her that very slowly, and with a thousand gingerly caressing folds, clung to her from within.

Surely there had been a time when she had been closer to life and had felt it more distinctly, as though touching it with her own hands, feeling it bodily. But for a long time now she had ceased to know what it was like; all she knew was that at some point in time something had come between her and life, leaving a barrier between. And she had never known what it was, whether a dream or some day-time sense of creeping anxiety, whether there had been something she had seen that had frightened her or if it was just that she was afraid of seeing things with her own eyes. She had not known it until today. For in the meantime her dim everyday existence had overlaid those old impressions and blurred them as even a light persistent breeze blots out traces in sand. Only the monotony of it had been with her, a sort of humming within her, now fainter, now louder. She no longer knew any intense pleasure or intense suffering; there was nothing that stood out in relief from the rest of her life, and gradually it had all become a mere blur. The days went by one like the other; and, one like the other, the years advanced. She still could feel that each year took something away from her and added something to her and that she was slowly changing with them; yet none of them stood out distinct from the others. Her sense of herself was now vague and fluid, and when she probed her own being all she could discover was the shifting of veiled, indefinite forms, as if she were touching something that stirred under a blanket, without being able to identify it. Gradually it became more and more as though she were living under a woollen blanket herself, or under a bell-shaped cover made of thin horn, which was becoming more and more opaque. Things around her were retreating further and further into the distance, losing their individual features, and her sense of herself seemed to be sinking into the distance too. Between her feelings and herself there was now a vast empty space, and in this void her body lived; it recognised the things around it, it smiled, it was animate, but whatever happened was without coherence or meaning, and often now a gluey disgust oozed soundlessly through this world of hers, smearing all sensations as with a mask of pitch.

And it was only when this strange emotion began to work in her, which had reached its peak today, that she had begun to wonder whether everything might not yet be again the way it had once been. And later she had even wondered whether this might not be love. Love? A long time it would have been on the way, and slow in coming; slow it would have been on its way. And yet even such slowness was too swift for the rhythm of her life; for the rhythm of her life was slower still, it was very slow, it was now no more than a languid opening and closing of the eyes, with, in the interval, a momentary glance that could not focus on things, that slid off and away from them, slid slowly away, untouched by anything. It was with such a gaze that she had seen it coming, and that was why she could not believe it was love.

She dreaded him as obscurely as she dreaded all things alien to her, an aversion without the sharp edge of hatred, merely as if he were a distant country beyond the frontier where one's own land merges softly and mournfully with the sky. But since that time she realised that all happiness had gone out of her life because something made her feel abhorrence of all that was not herself; and whereas formerly she had felt like someone who does not know the inner meaning of her own actions, now it seemed to her that she had merely forgotten that meaning and might perhaps begin to remember it. And the notion of something marvellous that would then come about tormented her like a memory drifting just below the surface of consciousness—a sense of something important she had forgotten. And all this began at the time of Johannes' return, when in the very first instant she recalled, without knowing why, how Demeter had once struck him and how Johannes had smiled.

Since then she felt as if someone had come who possessed whatever it was she lacked, carrying it with him as he went quietly on his way through the twilit wilderness of her life. It was simply that he was there, going on his way, and that as he looked at things they slowly and falteringly began to fall into a pattern before her eyes. It seemed to her sometimes, when he smiled in a startled way at himself, that it was as if he were breathing the world in and holding it in his body, feeling it within him, and then when he set it down before him again, very gently and carefully, he appeared to her like a circus-performer juggling with his hoops all alone, just for himself; it was no more than that. And yet it was anguish to her, in the intensity of her own unseeing imagination, to think how beautiful everything might well be for him; she was jealous of something she merely imagined he might be feeling. For although the ordered picture of the world continually crumbled away under her gaze, and although what she felt for things was only the avid love that a mother feels for a child she lacks the strength to guide, still, at times now her languor would begin to vibrate like a string, like a note sounding at once deep within the ear and somewhere in the world, rising in a great vault, kindling a light . . . a light and people whose gestures were a long-drawn yearning, lines extending far, far away and meeting far, far away in the infinite.

He said these were ideals, and that gave her the courage to believe it might all come true. And perhaps all she was doing was trying to stand up straight: but it was still painful, as if her body were sick and incapable of supporting her.

And it was then too that all her other memories began to come back to her, all except one. They all came, and she did not know why, and only had a vague sense that one was still missing and that it was only for the sake of that one missing memory that all the others had come. And the idea grew in her that Johannes might be able to help her to find it, and that her whole life depended on remembering this one forgotten thing. And she also realised that what gave her the feeling was not some strength in him, but his quietness, his weakness, that quiet invulnerable weakness of his that was a vast background to all he did, an empty landscape where he was alone with whatever happened to him. But that was as far as her understanding would take her, and she was perturbed and she suffered because whenever she thought herself close to recovering that memory, all she remembered was an animal. What often came to her mind when she thought of Johannes was animals—or Demeter—and she obscurely felt that he and she had a common enemy and tempter in Demeter. For her he was like a huge, rampant growth overshadowing her memory, sucking the strength out of it. And she did not know whether all this was caused by the thing she had forgotten or whether it was a hint of some meaning that must yet take on shape. Was *this* love? Something in her was on the move; something was drawing her onward. She herself did not know what it was. It was like walking along a road apparently towards a destination, but with a premonition that gradually made one's footsteps falter—a premonition that at some point before the end one would suddenly find an entirely different road and recognise it for one's own.

But he did not understand that; he did not know how difficult it was for her, this wavering sense of a life that was to arise for him and her, based on something still quite unknown to her, whereas he desired her in all simple reality as his wife or lover. She could not comprehend that; to her it seemed meaningless and at that moment almost vile. She had never experienced any direct and simple desire; but never at any other time had men seemed to her so absolutely a mere pretext, one that no time should be wasted on, a token of something else that was no more than elusively embodied in them. And suddenly she withdrew into herself and crouched there in her own darkness, staring at him, and with amazement, for the first time, felt this withdrawal to be like a sensual contact and abandoned herself to it with a lecherous awareness of doing so right before his eyes and yet out of his reach. Something in her bristled, soft and electric as a cat's fur—bristled with antagonism to him. And she let her 'no' roll out of her hiding-place, right to his feet, following it with her eyes as if it were a little glittering marble. . . . And then, when he was about to crush it under his heel, she screamed.

And now, when there at last the leave-taking was, erect and inexorable between them, walking between them as they walked together for the last time, all at once it happened: suddenly, fully defined and clear, that utterly lost, forgotten thing came back to Veronica's memory. She recognised it only with her feelings, without knowing how she did so, and she was a shade disappointed because there was nothing in it to tell her why it mattered; but it was like entering into a refreshing coolness.

She could feel that once before in her life something about Johannes had given her a sudden fright just like this; but she could not understand what the connection was, why it should have meant so much to her, or what it was to mean for the future—only it all at once seemed as if she were again in the same point on her road, at the very place where she had lost him once before. And she realised that here and now, at this moment, the real experience, her experience of the real Johannes, had passed its zenith and was over.

At this moment she felt as if everything were falling apart. Although they were standing close together, for her things were all at a slant, so that he and she seemed to be sliding further and further away from each other. Veronica looked at the trees by the side of the road, and they seemed to be standing straighter and stiffer than was natural. And only now did she feel the full weight of the 'no' she had uttered in bewilderment and merely in premonition of all this, and realised that it was because of that 'no' that he was going away, without wanting to go. And for a while she felt inwardly as deep and heavy as if there were two bodies lying beside each other, each body separate and sad, and each of them merely what it was in itself; and she knew it was because what she felt had almost turned into abandonment after all. And something came over her that made her small and weak, reducing her almost to nothingness, until she was like a small dog whimpering and limping on three legs, or like a tattered pennant fluttering but droopingly in a very faint breath of wind: so utterly did it dissolve her. And there was a yearning in her to hold him—a yearning that was like the softness of a broken-shelled snail faintly twitching in its search for another, yearning to stick to it tightly even as it dies.

But then she looked at him, and she herself hardly knew what she was thinking, except for an inkling that the only thing she did know about it all—this sudden memory that was there now, lying in her all shining, solitary—was very far from being anything that had a meaning in itself: it was something that some great fear had once prevented from coming to perfection, and since then it had lain within her, hardened and encapsulated, blocking the way for something that might have developed in her, and it must fall out of her like a foreign body. For even now her feeling for Johannes was beginning to ebb and flow away from her—something that had long lain as though dead, impotent, captive beneath that feeling, had broken loose, a broad liberating flood that swept the feeling away with it. And instead of her feeling for Johannes, something else, far in the distances at last revealed within her, grew like a dome, a radiance floating into the heights, effortlessly, unendingly exalted, a random glitter apprehended as if through webs of dream.

And the talk that was going on between their outer selves grew halting, their interchanges briefer. And while they were still struggling with it, Veronica could feel how in the gaps between their words it was turning into something else, and she realised with finality that he had to go away, and she said no more. All they had been saying and trying to say seemed to her futile, since it was decided that he must go and would never return. And because she realised that she no longer had any wish at all to do what she might perhaps otherwise even now have done, whatever was left of it all abruptly assumed a rigid and incomprehensible look. She knew of no meaning and no reason for this sudden change; it was a quick, hard fact, definite as a cast die.

And as he was still standing there before her amid the tangle of his words, she began to feel how inadequate his presence was, how irrelevant it was that he was really there with her. The reality of it weighed heavily on something in her that was striving to soar and bear away with it the memory of him. At every point she was impeded by his living presence as one might stumble against a dead body, stiff and hostile in its resistance to any effort to shift it. And when she noticed how intently he was still gazing at her, Johannes seemed like a big animal that was lying upon her in exhaustion and which she could not shake off. And once more she felt that memory of hers within her like a small hot object that she clutched tight in her hands, and suddenly something almost made her put out her tongue at him—a sensation strangely midway between flight and enticement, almost like a she-animal's reaction when, hard-pressed, she snaps at her pursuer.

Now the wind began to rise again, and on it her feelings widened out, floating free of all that was hard, resistant, and full of hate—not that she abandoned that, but it went deep down into her, drawn in like something very soft, until there was nothing left of it but a forlorn dismay in which she seemed to be wrapped: and it was as if in leaving it behind she also left herself behind. And everything else, all around her, was tremulous with premonitions. The opacity that had hitherto lain heavily upon her life, like a dark mist, was now stirring. It was as if the outlines of objects long sought in vain had become recognisable through a veil, only to vanish again. And although nothing of this appeared so clearly that her fingers could have grasped it, everything sliding away elusively between the quiet, fumbling words she and Johannes spoke while here was nothing really to say, yet all the words that must now remain unspoken seemed already visible from a long way off, like things in a landscape seen from a high promontory, and all shone with that queerly vibrant meaning which condenses everyday events into significance when they are re-enacted on a stage, rising up as pointers along some road not delineated on flat and stony ground. What had spread over the world was like a very sheer silken mask, bright and silver-grey, flickering as though at any moment it might tear. And she kept her gaze fixed on it until her eyes dazzled, unable to focus, as if she were being shaken by gusts of some invisible force.

So they stood side by side. And as the wind came blowing more and more strongly along the road and was like some marvellously soft and fragrant animal laying itself upon things, on her face, on the nape of her neck, in her armpits . . . breathing everywhere, its soft velvety fur overlaying everything and, at every breath she drew, pressing tighter on her skin . . . both her horror and her expectation dissolved in a languid warmth that began to circle round her, mute and blind and slow, like blood blown by the wind. And suddenly she could not help thinking of something she had once been told: that millions of infinitesimal living entities have their habitation on every human being and that with every drawn breath and every breath exhaled there are incalculable rivers of life that come and go. She lingered for an instant in astonishment at this thought, feeling a warmth and a darkness as though being borne along in a huge crimson wave. But then she sensed another presence within this sweltering bloodstream.

She looked up, and there he stood before her, his hair blown towards her in the wind, the quivering tips of it almost touching her own. And now she was overtaken by a wild, shrieking desire that was like two swarms of birds plunging and intermingling as they fly, and she would gladly have torn her life out of her body and poured it all over him out of the sheltering, burning darkness of drunken turmoil. But their bodies stood there stiff and unyielding, with closed eyes, merely allowing it all to happen secretly, as though they must not know of it. And they grew more and more tired and empty, stooping slightly, and then it was all very gentle and quiet and there was a deep and tender hush as though they were silently bleeding to death, the blood running into each other's veins.

And as the wind rose it seemed to her as though his blood were mounting from the earth on which they stood, mounting under her skirts, filling her body with stars and chalices, blue and yellow, and there was a light touch as of delicate tendrils and a very still, voluptuous delight such as flowers may feel when they conceive by the wind.

And when the sun was setting, sending its rays through the hem of her skirts, she was still standing there, quiescent and without a word and abandoned to this light, as shameless as though she knew everyone could see. And as in some far off oblivion she had a sense, even now, of that greater yearning which was yet to be fulfilled. But at this moment all that was as muted and sad as if far, far off there were bells ringing. And so the two of them stood there, side by side, grave and tall—two enormous animals, their backs bowed, outlined against the evening sky.

The sun had set. Veronica walked back, alone and meditative, along the path between meadows and fields.

From this leave-taking, as though from a broken husk on the ground, there had risen a sense of her own existence; it was suddenly so firm and solid that she felt like a knife plunged into that other person's life. Everything was clearly defined: he had gone away and was going to kill himself. She did not question it; it was simply a thing as majestically oppressive as some ponderous, dark form lying on the earth. It seemed as irrevocable as a dividing-line sliced through time, with everything that was previous to it eternally fixed and petrified. This day leapt out from the row of all the other days with the sudden flash of a drawn sword; indeed, it was as if she positively could see her soul's relationship to that other soul, a relationship that had now become final and unalterable, before her in mid-air like the broken branch of a tree pointing upwards into eternity.

At moments she felt tenderness for Johannes, to whom she owed this; and then again she would feel nothing, only the sense of her own walking. What urged her on was the knowledge that her destiny was solitude and nothing else; and with this she walked on between meadows and fields.

The world grew small in the dusk. And gradually Veronica began to be borne along by a strange pleasure that was like cruelly thin air: she inhaled it with twitching nostrils till it filled her lungs and buoyed her up; her arms reached out into the distance, and her steps became so light that her feet lost touch with the ground and she was carried away high over the woods.

She felt so volatile, she was almost sick with delight. Nor did this tension release her until she put her hand on the outer door of the house. It was a small, solid, rounded door. When she locked it after her it was like an impenetrable barrier, and she stood in the darkness as though at the bottom of a still, subterranean pool of water. Slowly she took a few paces ahead, feeling the proximity of the cool enclosing walls, though she did not touch them. It was a queerly secret, furtively-familiar feeling; she knew that now she was home.

Then she quietly did all that she had to do, and the day drew to its end like all the other days. From time to time the thought of Johannes loomed up among her other thoughts, and then she would glance at the clock and guess where he must be by now. Once, however, she made an effort not to think of him for a long time, and when she did think of him again she realised that now the train must be travelling through the mountain valleys southwards into the night, and an unknown landscape shut her out, leaving her behind in darkness.

She went to bed and soon fell asleep. But she slept lightly and impatiently as someone for whom the next day there is something extraordinary in store. Under her eyelids there was a perpetual radiance, and towards morning it grew still brighter, seeming to expand, until it became immeasurably vast. When Veronica awoke she knew: it was the sea.

By now he must be in sight of the sea, and there was nothing more that he need do except carry out his resolve. She imagined that he would take a boat and row far out and —then there would be a shot. But she did not know when this would be. She began guessing and trying to work it out in various ways. Would he go straight from the railway-station to find a boat? Or would he wait until evening? Till evening, when the sea was a great expanse of utter calm, gazing at one as though with enormous eyes? All day she went about in such uneasiness that it was as though her skin were all the time being pricked with tiny pins. Now and then, from here or there—perhaps out of a gilded frame glittering on a wall, or out of the darkness of the stairwell, or out of the white linen that she was embroidering—Johannes' face would loom up. Pale, with purplish lips, bloated and distorted from being in the water. . . . Or merely a black lock of hair over a shattered forehead. And now and then she was invaded by drifting fragments of tenderness that came as though on the returning tide. And when it was evening she knew that now it must be over.

Yet somewhere in the remote depths of her being there was a vague thought that it was all senseless: this expectation of hers and this way in which she was treating things unknown to her as though they were reality. From time to time the notion would flit through her mind that Johannes was not dead, and it was as if something were snatching at a large soft blanket, and for an instant such a fragment of reality would leap up, only to collapse again. Then she would feel the evening outside gliding around the house, and felt how silent and how ordinary it all was. And it was like thinking: Once there was a night; it came and went. She knew it. But then this feeling died away. Slowly a profound peace sank over her, and a sense of mystery, sinking in innumerable folds.

And so the night came, this one night of her life when all that had ever taken form under the twilit blanket of the long malaise that her existence was, all that had been dammed off from reality, became like a drop of acid corroding everything, spreading into weird patterns of unimaginable experience; and now at long last it had the force to break through into her consciousness.

Driven by some urge that she could not account for, she lit all the candles in her room and sat there among them, unmoving in the centre of it. Then she took out a portrait of Johannes and set it before her. But it no longer seemed that what she had been waiting for had anything to do with Johannes and his fate; nor did it seem to be within her either, as anything she imagined. What she all at once realised was that it was some sense of her surroundings that had changed, expanding into an unknown territory halfway between dream and waking.

The space between herself and the objects around her

ceased to be emptiness; instead there was a strange network of relations. All the objects were in their places—the table, the wardrobe, the clock on the wall—as solidly there as though nothing could ever shift them; and they were all as though heavily loaded with themselves, distinct from her and as firmly locked into themselves as a clenched fist. And yet at moments it was as though they were within her, or they gazed at her as if they had eyes, gazing out of some space that lay like a sheet of glass between herself and her room. And they were there as though for many years they had been waiting only for this one evening in order to find themselves, curving and bulging, arching high, with something emanating from them that was a kind of excess—until the sense of the moment rose like a hollow cube around Veronica and she herself became a silent room full of flickering candles, herself a room enclosing everything. And sometimes she was overcome with exhaustion after so much tension, and then it seemed that she was no more than a shining; and a radiance would flare up in her limbs, and she would feel it like a weight upon her and grow tired under the load of her own being, as one grows tired in the circle of light under a softly humming lamp. And her thoughts moved through this radiance and out into the bright sleepiness, like thin-tipped tendrils, a now visible pattern of delicate capillaries. And everything became more and more silent; veils sank about her, softly as drifts of snow floating down before the illumined windows of her conscious mind; and now and then there was a crackling, jagged flash of great light. . . . But after a while she rose once more to the limits of this strangely tense state of wakefulness, and all at once she had the distinct awareness: this is what Johannes is like now, he is within this other dimension of reality, within this kind of transformed space.

Children and dead people have no souls. But the soul that living people have is what prevents them from loving, no matter how much they may want to; it is that which, in all love, withholds a residue. Veronica was in this moment aware that the thing that cannot be given away by even the greatest love is the very thing that endues all emotions with direction, steering them away from whatever clings to them with timorous faith, the one thing that endues all emotions with something that is inaccessible to even the most dear beloved: something that is always ready to turn away and leave. It is something that even as it comes towards the beloved will smile and, as though keeping some secret pledge, turn and glance back the other way. But children and dead people are either not yet anything or no longer anything, and so it seems possible to believe that they may yet become everything, or that they have been it; they are like the hollowed-out reality of empty vessels, lending their shape to dreams. Children and dead people have no soul—no soul of such a kind. Nor have animals. To Veronica animals were terrifying, a menace in their ugliness; yet in their eyes there was that pin-bright glint of here and now, the falling droplet of oblivion.

To those who are searching without any definite aim the soul is something like that. All her sombre life long Veronica had been in dread of one kind of love and had yearned for another kind; in dreams it is sometimes the way she yearned for it to be. The things that really happen take their course in the full strength of what they are, hugely, draggingly, and yet like something that is within the person to whom they happen. It hurts, but just the way it does when one hurts oneself; it is humiliating, yet a humiliation like that floats away like a cloud drifting nowhere, and there is no one there to see it; such a humiliation floats like the blissful floating of a dark cloud. . . . So she wavered between Johannes and Demeter. . . . And dreams are not within one, nor are they rags and tatters of reality; somewhere there is a totality of feeling where they are at home and grow high, arching into a dome, hovering, weightless, like one fluid in another. In dreams one abandons oneself to a beloved the way one fluid merges with another; there is an altered sense of space, for the awakened soul is a hollow space within space and cannot ever be filled—the soul causes the space around it to warp and become like ice that is full of bubbles.

Veronica could now recall that she had sometimes dreamed. Never before tonight had she realised that. All she had known was that at times when she had wakened it had been as if she had become accustomed to some other rhythm, and she had then collided with the confining walls of her conscious mind; and yet somewhere there was a chink through which she could still see brightness . . . only a chink, yet she could sense the vastness of the space that lay beyond. And now it occurred to her that she must have dreamt often. And she gazed through the substance of her waking life and saw the life and pattern of her dreams, just as with the returning memory of conversations and actions long ago there also returns the memory of a pattern of emotions and thoughts that has long been overlaid. It is as one may often have remembered words that were spoken in the past, and then, after many years, one suddenly recalls too that all during that conversation there had been bells chiming, chiming. . . . Such were the talks she had had with Johannes, and such with Demeter. And underlying all those spoken words she now began to recognise the dog, the rooster, and a clenched fist striking a face. . . . And then there was Johannes speaking of God. Slowly, clingingly, as a snail moves, his words slid over it all.

Veronica too had always known, somewhere in the realm of all that is indifferent: there is an animal, its skin malodorous, loathsomely slimy, an animal that everyone knows. But in her mind it was merely a restless, vaguely outlined dark thing that sometimes went sliding along under her waking consciousness, or a forest, endless and tender as a man asleep.

In her it had nothing of the animal about it, except for certain lines of its effect upon her soul, as it were lines extended beyond their proper length. . . . And then Demeter would say: 'I only need to bend down' . . . and Johannes would say, right in the middle of the day: 'Something in me has sunk deeper, grown longer'. . . . And there would be a very soft, pallid wish in her that Johannes might be dead.

And—in some vague way, even while she was still awake —there was a mad, quiet way she had of looking at him when she would let her glances slide softly into him like needles, deeper and deeper, a way of watching to see whether some tremor of his smile, some twist of his lips, some tormented gesture, might not all at once be as a gift offered to her, as though someone dead were rising before her in all the incalculable fullness of life suddenly become real. Then his hair was a thicket and his fingernails were large glimmering discs. She saw fluid clouds in the whites of his eyes, and small mirroring pools. He lay there before her as hideous as if his body were wide open to her, with frontiers all disarmed; but his soul was still hidden in some ultimate feeling that was a feeling only of itself. And if he spoke of God, she would think: By 'God' he meant that *other* feeling, perhaps the feeling of some dimension in which he would wish to live.

Those thoughts of hers were a sign of something diseased in her. But besides this she also thought: Surely an animal would be like that other dimension, gliding past so very close, like things seen through water in one's eyes, spreading in large vague patterns, and yet small and far off when one regards it as something exterior to oneself. Why is it right in a fairy-tale to think in this way of animals that keep guard over princesses? Was that morbid? In this night she felt herself and these images all bright, floating upon a premonitory fear of going under again. Her waking life, that creeping life of hers by day, would once more founder. She knew that. And she saw that everything would then be disease, and full of impossibilities. But if she could manage to hold on to those details that went on growing longer and longer, holding them in her hand like bundles of sticks in spite of the repulsion they caused as soon as they became glued together into a real whole. . . . In this night her thoughts were able to reach the idea of a haleness that was tremendous as mountain air, a state in which she might master all her emotions with the utmost ease.

Like rings torn apart by some great tension this happiness went whirling through her mind. 'Now you are dead' was what her love dreamt, and all she meant by that was this strange feeling that had come between herself and the exterior world, a feeling in which the image of Johannes was alive for her. But the hot flickerings of the candlelight burnt their reflections into her lips. And all that happened in this night was no more than such a shining reflection of reality, and, flickering somewhere in her body and seeping away between fragments of her feelings, it cast its vague shadows into the outer world. Then it was as if she could feel Johannes very close to her, just as close to her as she was herself. He was subject then to all her wishes, and her tenderness passed through him unimpeded as the waves pass through those soft, crimson medusas that float in the sea. But at moments her love merely lay as a wide and unmeaning expanse upon him like the sea, exhausted now, and sometimes as the sea perhaps lay over his corpse now, huge and gentle as a cat purring tenderly in its dreams. And then the hours poured like murmuring water. . . .

And even as she started up she felt grief for the first time. There was coolness in the air, the candles had burnt down, and only one was still giving light. In the place where Johannes had been used to sit there was now a gaping hole in the room, and all her thoughts could not fill it up. And suddenly even the last candle went out too, silently, like a last departing guest shutting the door softly after him. Veronica was alone in darkness.

Small, humble sounds went straying through the house, the stairs heaved timorously, shaking off the pressure of the footsteps that had passed over them, and somewhere a mouse nibbled, and then there was the ticking of a deathwatch beetle in the wainscot. When somewhere a clock chimed, she began to be afraid. She was afraid of the unceasing life of this thing that, while she was sleepless with fatigue, went busily, unrestingly, through all the rooms, audible now through the ceiling, now through the floor, from far below. Like a killer who will strike his victim blow after blow, stabbing and slashing without knowing what he is doing, striking simply because something goes on jerking and twitching, she would gladly have seized hold of that unceasing faint sound and have choked it into silence. And all at once she was aware of her aunt asleep, in that room right at the back of the house, her stern, leathery face all wrinkles; and all the furniture stood there dark and heavy and flaccid; and once more she felt afraid of this alien life closing in around her.

Yet there was something—scarcely a real support, merely something that made her sink more slowly, sinking with her—that still held her. She had begun dimly to realise that it was not Johannes but herself that she experienced with such palpable sensuality. And by now her imaginings were overlaid by a resistance that came to her from the day's reality, from shame, from her aunt's matter-of-fact talk, from Demeter's scorn: a constriction, a closing down, now even an abhorrence of Johannes, a vague, increasing compulsion to take it all like a sleepless night. And even that long-sought-for memory seemed to have slipped stealthily away during these hours, until now it lay far off in the distance, once more tiny and insignificant, without ever having caused even the smallest change in her life. But just as a man will go about his business, pale and with dark rings under his eyes, after things have happened that he would never speak of to anyone, and feel his oddity and weakness amid all that is strong and reasonable in life as something like the thin thread of a quietly meandering tune: so it was with Veronica. Despite her grief there was a faint, teasing delight within her, which hollowed out her body until it became soft and tender, the merest husk around her.

Suddenly she felt an urge to undress: just for herself, just for the sake of feeling close to herself, alone with herself in a darkened room. The quiet rustle of her clothes sinking to the floor excited her. It was tenderness that went out from her body, as though venturing a few paces into the darkness, perhaps in search of someone, and then faltered and hurried back to cling to the body that it belonged to. And when Veronica picked up her clothes again, slowly, with lingering pleasure in the action, these skirts that still held in their dark folds the little pools of her body's warmth encased her, swelling out like bells, rotund dark caverns, hiding-places where she lurked; and when now and then her body secretly pressed against these coverings around it a tremulous ripple of sensuality went through it, like a hidden light moving restlessly through a house behind closed shutters.

It was this room. Involuntarily Veronica's gaze turned to the place where the looking-glass hung on the wall, but she could not find her own image. She saw nothing . . . perhaps a vague and sliding gleam in the darkness, but even that might have been an illusion. Darkness filled the house like a heavy liquid. It seemed that she herself was nowhere in it. She began to walk about, but everywhere there was only this darkness, nowhere herself; and yet she felt nothing but herself, and wherever she went she both was and was not, just as unuttered words are sometimes really there while silence reigns.

So it was that she had once talked with angels when she lay ill. They had stood around her bed, and from their wings, even though they did not move, there came a high, thin, sustained note that cut through everything. And all things fell apart then like brittle stone, and the whole world lay there before her, sharp-edged, like broken sea-shells, and only she remained whole, drawing herself ever more tightly into her own body. Consumed by fever, fine-drawn and thin as a withered rose-petal, she felt herself to have become transparent; and she felt as though her body were everywhere at once and at the same time contracted to such minuteness that it was as if she were holding it in her own tightly shut hand. And all around her stood those men with rustling wings—a faint crackle as of hair standing on end. For the others nothing of all this seemed to be there; they were shut out from it by that high, thin ringing, as by a glittering trellis through which one can see out but no one can see in. And Johannes spoke to her, the way one speaks to people who must be treated with indulgence and whom one does not take seriously. And in the next room Demeter was pacing up and down; she could hear his scornful footsteps and his huge, hard voice. And all the time she felt only that angels were there, standing around her, men with marvellously plumed hands, and while the others thought she was ill, they themselves, wherever they were, seemed to be outside, kept out by a magic circle drawn around her. And at that time it seemed to her she had achieved everything in the world. But it was only a fever, and when it passed off she realised that it must be so.

Now, however, there was a touch of that bygone illness in the sensual feelings she had about herself. Carefully withdrawing into herself, making herself small, she avoided touching the objects in the room, feeling their presence even from a distance. There was a quiet ebbing away of hope, collapse in which all that was exterior became as though burst wide open, empty, and beyond it everything became soft and still as behind curtains of mouldering silk. Gradually a mild, grey early-morning light began to fill the house. She stood at the window upstairs, watching the break of day, the people going to market. Now and then a word struck upwards, towards her, and then she would lean back into the gloom as though to avoid it.

And softly something wrapped itself round Veronica: a yearning without goal or desire, aimless as the dim aching in her womb before the recurring days. Strange thoughts crossed her mind: to love herself and only herself like this—it was like being able to do anything at all in front of some other person; and when among these thoughts the memory forced its way up—now like a hard, hideous face—the memory that she had killed Johannes, it no longer frightened her. She only caused pain to herself when she saw him; it was like seeing herself from inside, full of loathsomeness and intestines coiled like big worms. At the same time she could see herself looking at herself like that, and it was horror to her. Yet even in this horror of herself there was something ineradicable that pertained to love.

She was overcome now by a liberating fatigue and, drooping, she was wrapped in what she had done as in cool fur, all mournful and caressing, a stillness where she was all by herself, a gentle, gleaming light . . . as though even in her pain there were something that she loved, and even in grief she smiled.

And the brighter the day grew, the more it seemed improbable that Johannes could be dead: that was no more now than a hushed companionship from which she was abstracting herself. With no more than the remotest relevance to him, in which she herself did not believe, it was as if some last frontier dividing them had opened wide. She felt a lustful softness and an ineffable nearness, a proximity less of the body than of the soul. It was as if she were gazing at herself out of his eyes and with every movement feeling not only herself being touched by him but also in some indescribable way his sense of touching her; it was like a mysterious spiritual union. At some moments she thought to herself that he was her guardian angel. He had come and gone again after she had perceived his presence, and yet henceforth he would always be with her, he would be watching her when she undressed, and wherever she went she would carry him next to her body, under her skirts; and his gaze would be as gentle as a persistent faint weariness. She did not think this or feel this about the real Johannes, who was a matter of indifference to her; rather it was something wanly grey and tense in her, and her wandering thoughts stood out against it in relief, like dark figures brightly outlined against a wintry sky. What she reached was a mere fringe of something, all groping tenderness. It was a quiet state of being singled out and lifted up . . . a sense of becoming stronger and yet of being not there at all . . . it was nothing and yet everything. . . .

She sat quite still, toying with her thoughts. There is a world that is aloof and apart from this, a different world . . . or perhaps only a sadness . . . like walls painted by fever and delusions, and between those walls the words spoken by the sane and healthy have no resonance, but fall to the ground, meaningless . . . like carpets on which they cannot walk, so heavy is their tread. A very thin, echoing world she was walking through with him, and on all she did there silence followed, and all she thought went sliding on for ever, like a whispering in a maze of corridors.

And when at last it was broad daylight, a clear and pallid day, the letter came—such a letter as had been bound to come. Veronica realised that at once: this letter had been bound to come. There was a thundering at the door that went tearing through the silence of the house as a great boulder crashes through a thin blanket of snow. Through the open door wind and light swept in.

The letter said: 'What are you that I did not kill myself?

I am like one who has found his way out into the street. I have got out and cannot go back. The bread I eat, the dark brown boat hauled up on the beach, the boat that was to take me out to sea, everything around me, all that is muted, blurred, all the plenitude of warmth, the flux, the noisiness and aliveness around me—it all holds me fast. We shall talk about this. Everything is outside, quite simple and unrelated, all loosely heaped like a pile of rubble, but it holds me, I am like a post rammed into the ground and taking root again. . . .'

There were other things in the letter as well, but she could see only this: 'I have found the way out into the street.' And though it had been bound to happen, there was also, even if scarcely perceptible, a hint of derision in that callous leap into safety, away from her. It was nothing, nothing at all, merely as when there is a sudden chill in the air at dawn and someone begins to talk in a loud voice because it is now day. For everything had happened, once and for all, to him who had come soberly to his senses and was henceforth an onlooker. From that moment on, for a long time, Veronica neither thought nor felt anything; around her there was nothing but a fast, gleaming tranquillity on which no ripple stirred, pale and lifeless as ponds lying silent in early morning light.

When she roused herself to thought again, it was once more as if she were under a heavy cloak that hindered her movements; and her thoughts became confused, like hands struggling senselessly with a covering they cannot throw off. She could not find the way into simple reality. That he had not shot himself did not become the fact that he was alive; it turned into something within herself, something that grew dumb, sinking down into the depths. Something in her grew dumb and sank away again, down into that murmurous multitudinous clamour out of which it had only just risen. Now all at once she again heard those voices on every side.

It was that narrow corridor through which she had once gone running, and then crawling, until there was the place where it widened out, and there was a quiet rising and a standing erect; and now it had closed in on her again. In spite of the silence she felt as though there were people all round her, talking to each other all the time in low voices. She could not distinguish what they were saying. There was something wonderfully mysterious in not understanding what they were saying to each other. Her senses were stretched taut like very thin membranes, and those voices, beating against them, rustled like twigs in a tangled thicket.

Unknown faces loomed up. They were all faces she did not know: she was well aware that they were her aunt, her girl friends, acquaintances, Demeter, Johannes . . . and yet they remained the faces of strangers. Suddenly she was afraid of them, like someone in fear of being treated with much severity. She made an effort to think of Johannes, but she could no longer even imagine what he had looked like only a few hours earlier. His face blurred and merged with the others. She recalled that he had gone away from her, was far away, lost as in a crowd, and she could not shake off the feeling that from somewhere in that crowd his hidden eyes were watching her with a cunning look. She drew herself together, to make herself very small, to be invisible to that gaze. She tried to close herself up. But all she could feel was a faint and gradually dissolving awareness of herself.

And then by degrees she lost the sense of ever having been anything else. She could scarcely distinguish herself any longer from other people, and all these faces were now hardly distinguishable from each other, emerging and again merging with each other; they were repulsive to her as unkempt hair, and yet she entangled herself in them, she spoke in answer to words of theirs that she could not understand, and her only need was to keep herself busy. There was a restlessness in her that was trying to get out from under her skin,

bursting out like thousands of tiny animals. And ever anew
the old faces loomed up and the whole house was filled with
this restlessness.

She jumped up and walked a few steps. And suddenly all
was silence. She called out, and nothing answered. She
called out once again, and she could scarcely hear herself.
She gazed around her questingly, and there was everything
standing in its place as always, motionless. And all she could
feel was that she herself existed.

What came next was first of all a few short days through
which she lived as in a swoon. Sometimes she made a
desperate attempt to remember what it had been that she
had felt, that one time, as if it were something real, and what
it could have been that she had felt, that one time, as if it
were something real, and what it could have been that she
had done to make everything happen the way it had.

In these days Veronica roamed uneasily about the house;
sometimes she rose at night and wandered upstairs and
downstairs. But all she sensed was, now and then, the
whitewashed bareness as room after room mounted before
her in her candle's flickering light, with rags and tatters of
darkness still clinging to it; she sensed it as something that
stood tall and immobile against the walls and seemed to
scream with lust. When she imagined how the floor ran along
under her bare feet she would stop and for minutes on end
stand quite still, thinking, as though she were trying to focus
on a definite spot in a fast-running stream just below her.
Then her head would spin with all the thoughts that she
could no longer grasp. And only when her toes curled as in a
cramp, locking into the cracks between the floorboards and
coming into contact with the fine soft dust that lay there, or
when her soles felt the small rough patches of dirt on the
floor, she felt relieved, as if someone had slapped her naked
body.

Gradually she came to feel only what was present around her, and the memory of that night was of something she did not expect to experience again. The memory was only that shadow she had gained, a shadow of pure delight that fell on the reality in which she lived. Sometimes she would tiptoe to the door of the house, when it was locked for the night, and listen until she could hear the footsteps of a man walking past outside. The thought that she was standing there in nothing but a nightdress, almost naked in this loose garment that was open below, while outside a man walked past, so close, separated from her only by the thickness of a wooden board—this thought almost convulsed her. But what was for her most mysterious of all was that even out there there was some part of her too: for a ray of light from her candle fell through the narrow key-hole, and surely the trembling of her hand must send it quivering and flickering over the clothes of the passer-by.

And once, as she was standing like this, she suddenly thought of how she was now alone in the house with Demeter and his embrangled vices. It startled her. After this it happened that they would more often encounter each other on the stairs. They would pass the time of day and exchange a few non-committal words. Only once he stopped, close to her, and each of them searched for something else to say. Veronica looked at his knees, in his tight riding-breeches, and at his lips, which were like a short, wide, bleeding incision, and she wondered what Johannes would be like now that he would surely be coming back again. And at that very moment she saw the tip of Demeter's beard outlined— immeasurably huge—against a pallid window-pane. And after a while they went their separate ways, still without having spoken.

THREE WOMEN

Grigia

There is a time in life when everything perceptibly slows down, as though one's life were hesitating to go on or trying to change its course. It may be that at this time one is more liable to disaster.

Homo had an ailing little son. After this illness had dragged on for a year, without being dangerous, yet also without improving, the doctor prescribed a long stay at a spa; but Homo could not bring himself to accompany his wife and child. It seemed to him it would mean being separated too long from himself, from his books, his plans, and his life. He felt his reluctance to be sheer selfishness, but perhaps it was rather more a sort of self-dissolution, for he had never before been apart from his wife for even as much as a whole day; he had loved her very much and still did love her very much, but through the child's coming this love had become frangible, like a stone that water has seeped into, gradually disintegrating it. Homo was very astonished by this new quality his life had acquired, this frangibility, for to the best of his knowledge and belief nothing of the love itself had ever been lost, and during all the time occupied with preparations for their departure he could not imagine how he was to spend the approaching summer alone. He simply felt intense repugnance at the thought of spas and mountain resorts.

So he remained alone at home, and on the second day he received a letter inviting him to join a company that was about to re-open the old Venetian gold-mines in the Val Fersena. The letter was from a certain Mozart Amadeo

Hoffingott, whom he had met while travelling some years previously and with whom he had, during those few days, struck up a friendship.

Yet not the slightest doubt occurred to him whether the project was a sound one. He sent off two telegrams, one to tell his wife that he was, after all, leaving instantly and would send his address, the other accepting the proposal that he should join the company as its geologist and perhaps even invest a fairly large sum in the re-opening of the mines.

In P., a prosperous, compact little Italian town in the midst of mulberry-groves and vineyards, he joined Hoffingott, a tall, handsome, swarthy man of his own age who was always enormously active. He now learnt that the company was backed by immense American funds, and the project was to be carried out in great style. First of all a reconnaissance party was to go up the valley. It was to consist of the two of them and three other partners. Horses were bought, instruments were due to arrive any day, and workmen were being engaged.

Homo did not stay in the inn, but—he did not quite know why—in the house of an Italian acquaintance of Hoffingott's. There he was struck by three things. The beautiful mahogany beds were indescribably cool and soft. The wallpaper had an indescribably bewildering, maze-like pattern, at once banal and very strange. And there was a cane rocking-chair. Sitting in that chair, rocking and gazing at the wallpaper, one seemed to turn into a mere tangle of rising and falling tendrils that would grow within a couple of seconds from nothingness to their full size and then as rapidly disappear into themselves again.

In the streets the air was a blend of snow and the South. It was the middle of May. In the evening the place was lit by big arc-lights that hung from wires stretched across from house to house, so high that the streets below were like ravines of deep blue gloom, and there one picked one's way along, while away up in the universe there was a spinning and hissing of white suns. By day one looked out over vine-yards and woods. It was still all red, yellow, and green after the winter, and since the trees did not lose their leaves, the fading growth and the new were interlaced as in graveyard wreaths. Little red, blue, and pink villas still stood out very vividly among the trees, like scattered cubes inanimately manifesting to every eye some strange morphological law of which they themselves knew nothing. But higher up the woods were dark, and the mountain was called Selvot. Above the woods there was pasture-land, now still covered with snow, the broad, smooth, wavy lines of it running across the neighbouring mountains and up the steep little side-valley where the expedition was to go. When men came down from these mountains to sell milk and buy polenta, they sometimes brought great lumps of rock-crystal or amethyst, which was said to grow as profusely in many crevices up there as in other places flowers grow in the field, and these uncannily beautiful fairy-tale objects still further intensified his impression that behind the outward appearance of this district, this appearance that had the flickering remoteness and familiarity the stars sometimes have at night, there was hidden something that he yearningly awaited. When they rode into the mountain valley, passing Sant' Orsola at six o'clock, by a little stone bridge across a mountain rivulet overhung with bushes there were, if not a hundred, at least certainly a score of nightingales singing. It was broad daylight.

When they were well in the valley, they came to a fantastic place. It hung on the slope of a hill. The bridle-path that had brought them now began sheerly to leap from one huge flat boulder to the next, and flowing away from it, like streams meandering downhill, were a few short, steep lanes disappearing into the meadows. Standing on the bridle-path, one saw only forlorn and ramshackle cottages; but if one looked upward from the meadows below it was as though one had been transported back into a pre-historic lake-village built on piles, for the front of each house was supported on tall beams, and the privies floated out to one side of them like litters on four slender poles as tall as trees. Nor was the surrounding landscape without its oddities. It was a more than semicircular wall of high, craggy mountains sweeping down steeply into a crater in the centre of which was a smaller wooded cone, and the whole thing was like a gigantic empty pudding-mould with a little piece cut out of it by a deep-running brook, so that there it yawned wide open against the high flank of the slope on which the village hung. Below the snow-line there were corries, where a few deer strayed in the scrub, and in the woods crowning the round hill in the centre the blackcock were already displaying. The meadows on the sunny side were flowered with yellow, blue, and white stars, as big as thalers emptied out of a sack. But if one climbed another hundred feet or so beyond the village, one came to a small plateau covered with ploughed fields, meadows, hay-barns and a sprinkle of houses, with a little church, on a bastion that jutted over the valley, gazing out over the world that on fine days lay far beyond the valley like the sea beyond the mouth of a river: one could scarcely tell what was still the golden-yellow distance of the blessed plain and where the vague cloud-floors of the sky had begun.

It was a fine life they led there. All day one was up in the mountains, working at old blocked mine-shafts, or driving new ones into the mountainside, or down at the mouth of the valley where a wide road was to be built: and always one was in gigantic air that was already soft, pregnant with the imminent melting of the snow. They poured out money among the people and held sway like gods. They had something for them all to do, men and women alike. The men eyth organised into working parties and sent them up the mountains, where they had to spend the week; the women they used as porters, sending them in columns up the almost impassable mountainside, bringing provisions and spare parts. The stone schoolhouse was turned into a depot where their stores were kept and whence they were distributed. There a commanding male voice rapped out orders, summoning one by one the women who stood waiting and chattering, and the big basket on each woman's back would be loaded until her knees gave and the veins in her neck swelled. When one of those pretty young women had been loaded up, her eyes stared and her lips hung open; then she took her place in the column and, at a sign, these now silent beasts of burden slowly began to set one foot before the other up the long, winding track into the heights. But it was a rare and precious burden that they bore, bread, meat, and wine, and there was no need to be too scrupulous about the tools either, so that besides their wages a good deal that was useful found its way to their own households, and therefore they carried the loads willingly and even thanked the men who had brought these blessings into the mountains. And it was wonderful to feel: here one was not, as everywhere else in the world, scrutinised to see what sort of human being one was—whether one was reliable, powerful and to be feared, or delicate and beautiful—but whatever sort of human being one was, and no matter what one's ideas about life and the world were, here one met with love because one had brought blessings. Love ran ahead like a herald, love was made ready everywhere like a bed freshly made up for the guest, and each living being bore gifts of welcome in their eyes. The women could let that be freely seen, but sometimes as one passed a meadow there might be an old peasant there, waving his scythe like Death in person.

There were, indeed, peculiar people living at the head of this valley. Their forefathers had come here from Germany, to work in the mines, in the times when the bishops of

Trent were mighty, and they were still like some ancient
weathered German boulder flung down in the Italian
landscape. They had partly kept and partly forgotten their
old way of life, and what they had kept of it they themselves
probably no longer understood. In the spring the mountain
torrents wrenched away the earth from under them, so that
there were houses that had once stood on a hill and were now
on the brink of an abyss; but nobody lifted a finger to
contend with the danger, and by a reverse process the new
age was drifting into their houses, casting up all sorts of
dreadful rubbish. One came across cheap, shiny cupboards,
oleographs, and humorous postcards. But sometimes too
there would be a saucepan that their forbears might well
have used in Luther's time. For they were Protestants; but
even though it was doubtless no more than this dogged
clinging to their beliefs that had prevented their being
Italianised, they were certainly not good Christians. Since
they were poor, almost all the men left their wives shortly
after marrying and went to America for years on end; when
they came back, they brought with them a little money they
had saved, the habits learned in urban brothels, and the
irreligion, but not the acuity, of civilisation.

Right at the beginning Homo heard a story that interested
him extraordinarily. Not long before—it might have been
some fifteen years previously—a peasant who had been
away for a long time came home from America and bedded
with his wife again. For a while they rejoiced because they
were reunited, and they lived without a care until the last
of his cash had melted away. Then, when the rest of his
savings, which had been supposed to come from America,
still failed to arrive, the peasant girded himself up and—as
all the peasants in this district did—went out to earn a living
as a peddler, while his wife continued to look after the
unprofitable smallholding. But he did not come back.
Instead, a few days later, on a smallholding some distance

from the first, the peasant returned from America, reminded his wife how long it had been, exactly to the day, asked to be given a meal exactly the same as that they had had on the day he left, remembered all about the cow that no longer existed, and got on decently with the children sent him by Heaven during the years when he was away. This peasant too, after a period of relaxation and good living, set off with peddler's wares and did not return. This happened a third and a fourth time in the district, until it was realised that this was a swindler who had worked with the men over there and questioned them thoroughly about their life at home. Somewhere he was arrested and imprisoned, and none of the women saw him again. This, so the story went, they all were sorry about, for each of them would have liked to have him for a few days more and to have compared him with her memories, in order not to have to admit she had been made a fool of; for each of them claimed to have noticed something that did not quite correspond to what she remembered, but none of them was sufficiently sure of it to raise the matter and make difficulties for the husband who had returned to claim his rights.

That was what these women were like. Their legs were concealed by brown woollen skirts with deep borders of red, blue, or orange, and the kerchiefs they wore on their heads and crossed over the breast were cheap printed cotton things with a factory-made pattern, yet somehow, too, something about the colours or the way they wore these kerchiefs suggested bygone centuries. There was something here that was much older than any known peasant costume; perhaps it was only a gaze, one that had come down through the ages and arrived very late, faint now and already dim, and yet one felt it clearly, meeting one's own gaze as one looked at them. They wore shoes that were like primitive dug-out canoes, and because the tracks were so bad they had knife-sharp iron blades fitted into the soles, and in their blue or brown stockings they walked on these as the women walk in Japan. When they had to wait, they sat down, not on the edge of the path, but right on the flat earth of the path itself, pulling up their knees like Negroes. And when, as sometimes happened, they rode up the mountains on their donkeys, they did not sit on their skirts, but rode astride like men, their thighs insensitive to the sharp wooden edges of the baggage-saddles, their legs again raised indecorously high and the whole upper part of the body faintly swinging with the animal's movement.

And they had, besides, a bewilderingly frank friendliness and kindliness. "Do you come in," they would say, with all the dignity of great ladies, if one knocked at their rustic doors. Or if one stood chatting with them for a while in the open air, one of them might suddenly ask with extreme courtesy and reserve: "Shall I not hold your coat for you?" Once, when Homo said to a charming fourteen-year-old girl: "Come in the hay"—simply because 'the hay' suddenly seemed as natural to him as fodder is to cattle—the childish face under the pointed, ancestral kerchief showed not the slightest dismay: there was only a mirthful puffing and flashing, a tipping this way and that on the rocking shoe-boats, and almost a collapse on to her little bottom, with her rake still on her shoulder, the whole performance conveying, with winsome clumsiness, comic-opera astonishment at the man's intensity of desire.

Another time he asked a tall, Valkyrie-like peasant woman: "Well, and are you still a virgin?" and chucked her under the chin—this time, too, merely because such jests need a touch of virile emphasis.

But she let her chin rest quietly on his hand and answered solemnly: "Yes, of course. . . ."

Homo was taken aback. "You're still a virgin!" he repeated, and laughed.

She giggled.

"Tell me!" he said, drawing closer and playfully shaking her chin.

Then she blew into his face and laughed. "Was once, of course!"

"If I come to see you, what can I have?" he went on with his cross-examination.

"Whatever you want."

"Everything I want?"

"Everything."

"Really everything?"

"Everything! Everything!" and her passion was so brilliantly and passionately acted, that the theatrical quality of it, up here, nearly 5,000 feet above sea-level, left him quite bewildered.

After this he could not rid himself of the feeling that this life, which was brighter and more highly spiced than any life he had led before, was no longer part of reality, but a play floating in the air.

Meanwhile summer had come. When he had received the first letter and recognised his ailing little boy's childish handwriting, the shock of happiness and secret possession had flashed right through him, down to the soles of his feet. Their knowing where he was seemed to give everything tremendous solidity. He was here: oh, now everything was known and he had no more need to explain anything. All white and mauve, green and brown, there were the meadows around him. He was no phantom. A fairy-tale wood of ancient larches, feathery with new green, spread over an emerald slope. Under the moss there might be living crystals, mauve and white. The stream in the midst of the wood somewhere ran over a boulder, falling so that it looked like a big silver comb. He no longer answered his wife's letters. Here, amid the secrets of Nature, their belonging together was only one secret more. There was a tender scarlet flower, one that existed in no other man's world, only in his, and

thus God had ordered things, wholly as a wonder. There
was a place in the body that was kept hidden away, and no
one might see it lest he should die: only one man. At this
moment it seemed to him as wonderfully senseless and
unpractical as only profound religious feeling can be. And
only now did he realise what he had done in cutting himself
off for this summer and letting himself drift on his own tide,
this tide that had taken control of him. Among the trees
with their arsenic-green beards he sank down on one knee
and spread out his arms, a thing he had never done before
in all his life, and it was as though in this moment someone
lifted him out of his own embrace. He felt his beloved's hand
in his, her voice sounded in his ear, and it was as though
even now his whole body were answering to a touch, as
though he were being cast in the mould of some other body.
But he had invalidated his life. His heart had grown humble
before his beloved, and poor as a mendicant; only a little
more, and vows and tears would have poured from his very
soul. And yet it was certain that he would not turn back, and
strangely there was associated with his agitation an image of
the meadows in flower round about these woods, and despite
all longing for the future a feeling that here, amid anemones,
forget-me-not, orchids, gentian, and the glorious greenish-
brown sorrel, he would lie dead. He lay down and stretched
out on the moss. "How am I to take you across with me?" he
asked himself. And his body felt strangely tired, was like a
rigid face relaxing into a smile.

Here he was, having always thought he was living in
reality—but was there anything more unreal than that one
human being should for him be different from all other
human beings?—that among innumerable bodies there was
one on which his inmost existence was almost as dependent
as on his own body?—whose hunger and fatigue, hearing and
seeing, were linked with his own? As the child grew older, this
had grown—as the secrets of the soil grow into a sapling—

into earthly cares and comforts. He loved his child, but just as the boy would outlive them, so too the boy had earlier killed the other-worldly part of them. And suddenly he flushed hot with a new certainty. He was not a man inclined to religious belief, but at this moment he was illumined within. Thoughts cast as little light as smoky candles in this great radiance of emotion that he experienced; it was all simply one glorious word blazing with the light of youth: Reunion. He was taking her with him for all eternity, and in the moment when he yielded to this thought, the little blemishes that the years had wrought in his beloved were taken from her and all was, eternally, the first day of all. Every worldly consideration vanished, and every possibility of tedium and of unfaithfulness, for no one will sacrifice eternity for the sake of a quarter of an hour's frivolity. And for the first time he experienced love beyond all doubt as a heavenly sacrament. He recognised the Providence that had guided his life into this solitude and felt the ground with its gold and jewels beneath his feet no longer as an earthly treasure, but as an enchanted world ordained for him alone.

From this day onward he was released from a bondage, as though rid of a stiff knee or a heavy rucksack. It was the bondage of wanting to be alive, the horror of dying. It did not happen to him as he had always thought it would, when in the fullness of one's strength one seems to see one's end approaching, so that one drinks more deeply of life, savours it more intensely. It was merely that he felt no longer involved, felt himself buoyed up by a glorious lightness that made him supreme lord of his own existence.

Although the mining operations had not progressed according to plan it was indeed a gold-digger's life they were leading. A lad had stolen wine, and that was a crime against the community, the punishment of which could count on general approval. The lad was brought in with his wrists

bound. Mozart Amadeo Hoffingott gave orders that he
should constitute a warning to others by being tied upright
to a tree for a day and a night. But when the foreman came
with the rope, in jest portentously swinging it and then
hanging it over a nail, the lad began to tremble all over in
the belief that he was about to be hanged. And it was always
just the same—although this was hard to explain—when
horses arrived, either fresh horses from beyond the valley or
some that had been brought down for a few days' rest: they
would stand about on the meadow, or lie down, but would
always group themselves somehow, apparently at random,
in a perspective, so that it looked as if it were done accord-
ingly to some secretly agreed aesthetic principle, just like
that memory of the little green, blue, and pink houses at
the foot of Mount Selvot. But if they were up above, standing
around all night tethered in some high corrie in the mountains, three or four at a time tied to a felled tree, and one had
started out in the moonlight at three in the morning and
now came past the place at half-past four, they would all
look round to see who was passing, and in the insubstantial
dawn light one felt oneself to be a thought in some very slow-
thinking mind. Since there was some thieving, and various
other risks as well, all the dogs in the district had been bought
up to serve as guards. The patrols brought them along in
whole packs, two or three led on one rope, collarless. By now
there were as many dogs as men in the place, and one might
well wonder which was actually entitled to feel he was master
in his own house on this earth and which was only adopted
as a domestic companion. There were pure-bred gun-dogs
among them, Venetian setters such as a few people in this
district still kept, and snappy mongrels like spiteful little
monkeys. They too would stand about in groups that had
formed without anyone's knowing why, and which kept
firmly together, but from time to time the members of a
group would attack each other furiously. Some were half

starved, some refused to eat. One little white dog snapped at the cook's hand as he was putting down a plate of meat and soup for it, and bit one finger off.

At half-past four in the morning it was already broad daylight, though the sun was not yet up. When one passed the grazing-land high up on the mountain, the cattle were still half asleep. In big, dim, white, stony shapes they lay with their legs drawn in under them, their hindquarters drooping a little to one side. They did not look at the passer-by, nor after him, but imperturbably kept their faces turned towards the expected light, and their monotonously, slowly moving jaws seemed to be praying. Walking through the circle of them was like traversing some twilit, lofty sphere of existence, and when one looked back at them from above, the line formed by the spine, the hind legs, and the curving tail made them seem like a scattering of treble-signs.

There was plenty of incident. For instance, a man might break his leg, and two others would carry him into camp on their crossed arms. Or suddenly the shout of: "Take co-ver!" would ring out, and everyone would run for cover because a great rock was being dynamited for the building of the road. Once, at such a moment, a shower swept a few flickers of moisture over the grass. In the shelter of a bush on the far side of the stream there was a fire burning, forgotten in the excitement, though only a few minutes earlier it had been very important: standing near it, the only watcher left, was a young birch-tree. And still dangling by one leg from this birch was the black pig. The fire, the birch, and the pig were now alone. The pig had squealed even while one man was merely leading it along on a rope, talking to it, urging it to come on. Then it squealed all the louder as it saw two other men come delightedly running towards it. It was frantic at being seized by the ears and unceremoniously dragged forward. It straddled all four legs in resistance, but the pain in its ears forced it to make little jumps onward.

Finally, at the other end of the bridge, someone had grabbed a hatchet and struck it on the forehead with the blade. From that moment on everything went more quietly. Both fore-legs buckled at the same instant, and the little pig did not scream again until the knife was actually in its throat. There was a shrieking, twitching blare, which sank down into a death-rattle that was no more than a pathetic snore. All these were things Homo saw for the first time in his life.

When dusk fell, they all gathered in the little vicarage, where they had rented a room to serve as their mess. Admittedly the meat, which came the long way up the mountain only twice a week, was often going off, and not infrequently one had a touch of food-poisoning. But still all of them came here as soon as it was dark, stumbling along the invisible tracks with their little lanterns. For what caused them more suffering than food-poisoning was melancholy and boredom, even though everything was so beautiful. They swilled it away with wine. After an hour a cloud of sadness and ragtime hung over the room. The gramophone went round and round, like a gilded hurdy-gurdy trundling over a soft meadow spattered with wonderful stars. They no longer talked to each other. They merely talked. What should they have said to each other, a literary man of independent means, a business man, a former inspector of prisons, a mining engineer, and a retired major? They communicated in sign-language—and this even though they used words: words of discomfort, of relative comfort, of homesickness— it was an animal language. Often they would argue with superfluous intensity about some question that concerned none of them, and would reach the point of insulting each other, and the next day seconds would be passing to and fro. Then it would turn out that nobody had meant a word of it. They had only done it to kill time, and even if none of them had ever really known anything of the world, each of them

felt he had behaved as uncouthly as a butcher, and this filled
them with resentment against each other.

It was that standard psychic unit which is Europe. It was
idleness as undefined as at other times their occupation was.
It was a longing for wife, child, home comforts. And inter-
spersed with this, ever and again, there was a gramophone.
"Rosa, we're going to Lodz, Lodz, Lodz . . ." or: "Whate'er
befall I still recall. . . ." It was an astral emanation of powder
and gauze, a mist of far-off variety-shows and European
sexuality. Indecent jokes exploded into guffaws, each joke,
it seemed, beginning: "You know the one about the Jew in
the train. . . . " Only once somebody asked: "How far is it to
Babylon?" And then everyone fell silent, and the major put
on the "Tosca" record and, as it was about to start, said
mournfully: "Once I wanted to marry Geraldine Farrar."
Then her voice came through the horn, out into the room,
and this woman's voice that all these drunken men were
marvelling at seemed to step into a lift, and the next instant
the lift was flashing away up to the top with her, arriving
nowhere, coming down again, bouncing in the air. Her skirts
billowed out with the movement, with this up and down, this
long lying close to, clinging tightly to, one note, and again
there was the rise and fall, and with it all this streaming
away as if for ever, and yet again and yet again and again this
being seized by yet another spasm, and again a streaming
out: a voluptuous ecstasy. Homo felt it was that naked
voluptuousness which is distributed throughout all the things
there are in cities, a lust no longer distinguishable from
manslaughter, or jealousy, or business, or motor-car racing—
ah, it was no longer lust, it was a craving for adventure—no,
it was not a craving for adventure either, it was a knife
slashing down out of the sky, a destroying angel, angelic
madness—the war?

From one of the many long fly-papers trailing from the
ceiling a fly had dropped in front of him and was lying on

its back, poisoned, in the middle of one of those pools that the light of the paraffin-lamps made in the scarcely perceptible wrinkles in the oilcloth—pools with all that sadness of very early spring, as if a strong wind had swept over them after rain. The fly made a few efforts, each weaker than the last, to turn over, and from time to time a second fly that was feeding on the oilcloth ran to see how it was getting on. Homo also kept a careful watch—the flies were a great nuisance here. But when death came, the dying fly folded its six little legs together, to a point, and kept them straight up like that, and then it died in its pale spot of light on the oilcloth as in a graveyard of stillness that could not be measured in inches or decibels, and which was nevertheless there. Someone was just saying: "They say someone's worked out that all the Rothschilds put together haven't enough money to pay for a third-class ticket to the moon."

Homo murmured to himself: ". . . Kill, and yet feel the presence of God? . . . Feel the presence of God and yet kill?" And with a flick of his forefinger he sent the fly right into the face of the major sitting opposite, which caused another incident and thus kept them occupied until the next evening.

By then he had already known Grigia for some time, and perhaps the major knew her too. Her name was Lene Maria Lenzi. That sounded like Selvot and Gronleit or Malga Mendana, had a ring as of amethyst crystals and of flowers, but he preferred to call her Grigia, pronounced Greeja, after the cow she had, which she called Grigia, Grey One. At such times she would be sitting at the edge of her meadow, in her mauve-brown skirt and dotted kerchief, the toes of her wooden clogs sticking up into the air, her hands clasped over her bright apron, and she would look as naturally lovely as a slender little poisonous mushroom, while now and then she called out to the cow grazing lower down the hillside. There were actually only two things she called:

"Come a-here!" and: "Come a-up!" when the cow strayed too far. But if her cries were unavailing, there would follow an indignant: "Hey, you devil, come a-*here*!", and in the last resort she herself would go hurtling down the hillside like a flung stone, the next best piece of stick in her hand, to be aimed at the Grey One as soon as she was within throwing distance. Since, however, the cow Grigia had a distinct taste for straying valley-wards, the whole of this operation would be repeated with the regularity of pendulum-clockwork that is constantly dropping lower and constantly being wound higher again. Because this was so paradisically senseless, he teased her by calling her Grigia herself. He could not conceal from himself that his heart beat faster when from a distance he caught sight of her sitting there; that is the way the heart beats when one suddenly walks into the smell of pine-needles or into the spicy air rising from the floor of woods where a great many mushrooms grow. In this feeling there was always a residual dread of Nature. And one must not believe that Nature is anything but highly unnatural: she is earthy, edgy, poisonous, and inhuman at all points where man does not impose his will upon her. Probably it was just this that fascinated him in this peasant woman, and the other half of it was inexhaustible amazement that she did so much resemble a woman. One would, after all, be equally amazed, going through the woods, to encounter a lady balancing a tea-cup.

"Do you come in," she too had said, the first time he had knocked at her door. She was standing by the hearth, with a pot on the fire, and since she could not leave it, she made a courteous gesture towards the bench. After a while she wiped her hand on her apron, smiling, and held it out to her visitors: it was a well-formed hand, as velvety-rough as the finest sandpaper or as garden soil trickling between the fingers. And the face that went with the hand was a faintly mocking face, with delicate, graceful bones that one saw best in profile, and a mouth that he noticed very particularly. This mouth was curved like a Cupid's bow, yet it was also compressed as happens when one gulps, and this gave it, with its subtlety, a determined roughness, and to this roughness again a little trace of merriment, which was perfectly in keeping with the wooden shoes that the slight figure grew up out of as out of wild roots. . . . They had come to arrange some matter or other, and when they left, the smile was there again, and the hand rested in his perhaps a moment longer than when they had come. These impressions, which would have been so insignificant in town, out there in this solitude amounted to a shock, as though a tree had moved its branches in a way not to be explained by any stirring of the wind or a bird's taking flight.

A short time later he had become a peasant woman's lover. This change that had taken place in him much occupied his mind, for beyond doubt it was not something he had done, but something that had happened to him.

When he came the second time, Grigia at once sat down on the bench beside him, and when—to see how far he could already go—he put his hand on her lap and said: "You are the beauty of them all", she let his hand rest on her thigh and merely laid her own upon it. With that they were pledged to each other. And now he kissed her to set the seal upon it, and after the kiss she smacked her lips with a sound like that smack of satisfaction with which lips sometimes let go of the rim of a glass after greedily drinking from it. He was indeed slightly startled by this indecorum and was not offended when she rejected any further advances; he did not know why, he knew nothing at all of the customs and dangers of this place, and, though curious, let himself be put off for another day. "In the hay," Grigia had said, and when he was already in the doorway, saying goodbye, she said: "Goodbye till soon", and smiled at him.

Even on his way home he realised he was already happy about what had happened: it was like a hot drink suddenly beginning to take effect after an interval. The notion of going to the hay-barn with her—opening a heavy wooden door, pulling it to after one, and the darkness increasing with each degree that it closes, until one is crouching on the floor of a brown, perpendicular darkness—delighted him as though he were a child about to play a trick. He remembered the kisses and felt the smack of them as though a magic band had been laid around his head. Picturing what was to be, he could not help thinking of the way peasants eat: they chew slowly, smacking their lips, relishing every mouthful to the full. And it is the same with the way they dance, step after step. Probably it was the same with everything else. His legs stiffened with excitement at these thoughts, as though his shoes were already sticking in the earth. The women lower their eyelids and keep their faces quite stiff, a defensive mask, so as not to be disturbed by one's curiosity. They let scarcely a moan escape them. Motionless as beetles feigning death, they concentrate all their attention on what is going on within them.

And so too it was. With the rim of her clog Grigia scraped together into a pile the scrap of winter hay that was still there there, and smiled for the last time when she bent to the hem of her skirt like a lady adjusting her garter.

It was all just as simple and just as magical as the thing about the horses, the cows, and the dead pig. When they were behind the beam, and heavy boots came thumping along the stony path outside, pounding by and fading into the distance, his blood pulsed in his throat; but Grigia seemed to know even at the third footstep whether the foot-steps were coming this way or not. And she talked a magical language. A nose she called a neb, and legs she called shanks. An apron was for her a napron. Once when he threatened not to come again, she laughed and said: "I'll bell thee!"

And he did not know whether he was disconcerted or glad of it. She must have noticed that, for she asked: "Does it rue thee? Does it rue thee much?" Such words were like the patterns of the aprons and kerchiefs and the coloured border at the top of the stocking, already somewhat assimilated to the present because of having come so far, but still mysterious visitants. Her mouth was full of them, and when he kissed it he never knew whether he loved this woman or whether a miracle was being worked upon him and Grigia was only part of a mission linking him ever more closely with his beloved in eternity. Once Grigia said outright: "Thou'rt thinking other things, I can tell by thy look", and when he tried to pretend it was not so, she said: "Ah, all that's but glozing." He asked her what that meant, but she would not explain, and he racked his brains over it for a long time before it occurred to him that she meant he was glossing something over. Or did she mean something still more mysterious?

One may feel such things intensely or not. One may have principles, in which case it is all only an aesthetic joke that one accepts in passing. Or one has no principles, or perhaps they have slackened somewhat, as was the case with Homo when he set out on his journey, and then it may happen that these manifestations of an alien life take possession of whatever has become masterless. Yet they did not give him a new self, a self for sheer happiness become ambitious and earth-bound; they merely lodged, in irrelevantly lovely patches, within the airy outlines of his body. Something about it all made Homo sure that he was soon to die, only he did not yet know how or when. His old life had lost all strength; it was like a butterfly growing feebler as autumn draws on.

Sometimes he talked to Grigia about this. She had a way of her own of asking about it: as respectful as if it were something entrusted to her, and quite without self-seeking. She

seemed to regard it as quite in order that beyond the mountains there were people he loved more than her, whom he
loved with his whole soul. And he did not feel this love
growing less; it was growing stronger, being ever renewed.
It did not grow dim, but the more deeply coloured it became,
the more it lost any power to decide anything for him in
reality or to prevent his doing anything. It was weightless
and free of all earthly attachment in that strange and
wonderful way known only to one who has had to reckon up
with his life and who henceforth may wait only for death.
However healthy he had been before, at this time something within him rose up and was straight, like a lame
man who suddenly throws away his crutches and walks on
his own.

This became strongest of all when it came to hay-making
time. The hay was already mown and dried and only had
to be bound and fetched in, up from the mountain meadows.
Homo watched it from the nearest height, which was like
being high in a swing, flying free above it all. The girl—
quite alone in the meadow, a polka-dotted doll under the
enormous glass bell of the sky—was doing all sorts of things
in her efforts to make a huge bundle. She knelt down in it,
pulling the hay towards her with both arms. Very sensually
she lay on her belly across the bale and reached underneath
it. She turned over on her side and stretched out one arm as
far as she could. She climbed up it on one knee, then on
both. There was something of the dor-beetle about her,
Homo thought—the scarab, of course. At last she thrust her
whole body under the bale, now bound with a rope, and
slowly raised it on high. The bundle was much bigger than
the bright, slender little human animal that was carrying it
—or was that not Grigia?

When, in search of her, Homo walked along the long row
of hay-stooks that the peasant women had set up on the level
part of the hillside, they were resting. He could scarcely

believe his eyes, for they were lying on their hillocks of hay like Michelangelo's statues in the Medici chapel in Florence, one arm raised to support the head, and the body reposing as in flowing water. And when they spoke with him and had to spit, they did so with much art: with three fingers they would twitch out a handful of hay, spit into the hollow, and then stop it up again. One might be tempted to laugh; only if one mixed with them, as Homo did when he was in search of Grigia, one might just as easily start in sudden fright at this crude dignity. But Grigia was seldom among them, and when at last he found her, she would perhaps be crouching in a potato-field, laughing at him. He knew she had nothing on but two petticoats and that the dry earth that was running through her slim, rough fingers was also touching her body. But the thought of it was no longer strange to him. By now his inner being had become curiously familiar with the touch of earth, and perhaps indeed it was not at the time of the hay-harvest at all that he met her in that field: in this life he was leading there was no longer any certainty about time or place.

The hay-barns were filled. Through the chinks between the boards a silvery light poured in. The hay poured out green light. Under the door was a wide gold border.

The hay smelt sour—like the Negro drinks that are made of fermented fruits and human saliva. One had only to remember that one was living among savages here, and the next instant one was intoxicated by the heat of this confined space filled to the roof with fermenting hay.

Hay bears one up in all positions. One can stand in it up to the knees, at once unsure of one's footing and all too firmly held fast. One can lie in it as in the Hand of God, and would gladly wallow in God's Hand like a little dog or a little pig. One may lie obliquely, or almost upright like a saint ascending to heaven in a green cloud.

Those were bridal days and ascension days.

But one time Grigia declared it could not go on. He could not bring her to say why. The sharpness round the mouth and the little furrow plumb between the eyes, which before had appeared only with the effort of deciding which would be the nicest barn for their next meeting, now boded ill weather somewhere in the offing. Were they being talked about? But the other women, who did perhaps notice something, were always as smiling as over a thing one is glad to see. There was nothing to be got out of Grigia. She made excuses and was more rarely to be found, and she watched her words as carefully as any mistrustful farmer.

Once Homo met with a bad omen. His puttees had come undone and he was standing by a hedge winding them on again, when a peasant woman went by and said in a friendly way: "Let thy stockings be—it won't be long till nightfall." That was near Grigia's cottage. When he told Grigia, she made a scornful face and said: "People will talk, and brooks will run", but she swallowed hard, and her thoughts were elsewhere. Then he suddenly remembered a woman he had seen up here, whose bony face was like an Aztec's and who spent all her time sitting at her door, her black hair loose, hanging down below her shoulders, and with three healthy, round-cheeked children around her. Grigia and he unthinkingly passed by her every day, yet this was the only one of the local women whom he did not know, and oddly enough he had never asked about her either, although he was struck by her appearance: it was almost as though the healthiness of her children and the illness manifest in her face were impressions that always cancelled each other out. In his present mood he suddenly felt quite sure it was from here that the disturbing element must have come. He asked who she was, but Grigia crossly shrugged her shoulders and merely exclaimed: "She doesn't know what she says! With her it's a word here and a word over the mountains!" And she made a swift, energetic gesture, tapping her brow, as though she must instantly devalue anything that woman might have said.

Since Grigia could not be persuaded to come again into any of the hay-barns around the village, Homo proposed going higher up the mountain with her. She was reluctant, and when at last she yielded, she said, in a tone that afterwards struck Homo as equivocal: "Well, then, if go we must."

It was a beautiful morning that once again embraced the whole world; far beyond, there lay the sea of clouds and of mankind. Grigia was anxious to avoid passing any dwelling, and even when they were well away from the village she, who had always been delightfully reckless in all arrangements to do with their love-making, showed concern lest they should be seen by watchful eyes. Then he grew impatient and it occurred to him that they had just passed an old mineshaft that his own people had soon given up trying to put back into use. There he drove Grigia in.

As he turned to look back for the last time, there was snow on a mountain-peak and below it, golden in the sun, a little field of corn-stooks, with the white and blue sky over it all.

Grigia made another remark that seemed strangely pointed. Noticing his backward glance, she said tenderly "Better leave the blue alone in the sky, so it'll keep fine." But he forgot to ask what she meant by this, for they were already intent on groping their way further into darkness, which seemed to be closing around them.

Grigia went ahead, and when after a while the passage opened out into a small chamber, they stopped there and embraced. The ground underfoot seemed pleasantly dry and they lay down without Homo's feeling any of the civilised man's need to investigate it first by the light of a match. Once again Grigia trickled through him like soft, dry earth, and he felt her tensing in the dark, growing stiff with her pleasure. Then they lay side by side, without any urge to speak, gazing towards the little far-off rectangle beyond which daylight blazed white. And within him then Homo experienced over again his climb to this place, saw himself meeting Grigia beyond the village, then climbing, turning, and climbing, saw her blue stockings up to the orange border under the knee, her loose-hipped gait in those merry clogs, he saw them stopping outside the cavern, saw the landscape with the little golden field, and all at once in the brightness of the entrance beheld the image of her husband.

He had never before thought of this man, who was in the company's employ. Now he saw the sharp poacher's face with the dark, cunning eyes of a hunter, and suddenly remembered too the only time he had heard him speak: it was after creeping into an old mine-shaft where nobody else had dared to go, and the man's words were: "I got into one fix after another. It's getting back that's hard."

Swiftly Homo reached for his pistol, but at the same instant Lene Maria Lenzi's husband vanished and the darkness all around was as thick as a wall. He groped his way to the entrance, with Grigia clutching his sleeve. But he realised at once that the rock that had been rolled across the entrance was much heavier than anything he could shift unaided. And now too he knew why her husband had left them so much time: he himself needed time to make his plan and get a tree-trunk for a lever.

Grigia knelt by the rock, pleading and raging. It was repulsive in its futility. She swore that she had never done anything wrong and would never again do anything wrong. She squealed like a pig and rushed at the rock senselessly, like a maddened horse. In the end Homo came to feel that this was only in accordance with Nature, but he himself, a civilised man, at first could not overcome his incredulity, could not face the fact that something irrevocable had really happened. He leaned against the rocky wall, his hands in his pockets, and listened to Grigia.

Later he recognised his destiny. As in a dream he felt it descending upon him once again, through days, through weeks, through months, in the way sleep must begin when it will last a very long time. Gently he put one arm round Grigia and drew her back. He lay down beside her and waited for something. Previously he would perhaps have thought that in such a prison, with no escape, love must be sharp as teeth; but he quite forgot to think about Grigia. She had slipped away from him, or perhaps he from her, even though he could still feel her shoulder touching his. His whole life had slipped away from him, just so far that he could still tell it was there, but without being able to lay his hand upon it.

For hours they did not stir. Days might have passed, and nights. Hunger and thirst lay behind them, like one eventful stage of the journey, and they grew steadily weaker, lighter, and more shut into themselves. Their half-consciousness was wide seas, their waking small islands. Once he started up, with glaring awareness, into one such small waking: Grigia was gone. Some certainty told him that it must have been only a moment earlier. He smiled . . . telling him nothing of the way out . . . meaning to leave him behind, as proof for her husband. . .! He raised himself up on his elbow and looked about him. So he too discovered a faint, glimmering streak. He crawled a little nearer, deeper into the passage— they had always been looking in the other direction. Then he realised there was a narrow crevice there, which probably led out, obliquely, into the open air. Grigia had slender bones, yet even he, if he made an immense effort, might perhaps be able to worm his way through. It was a way out. But at this moment he was perhaps already too weak to return to life, or he had no wish to, or he had lost consciousness.

At this same hour, all efforts having proved unavailing and the futility of the undertaking having been recognised, Mozart Amadeo Hoffingott, down in the valley, gave orders for work to cease.

The Lady from Portugal

In some old charters they were called the seigniors delle Catene, in others Herren von Ketten, both of which mean: of the Chains. They had come down from the North, stopping at the very threshold of the South. They proclaimed their loyalty now to the Guelph, now to the Ghibelline cause, as it suited them, and at bottom regarded themselves as owing no allegiance to anything or anyone but themselves.

It was to one side of the great highway leading across the Brenner Pass into Italy, somewhere between Brixen and Trent, on an almost sheer, lone crag, that their castle stood, with a wild torrent coursing five hundred feet below it, raging so deafeningly that if a man put his head out of one of the windows, he could not have heard even the pealing of church bells in the room behind him. It was an impenetrable curtain of solid noise, through which no sound of the outer world could pass into the castle of the seigniors delle Catene. Only the gaze was unimpeded and, piercing that protective curtain, plunged headlong into the deep encircling panorama.

All the lords delle Catene or von Ketten had the reputation of being keen and alert, and there was no advantage that escaped them as far as their arm could reach. And they were cruel as knives that always cut deep. They never turned red with anger or rosy with joy: in their anger they darkened, and in their joy they shone like gold—a shining as perfect and as rare. All of them, without exception through the years and the centuries, were said also to resemble each other in this: that white threads early mingled with the brown hair of head and beard, and that every one of them died before his sixtieth year; and in this too, that the enormous strength each sometimes displayed seemed not to have its seat and origin in his body, which was slender and of medium stature, but to emanate from the eyes and forehead. This, however, was merely the legend among their overawed neighbours and their villeins. They took whatever they could get, going about it honestly or accomplishing it by violence or cunning as the case might be, but always imperturbably, inexorably. Each lived out his short life without haste, and for each the end was swift, death cutting him down when he had accomplished his task.

It was the custom among the Kettens not to form ties of marriage with any of the nobility who held the surrounding manors, but to seek their brides far off, and rich brides too, in order not to be hindered in making their alliances and carrying on feuds as they chose. The Herr von Ketten who had brought home a beautiful Portuguese bride twelve years earlier was now in his thirtieth year. The marriage had been celebrated in her country, and the very youthful bride was expecting her confinement by the time the jingling procession of attendants and menials, horses, maid-servants, baggage-mules, and dogs crossed the boundary of the Catene land. The year had passed like one long honeymoon. For all the Catene were brilliant cavaliers, yet they proved it only in the one year of their lives when they went wooing. The brides they chose were beautiful, for they wanted handsome sons, and without courtly graces they could not have won such wives abroad, where they did not count for so much as at home. But they themselves did not know whether it was in that one year that they revealed their true selves, or only in all the other years.

A messenger came to meet the cavalcade, bearing weighty news; and though the bright-coloured garments and pennants still resembled a great butterfly, Herr von Ketten himself was changed. When he had galloped back to rejoin the company, he continued to ride slowly beside his wife as though he would not allow any other concern to press him, but his face had altered and was now forbidding as a bank of storm-clouds. Then suddenly, at a turn in the road, the castle towered up before them, scarcely a quarter of an hour's journey ahead, and with an effort he broke his silence.

He told his wife he wished her to turn back and return to her native country The cavalcade came to a halt. The Portuguese lady pleaded and insisted that they should ride on, urging that there would still be time to turn back when the reasons had been heard.

The Bishops of Trent were mighty lords, and the Imperial courts pronounced in their favour. For generations the Kettens had been at feud with them over a question of territory, and sometimes they had invoked the law against each other, sometimes their demands and counter-demands had led to bloodshed, but always it had been the seigniors von Ketten who had been obliged to yield to their opponents' superior strength. In this one matter the gaze that missed no other chance of advantage waited in vain to glimpse it. And father handed on the task to son, and through the generations their pride continued to wait, and never relented.

It was for this Herr von Ketten now that the luck seemed to have changed. He was dismayed to realise how nearly he had missed his chance. A strong party among the nobility was in rebellion against the Bishop, and it had been decided to make a surprise attack and take him prisoner. Ketten's return home might tip the scales in favour of the rebel party. Having been absent for more than a year, Ketten did not know how strong the Bishop's position was; but he did know this would be a long and fearful struggle that would last for years and that the outcome was uncertain, and he also knew it would be impossible to count on each of their party to the bitter end if they did not succeed in taking Trent at the very beginning. He resented it that his beautiful wife had, by her mere existence, almost caused him to miss the opportunity. True, as he rode at her side, keeping one pace to the rear, he delighted in her as much as ever; and she was still as mysterious to him as the many pearl necklaces that she possessed. A man could have crushed such little things like peas, weighing them in the hollow of his sinewy hand—so it seemed to him, as he rode beside her—and yet there they lay, incomprehensibly invulnerable. It was only that this enchantment had been displaced by the news he had received, had been thrust aside like winter's muffled dreams when all at once the boyishly naked, first, sunlight-solid days are there again. Years in the saddle lay ahead, and in them wife and child turned to strangers, vanished from ken.

But meanwhile the cavalcade had reached the foot of the cliff on which the castle stood, and the lady from Portugal, having listened to all he had to say, once more declared that she would remain with him. How fiercely the castle reared into the height! Here and there on the rock-face a few stunted trees sprouted like sparse hair. The rising and falling of the line of wooded mountains was so violent that no one could have imagined that savagery who knew only the waves of the sea. The air was full of some spicy chill, and it was all like riding into a huge cauldron that had burst, spilling everywhere this alien green that it contained. But in the forest there was the stag, the bear, the wild boar, the wolf, and perhaps the unicorn. Further beyond, there was the realm of chamois and eagle. Unfathomed gorges harboured dragons. Many days' journey wide, many days' journey deep this forest was, where the only tracks were those where wild beasts made their way; and high above, where the crags towered, the realm of spirits began. There demons lurked amid the storm and the clouds. No Christian had ever set

foot there, or if ever one had the audacity to try to scale those
heights, ill-luck followed—stories that the maids told in
hushed voices round the fire in winter, while the serving-men
smirked in silence and shrugged their shoulders, because a
man's life is full of dangers, and such adventures can easily
befall one. But of all the tales the lady from Portugal heard,
there was one that seemed strangest. Just as no one had ever
yet reached the place where the rainbow ends, so too, they
recounted, no one had ever yet succeeded in looking out
over these great stone walls: there were always more walls
beyond, and between them there were ravines like outspread
blankets full of stones, stones as big as a house, and even the
finest gravel underfoot was no smaller than a man's head. It
was a world that was not really a world at all. Often in her
dreams of this country, whence came the man she loved, she
had imagined it as being of his own nature, and she had
imagined the man's nature according to all that he had told
her of his native country. Weary of the peacock-blue sea,
she had expected a land tense with the unexpected, like the
string of a drawn bow. Then, when she came face to face
with the secret, she found it unimaginably hideous and
longed to escape. The castle was like an agglomeration of
hen-houses: stone piled on rock . . . dizzy walls where mould
and lichen grew . . . here rotting beams, there unseasoned,
unhewn tree-trunks . . . farming tools and war-gear, stable
chains and axle-trees. But now that she was here, it was here
that she belonged, and perhaps what she saw was not really
hideous, perhaps it had a beauty of its own, like a man's
ways, to which one had to become accustomed.

Herr von Ketten watched his wife riding up the mountainside and could not bring himself to stop her. He felt no
gratitude. Her action was something that neither bested his
will nor yielded to it, but eluded him, luring him on into
some other realm, making him ride after her in awkward
silence, helpless as a lost soul.

Two days later he was again in the saddle.

And eleven years later it was still the same. Too rashly attempted, the attack on Trent had failed, costing the nobles a third of their force at the very start, and with it more than half their boldness. Herr von Ketten, though wounded in the retreat, did not at once return home. For two days he lay hidden in a peasant's hut, and then he rode from castle to castle, trying to reawaken his allies' fighting-spirit. Having come too late to take part in their councils and preparations, after this setback he clung to the plan as a dog will cling to a bull's ear. He expounded to the other knights what lay in store for them if the Bishop's forces made a counter-attack before their own ranks were closed again; he urged on the faint-hearted and the miserly, squeezing money out of them, bringing up reinforcements, providing arms—and finally was chosen to be their captain in the field. At first his wounds still bled so profusely that he had to change the bandages twice a day; and, riding and counselling and trying to make up for his earlier absence, he gave no thought to his lovely Portuguese bride, who was surely anxious for him.

It was not until five days after he was wounded that he came to her, and then he remained only one day. She looked at him without asking questions, yet keenly, as one may follow the flight of an arrow, wondering if it will strike its mark.

He gathered his men together, down to the meanest lad on whom he could lay hands, manned the castle to withstand a siege, issued commands, and saw to everything. That day was all a shouting of men-at-arms, a neighing of horses, hauling of beams, clang of iron and stone. In the night he rode away. He was kind and tender as to some noble creature that one admires, but his gaze went straight ahead as if from under a helmet, even when he wore none. At their leave-taking the lady from Portugal, suddenly overwhelmed by a woman's feelings, pleaded to be allowed, at least now, to bathe his wounds and bind them up afresh. But he refused and took leave of her more hastily than was necessary, laughing as he did so. And then she also laughed.

The way the enemy fought out this campaign was violent wherever it could be so, as befitted the hard man of noble blood who wore the episcopal robes; but it was perhaps from these long womanish robes that he had also learnt to be supple, deceitful, and stubborn. Wealth and extensive possessions gradually proved what they could do, and ground was yielded only inch by inch, always only at the last moment, when rank and influence no longer sufficed to engage the help of allies. It was a way of fighting that avoided decisive action. As soon as resistance stiffened, there was a withdrawal; wherever it seemed to be slackening, there would be an onslaught. So it happened that sometimes a castle would be overrun and, if it had not been abandoned in time, all the inmates put to the sword. But at other times troops might be encamped in a district for weeks and nothing worse would happen than that some peasants' cow would be stolen or a few hens would have their necks twisted. The weeks lengthened into summer and winter, and the seasons revolved into years. Two powers were contending with each other, the one fierce and aggressive, but lacking in strength, the other resembling an indolent, soft, but dreadfully heavy body, made heavier still by the weight of time.

Herr von Ketten was well aware of all this. He had trouble in preventing the weakened, sullen forces of the knights from squandering the last of their strength in a sudden, hasty attack. He was always on the outlook for the exposed position, the turn of events, the unlikely constellation that only chance could bring about. So too his father had bided his time, and his father before him. And if one waits long enough, even the most unlikely event may come to pass. So he waited for eleven years.

For eleven long years he rode to and fro between the nobles' castles and his fighting-forces, keeping resistance alive. In a hundred skirmishes, again and again, he earned a name for reckless courage, in order that none might reproach him with being timid in leadership; and at times he even manœuvred both sides into a great bloody encounter, lest his allies' taste for battle should falter. But he too avoided decisive action, just as the Bishop did. More than once he received slight wounds, but he was never at home for more than twelve hours. He was battle-scarred and weather-beaten from his roving life. Doubtless he feared to stay at home longer, just as a tired man dare not sit down.

The restiveness of horses hitched to a tree, men's loud laughter, torchlight, flames of a camp-fire rising like a pillar, like a tree-trunk of golden dust in green-glimmering wood-land, the smell of rain, curses, boastful knights, dogs sniffing at the wounded, women's petticoats lifted high, scared peasants—such things were his amusements in these years. In the midst of it all he remained slender and graceful. White began to show among the brown hairs of his head, but his face was ageless. He had to find retorts to coarse jests, and did so like a man; but his eyes would remain quite still. Wherever discipline slackened, he restored order with an iron hand; but he did not raise his voice, he spoke quietly and briefly, and the soldiers feared him, for anger never seemed to take possession of him, it was something that streamed out of him like a light, and his face would grow quite dark. In battle he forgot himself. Then everything followed a single course—a wild slashing and blood-letting, a frenzied dance drunk with blood, he did not know what he was doing and yet he always did the right thing. For this his soldiers idolised him, and a legend arose that in his hatred of the Bishop he had sold his soul to the Devil, who dwelt

in his castle in the guise of a beautiful outlandish woman
that he visited there in secret.

The first time he heard this Herr von Ketten neither
frowned nor laughed: but his face became dark golden with
joy. Often, when he sat by the camp-fire or at some peasant's
hearth and the hard day behind him would seem to soften
in the warmth, as rain-stiffened leather will grow soft again,
he would think. He would think, at such times, of the Bishop
of Trent, who slept on fresh linen, was surrounded by
learned clerks, and had painters in his service, while he
himself roamed like a wolf, circling round the enemy. He
too could have that. He had installed a chaplain in his castle
so that the needs of the spirit might be provided for, and a
scrivener to read aloud, and a merry maid-in-waiting; a
cook had been brought from a great distance, so that the
castle's mistress need not hanker for the dishes she had
known at home; wandering scholars and students would
be given hospitality so that their conversation might
afford some days of distraction; costly stuffs and tapestries
came, so that the walls might be covered. Only he stayed
away.

For a whole year, in that far country and on the journey,
he had practised pretty speeches and flattery. For just as
every well-made thing, be it steel or strong wine, horse or
fountain, has a spirit of its own, so too the lords delle Catene
had, and were not lacking in wit. But during that time he
was far from his homeland and his essential being was something that he might ride towards for many weeks without
reaching it. And even now he would sometimes unthinkingly
make gallant speeches, but only so long as the horses were
being rested in the stables. He would arrive late at night and
ride away the next morning; or else he would be there
from when the bell rang for Matins till the Angelus. He
was as familiar to her as a thing long worn on one's person.
When you laugh, that familiar thing also laughs—is shaken

to and fro; when you walk, it goes with you; when your hand touches your own body, you feel the presence of that thing: but if you raise it up and contemplate it, it remains silent, it avoids your eyes. If he had ever remained longer, he would have had to be truly as he was. But he recalled that he had never said: I am this; or: I wish to be that. He had talked to her of hunting, of adventures and of things that he did. Nor had she ever done what young people so often do and asked him what he thought about this and about that, or said anything about what she would wish to be like when she was older; lively as she had been before, she had simply bloomed, silently, like a rose, and she had stood on the church steps ready to depart, as though on a mounting-block from which she would step into the saddle and ride into that other life.

He scarcely knew the two children she had borne him, but these two sons of his also loved him passionately—that remote father with whose fame their childish ears had rung since they could remember. It was a strange memory, that of the evening to which the second son owed his being. There she was, when he came home, in a soft light-grey robe patterned with dark grey flowers; her black hair was already plaited for the night, and her finely chiselled nose cast a sharp shadow into the smooth yellow of a book on which the lamplight shone, illumining the mysterious pictures it contained. It was like magic. Tranquilly the woman sat there, in her rich gown, the skirt flowing down in countless rippling folds—a figure rising out of itself and falling back into itself, like the water of a fountain. And is the water of a fountain anything that can be ransomed and redeemed, can it be set free by anything but magic or some miracle, and thus issue forth wholly out of its self-borne, swaying existence? Embracing the woman, might he not suddenly be brought up short by the force of some magical resistance? This was not so—but is tenderness not even more uncanny?

She looked at him, as he entered, like someone recognising an old cloak that one has not worn for a long time, has not even seen for a long time, and which remains a little strange, and yet one wraps it round oneself.

What intimate, familiar things, by contrast, did the strategies of war, and political cunning and anger and killing seem to him! An act is performed because some other act has preceded it. The Bishop relies on his gold pieces, and the captain on the nobility's powers of endurance. To command is a thing of clarity; such a life is day-bright, solid to the touch, and the thrust of a spear under an iron collar that has slipped is as simple as pointing one's finger at something and being able to say: This is *this*. But the other thing is as alien as the moon.

Secretly Herr von Ketten loved this other thing. He took no delight in ordering his household or increasing his wealth. And although he had for years been fighting about possessions not his own, his desire was not a reaching out for the satisfaction of gain; it was a yearning from his very soul. It was in their brows that the Catene's power lay; but all that their power produced was voiceless actions. Every morning that he climbed into the saddle he again felt the happiness of not yielding, and this was the very soul of his soul. But when he dismounted at evening, often a sullen weariness of all the violence he had been living with would sink upon him, as though that day he had been straining all his resources lest, through no doing of his own, he should suddenly be radiant with some inner beauty for which he had no name. The Bishop, that slippered priest, could pray to God when Ketten pressed him hard. Ketten could only ride through standing corn, feel the horse's stubborn, billowing movement under him, and conjure up good will with blows of his iron gauntlet. But he was thankful that it should be so. He was glad that a man could live and cause others to die without that other thing. Thus one could deny and drive off something that crept towards the fire when one stared into the flames, something that was gone the moment one straightened up, stiff from dreaming, and turned round. Herr von Ketten sometimes became entangled in the long, intertwining threads of his thoughts when he remembered the Bishop to whom he was doing all this, and it seemed to him that only a miracle could straighten it all out.

His wife would summon the old steward and roam through the forest with him when she was not sitting gazing at the pictures in her books. Forest opens up before one, but its soul withdraws. She would press through the undergrowth, clamber over boulders, come upon tracks and spoors, and catch glimpses of animals, but she never came home having had more than such small adventures, difficulties overcome, curiosities satisfied, things from which all the life vanished as soon as one emerged from the forest. And that green *fata morgana* of which she had heard tell before she came to this country—as soon as one was no longer entering into it, it closed again behind one's back.

Rather indolently, meanwhile, she kept some order in the castle. As for her sons, neither of whom had ever seen the sea—were they really her children? At times it seemed to her they were young wolves. Once she was brought a wolf-cub that had been taken in the forest. And she looked after him too. He and the great hounds treated each other with uneasy tolerance, letting each other be without exchanging any sign. When the wolf-cub crossed the castle yard, they would stand up and watch him pass, but they neither barked nor growled. And even if he cast a sidelong glance at them, he would keep straight on, scarcely slackening his pace, only a little more stiff-legged, lest he should show any fear. He followed his mistress everywhere. He gave no sign of affection or of familiarity, merely turning his intense gaze to her often —but his gaze said nothing. She loved this wolf for his sinewiness, his brown coat, and the silent ferocity and intensity of his gaze, which reminded her of Herr von Ketten.

At last the moment came for which a man must wait. The Bishop fell ill and died, and the cathedral chapter was without leadership. Ketten sold his goods and chattels, mortgaged his land, and employed all his means to equip a small army entirely his own. Then he negotiated. Faced with the choice between having to continue the old struggle against newly armed forces and coming to terms, the chapter decided for the latter; and it was inevitable that Ketten, the last captain remaining, strong and menacing, in the field, should make advantageous terms for himself, while the cathedral chapter extorted what compensation it could from weaker and more hesitant foes.

So there was an end to what, by the fourth generation, had become like the wall of a room, a wall one sees facing one every morning at breakfast and does not really see at all. All at once this wall was not there. Hitherto everything had been as in the lives of all foregoing Kettens, and all that remained to be done in this Ketten's life was to round things out and set them in order, an artisan's aim in life, no goal for a great lord.

And then, as he was riding home, a fly stung him.

His hand at once began to swell, and he became very tired. He dismounted at the tavern in a small, poverty-stricken village, and, sitting at the greasy wooden table, he laid his head down on it, overcome by drowsiness. When he woke, at evening, he was in a fever. He would nevertheless have ridden on if he had been in haste; but he was not in haste now. In the morning, when he tried to mount, he was so dizzy that he slipped and fell. The swelling had already spread up his arm to his shoulder. Having forced his armour on, he had to be unbuckled again, and while he was standing there, letting it be done, he was shaken by such a fit of

shivering as he had never known. His muscles twitched and
jerked so that his hands would not obey him, and the half-
unbuckled pieces of armour clattered like a loose roof-gutter
in a gale. He felt this was unworthy of him, and laughed,
with grimly set face, at his clattering; but his legs were weak
as a child's. He sent a messenger to his wife, another to a
surgeon, and yet another to a famous physician.

The surgeon, who was the first to arrive, prescribed hot
compresses of healing herbs and asked for permission to
use the knife. Ketten, who was now much more impatient to
reach home, bade him cut—until he had half as many fresh
wounds again as he had old ones. How strange it was to let
pain be inflicted on one and not defend oneself! For two
days he lay wrapped from head to toe in the healing herbal
compresses, and then had himself carried home. The journey
took three days, but this kill-or-cure treatment, which
might indeed have caused his death by exhausting his
remaining strength, seemed to have halted the malady:
when they arrived, he lay in a high fever from the poison in
his blood, but the infection had not spread further.

This fever was like a plain of burning grass, smouldering
on day after day, week after week. Daily the sick man
dwindled, being consumed in his own fire, but the evil
humours also seemed to be gradually consumed by it. More
than this even the famous physician could not say, and only
the lady from Portugal knew secret signs that she chalked on
his door and the bedposts. When, one day, there was almost
nothing left of Herr von Ketten, only something like a shape
filled with soft, hot ash, suddenly the fever diminished—
remaining a mere faint glimmer under the ashes.

If it was strange to suffer pain against which one did not
fight, what followed now was something that the sick man
did not experience like someone who was himself in the midst
of it. He slept a great deal, and was absent even when his
eyes were open. But when his consciousness returned, this

body without any will of its own, this body as warm and helpless as an infant's, was not his at all, and neither was this weak soul that the faintest breath of air could agitate. Surely he had already died and was all this time merely waiting somewhere, as though he might have to come back again. He had never known that dying was so peaceful. Part of his being had gone ahead into death, separating and scattering like a cavalcade of travellers. While the bones were still lying in bed, and the bed was there, his wife bending over him, and he, out of curiosity, for the sake of some diversion, was watching the changing expressions in her attentive face, everything he loved had already gone a long way ahead. Herr von Ketten and his moon-lady, his nocturnal enchantress, had issued forth from him and softly withdrawn to a distance: he could still see them, he knew that by taking a few great leaps he could still catch up with them, only he no longer knew whether he was already there with them or still here. Yet all this lay in some immense and kindly hand that was as benign as a cradle and which nevertheless weighed all things as in scales, imperturbable, unconcerned as to the outcome. Doubtless that was God. But even though he did not doubt it, it did not stir him either. He was waiting for whatever was to come, not even responding to the smile that hovered above him, and those caressing words.

Then the day came when all at once he knew this would be his last if he did not gather up all his will-power in order to remain alive. And it was on the evening of this day that the fever ceased.

When he felt this first stage of returning health like solid ground beneath him, he began to have himself carried out every day to the little green patch of ground on the rocky bluff that jutted, unwalled, above the precipice. Wrapped in blankets, he would lie there in the sun—now dozing, now waking, never sure whether he was asleep or awake.

Once, when he woke, the wolf was there. Gazing into those

bevelled eyes, he could not stir. He did not know how much time passed—and then his wife was there beside him, the wolf at her knee. He closed his eyes again, pretending he had not been awake at all. But when he was carried back to his bed, he asked for his crossbow. He was so weak that he could not draw it, and this amazed him. Beckoning to the servant, he bade him take the crossbow. "The wolf," he said. The man hesitated. But Herr von Ketten raged like a child, and that evening the wolf's pelt hung in the castle yard. When the Portuguese lady saw it and learnt only then, from the serving-men, what had happened, her blood froze. She went to his bedside. There he lay, pale as the wall behind him, and for the first time he looked her straight in the eyes again. She laughed and said: "I shall have a hood made of the pelt, and come by night and suck the blood from your veins."

Then he wanted to send away the chaplain, who once had said: "The Bishop can pray to God, and that is a threat to you"—and who had later, time after time, given him Extreme Unction. But this he could not do at once, for the Portuguese lady exerted herself on his behalf, begging him to have patience with the chaplain a short while longer, until he found another place. Herr von Ketten yielded. He was still weak and still spent much time drowsing in the sun, on the patch of grass.

Once—another time when he woke—there was the friend of her youth. He was standing beside the lady from Portugal, having come from her native country, and here in the North he seemed to resemble her. He saluted Herr von Ketten with a nobleman's courtesy, uttering words that, judging by his look and gestures, must have been all grace and cordiality. And the lord of Ketten lay in the grass like a dog, filled with shame.

Unless, indeed, that was not until the second time—for his mind sometimes wandered even now. It was a long time too before he noticed that his cap had become too big for him. The soft fur cap that had always sat so firmly on his head now, at a light touch, slipped down to where his ears stopped it from going further. The three of them were together, and his wife said: "Dear heaven! Your head has shrunk!"

His first thought was that he must have let his hair be cropped too short, though at the moment he could not remember when. Furtively he passed his hand over his head. But his hair was longer than it should have been, and matted since he had been ill. Then the cap must have stretched, he told himself. But it was still almost new—and how should it have stretched, lying unused in a chest? So he made a jest of the matter, remarking that in all the years when he had been living among men-at-arms, instead of with courtly cavaliers, his head might well have shrunk. He felt how awkwardly the jest came from his lips, and it did not even remove the question—can a skull become smaller? The strength in the veins may grow less, the fat beneath the scalp may melt away in fever: but what does that amount to? Now at times he would make a gesture as of smoothing his hair, or pretend to be wiping away sweat, or he would try to lean back into the shade unobtrusively and then, swiftly, using two fingertips as if they were a mason's compass, would measure his skull, placing his fingers now this way, now that. But no doubt remained: his head had become smaller, and if he fingered it from within, with his thoughts, it was even smaller, like two small thin shells fitted together.

There are, of course, many things that one cannot account for, but one does not carry them on one's own shoulders, feeling them every time one turns one's neck towards two people who are talking while one seems to be asleep. Although he had long forgotten all but a few words of that foreign language, once he caught the sentence: "You do not do what you would, and you do what you would not."

The tone seemed to be urgent rather than jesting—what could it mean?

Another time he leaned far out of the window, right into the rushing sound of the torrent; he now did this often, as a sort of game: the noise, as confused as wildly whirling hay, closed the ears, and when he returned out of that deafness, his wife's conversation with the other man suddenly stood out clearly, very small and far away. And it was an eager conversation. Their souls seemed to be in harmony with each other.

The third time it was simply that he followed the other two when they went out into the courtyard again in the evening. When they passed the torch at the top of the outside steps, their shadows must fall across the tops of the trees. He bent forward swiftly when this happened, but among the leaves the shadows all blurred into one.

At any other time he would have tried to drive the poison out of his body by calling for his horse and his men, or would have tried to burn it out in wine. But the chaplain and the scrivener gobbled and drank till the wine and food dribbled out of the corners of their mouths, and the young knight would clink the canikin with them, laughing like one setting two dogs at each other. Ketten felt a disgust for the wine that was swilled by these two clerks, mere oafs under their veneer of scholasticism. They would argue about the Millennium, and about learned doctoral questions, and would talk bawdy, now in German, now in Church Latin. A journeying humanist would translate whatever was needed to complement this gibberish and that of the Portuguese; he had sprained his ankle and had every intention of staying on until it was thoroughly strong again.

"He fell off his horse when a rabbit ran by," the scrivener said banteringly.

"He took it for a dragon," Herr von Ketten said with sullen mockery, standing nearby, unsure of himself.

"But then so did the horse!" the castle chaplain bellowed. "Else it would not have shied. And thus the magister understands better than the lord what comes from the horse's mouth!"

The drunken company guffawed at the lord's expense. Herr von Ketten looked at them hard, took a step towards them, and struck the chaplain in the face. He was a plump young peasant, and he turned very red, then deadly pale, but he remained seated. The young knight rose, smiling, and went in search of his friend, the lady of the castle.

"Why did you not stab him to the heart?" the rabbit-humanist hissed when they were alone.

"He is strong as two bulls," the chaplain answered, "and, moreover, Christian teachings are truly of such a nature as to afford consolation in such circumstances."

But the truth was that Herr von Ketten was still very weak, and his life was returning to him all too slowly. He could not reach the second stage of recovery.

The visitor did not resume his travels, and the mistress of the castle failed to understand her lord's hints. For eleven years she had been waiting for her husband, for eleven years years he had been her far-off beloved in an aura of fame and glory, and now he went about castle and courtyard, wasted and worn by illness, looking commonplace enough beside the other's youth and courtly grace. She did not give it much thought, but she was a little weary of this country that had promised things beyond the power of words to tell, and she could not bring herself, just because of a cross face, to send away her childhood friend, who had brought back to her the very fragrance of her homeland and thoughts that one could think with laughter. She had nothing to reproach herself with. She had been a shade more superficial during these last weeks, but that was pleasant, and she could now sometimes feel her face lighting up as it had done years before.

A soothsaying woman, whom he consulted, prophesied to Herr von Ketten: "You will be cured only when you accomplish a task." But when he pressed her to tell him what task, she fell silent, tried to slip away, and finally declared that that was hidden from her.

He could easily have put a quick, painless end to this visit, for the sanctity of life and the sacred laws of hospitality are of little account to one who has spent years as an unbidden guest among his enemies. But in his enfeebled convalescent state he was almost proud of being clumsy, and any cunning solution seemed to him as unworthy as the young man's frivolous readiness of tongue. Strange things happened to him. Through the mists of weakness that enveloped him his wife's ways seemed to him tenderer than they need be; it reminded him of earlier days, when sometimes, returning home to her love, he had wondered at finding it more intense than at other times. For his absence alone could not, he thought, be the cause. He could not even have said whether he was glad or sorry. It was just as in the days when he had lain so close to death. He could not make any move. When he gazed into his wife's eyes, they were like new-cut glass, and although what the surface showed him was his own reflection, he could not penetrate further. It seemed to him that only a miracle could change this situation. And one cannot make destiny speak when it chooses to be silent. One must simply harken for whatever is on its way.

One day when a company of them came up the mountainside together, they found the little cat at the gate. It was standing outside the gate as though it did not want to jump, cat-fashion, over the wall, but to enter as human beings did. It arched its back in welcome and rubbed itself against the skirts and boots of the towering beings who were strangely surprised by its presence. They let it in, and it was like receiving a guest. The very next day it was apparent that what they had opened the gate to was no mere kitten that had come to stay; it was almost as though they had adopted a small child. The dainty little creature's tastes were not for the delights of cellar and attic. It would not leave the human beings' company for a single moment. And it had a way of making them give up their time to it, which was all the less comprehensible in that there were so many other and grander animals at the castle, and the human beings also had their own affairs to occupy them. The fascination seemed positively to originate in their having to keep their eyes lowered, watching the little creature, for it was very unobtrusive in its ways and just a shade quieter, one might almost have said sadder and more meditative, than seemed appropriate to a kitten. It romped in the way it knew human beings expect a kitten to romp; it climbed on to their laps and was, it seemed, studiously charming to them, and yet one could feel that it was also somehow absent. And precisely this—this absence of whatever would have made it into an ordinary kitten—was like a second presence, a hovering double, perhaps, or a faint halo surrounding it. Not that any of them had the hardihood to put this into words. The lady from Portugal bent tenderly over the little creature lying on its back in her lap, in its childlike way beating its tiny paws at her playful fingers. Her young friend, laughing, bent low over too—over the kitten, over her lap. And this casual frolicking reminded Herr von Ketten of his illness, now nearly gone, as though the illness and its deathly gentleness had been transformed into that little animal's body and so were no longer merely within him, but there in the midst of them all. A serving-man said: "That cat is getting the mange."

Herr von Ketten was astonished that he had not noticed this himself. The serving-man spoke again: "It will have to be done away with before long."

Meanwhile, the kitten had been given a name taken from one of the fairy-tale books. It had become gentler and more sweet-natured than ever. Soon everyone began to see that it was ill and growing almost luminously weak. It spent more and more time resting in someone's lap, resting from the affairs of the world, its little claws clutching tight in mingled affection and anxiety. And now too it began to look at them, one after the other: at pale Ketten and at the young Portuguese sitting bent forward, his eyes intent on it or perhaps on the breathing movement of the lap where it lay. It looked at them all as though asking forgiveness for the ugliness of what it was about to suffer—in some myterious way for all of them. And then its martyrdom began.

One night the vomiting began, and the little animal continued to vomit until the next morning. When daylight returned, it lay languid and dizzy as though it had been beaten over the head. Perhaps it was merely that in their excess of love for it they had given the starving kitten too much to eat. However this might be, after that it could not be kept in the bedroom, but was given to the serving-man to look after. After two days the serving-men complained that it was no better; and indeed it was probable that they had put it outside in the night. And now it not only vomited but could not hold its stool, and nothing was safe from it. And this now was an ordeal, a grim trial of strength between that almost imperceptible halo and the dreadful filth, and it was decided—since it had meanwhile been discovered whence the little creature came—to have it taken back there: to a peasant's cottage down by the river, near the foot of the hill. This was a kind of deportation, done in the hope of evading both responsibility for the animal and ridicule for all the attention they paid to it. But it weighed on their conscience, and so they also sent milk and a little meat and even money in order to make sure that the peasants, to whom dirt did not matter so much, would look after the cat properly.

Nevertheless, the servants shook their heads over their master and mistress.

The serving-man who had carried the kitten down recounted that it had run after him when he left and that he had had to carry it back again. Two days later it was once more up in the castle. The hounds avoided it, the servants did not dare to drive it away for fear of the master and mistress, and when the latter set eyes on it, it was tacitly agreed that nobody would now refuse to let it die up here.

It was now very thin and lustreless, but the disgusting malady seemed to have passed off; now it was merely grow-ing thinner all the time, losing flesh almost before their very eyes. For two days everything was, to a heightened degree, just as it had been before: there was the slow, affectionate prowling about in the refuge where it was cared for; an absent-minded smiling with the paws while striking at a scrap of paper dangled before it; sometimes a faint swaying out of weakness, in spite of having four legs to support it— and on the second day it sometimes collapsed on to its side. In a human being this process of disembodiment would not have seemed so strange, but in the animal it was like a metamorphosis into a human being. They watched it almost with awe. None of these three people, each in his or her peculiar situation, could escape the thought that it was his or her own destiny that was being vicariously accom-plished in this little cat already half released from earthly bonds.

But on the third day the vomiting and filthiness began again. The serving-man stood by, and even though he did not dare to say it again aloud, his silence said it clearly enough: it will have to be put away. The Portuguese bowed his head as though struggling with some temptation, and then he said to his friend: "It is the only way." It seemed to him he had accepted his own death-sentence. And suddenly everyone looked at Herr von Ketten. He had grown white as the wall, and rose, and left the room. Then the lady from Portugal said to the serving-man: "Take it away."

The man took the sick animal away to his own place, and the next day it was gone. Nobody asked any questions. They all knew that he had killed it. All of them felt the oppression of unspeakable guilt; something had gone from among them. Only the children felt nothing, finding it quite natural that the serving-man should kill a dirty cat that nobody could play with any more. But now and then the hounds would snuffle at a patch of grass on which the sunlight fell in the courtyard, and their legs stiffened, their hair bristled, and they glanced sidelong. At one such moment Herr von Ketten and the lady from Portugal encountered each other. They stopped side by side, looking across at the dogs and finding nothing to say. The sign had been given—but how was it to be interpreted and what was to be done? A great dome of silence surrounded them both.

If she has not sent him away before nightfall, I must kill him—Herr von Ketten thought to himself. But night fell and still nothing had happened. Supper was over. Ketten sat looking grave, heated by a slight fever. After a while he went out into the courtyard, for the cool evening air, and he remained absent for a long time. He could not make the final decision that he had all his life found it so easy to make. Saddling horses, buckling on armour, drawing a sword—all of that, which had once been the very music of his life, now had a harsh, discordant ring; and fighting seemed a senseless, alien mode of action. Even the short way, the way of the knife, was now like an infinitely long road on which a man might die of thirst. But neither was it his way to suffer; he could feel that he would never be wholly well again if he did not wrench himself free of all this. And gradually another thought associated itself with these. . . .

As a boy he had always wanted to climb the unscaleable cliff on top of which the castle stood. The thought was a mad one, a suicidal one, but now it was gradually gaining in obscure conviction, as though it were a matter of trial by ordeal, or something like an approaching miracle. It was not he but the little cat from the world beyond, it seemed to him, that would return this way. Laughing softly to himself, he shook his head in order to make sure it was still on his shoulders, and at the same time he realised that he had already gone a long distance down the stony path to the bottom of the hill.

At the bottom, down by the torrent, he left the path and clambered over great boulders with the water dashing between them, then through the bushes and up to the cliff. In the moonlight little points of shadow revealed crevices where fingers and toes could find a hold. Suddenly a piece of stone broke loose under one foot: the shock ran through his whole body, right into his heart. He strained his ears. It seemed an eternity before the stone splashed into the water far below. He must already have climbed a third of the height. Then it distinctly seemed to him that he awoke and realised what he was doing. Only a dead man could reach the bottom now, and only the Devil himself could reach the top. He groped above him. With each grip his life hung by the ten thin straps of sinew in his fingers. Sweat poured from his face, waves of heat flashed through his body, his nerves were like stony threads. But it was strange to feel how in this struggle with death strength and health came flowing back into his limbs, as though returning into his body from some place outside him. And then the impossible was indeed accomplished. There was one overhanging ledge that had to be circumvented, and then his arm was thrust in through an open window. Doubtless there was no other place where he could have arrived but at this very window, yet it was only now that he knew where he was. He swung himself in, sat on the sill and let his legs dangle inside the room. With his strength his ferocity had also returned. He waited until he had regained his breath. No, he had not lost the dagger from his side. It seemed to him that the bed was empty. But he went on waiting until his heart and lungs were quite calm again. And more and more distinctly it seemed to him that he was alone in the room. He crept towards the bed: nobody had slept in it this night.

Herr von Ketten tiptoed through rooms, corridors, and doorways that no one else would have found at once without guidance—until he came to his wife's bed-chamber. Listening, he waited. There was no sound of whispering. He glided in. The lady from Portugal was breathing quietly in her sleep. He searched dark corners and fumbled along walls and, when he stealthily left the room again, he could almost have sung for joy, joy that shook the very fabric of his unbelief.

He roved through the castle, but now floorboards and flagstones echoed with his tread, as though he were in search of some joyful surprise. In the yard a serving-man called out to him, demanding to know who he was. He asked for the visitor and learned that he had ridden away at the rising of the moon. Herr von Ketten sat down on a pile of rough-hewn timber, and the watchman marvelled at how long he sat there.

All at once he was seized by the certainty that if he were to return to the Portuguese lady's chamber, she would no longer be there. He thundered on the door and went in. His young wife started up as though in her dreams she had been waiting for this, and she saw him standing before her fully dressed, just as he had gone out that evening. Nothing had been proved, nothing had been disposed of, but she asked no question, and there was nothing that he could ask. He pulled aside the heavy curtain hanging before the window, and beyond it there rose the curtain of torrential thunder behind which all the seigniors delle Catene were born and died.

"If God could become man, then He can also become a kitten," the lady from Portugal said.

And perhaps he should have laid his hand upon her mouth to hush this blasphemy, but they both knew that no sound of it could penetrate beyond these walls.

Tonka

I

At a hedge. A bird was singing. And then the sun was somewhere down behind the bushes. The bird stopped singing. It was evening, and the peasant girls were coming across the fields, singing. What little things! Is it petty if such little things cling to a person? Like burrs? That was Tonka. Infinity sometimes flows in drips and drops.

And the horse was part of it too, the roan that he had tied to a willow. It was during his year of military service. It was no mere chance that it was in that year, for there is no other time of life when a man is so deprived of himself and his own works, and an alien force strips everything from his bones. One is more vulnerable at this time than at any other.

But had it really been like that at all? No, that was only what he had worked it up into later. That was the fairy-tale, and he could no longer tell the difference. In fact, of course, she had been living with her aunt at the time when he got to know her. And Cousin Julie sometimes came visiting. That was how it had been. He remembered being disconcerted by their sitting down at the same table with Cousin Julie over a cup of coffee, for she was, after all, a disgrace to the family. It was notorious that one could strike up a conversation with Cousin Julie and take her back to one's lodgings that same evening; she would also go to the bawdy-houses whenever she was wanted. She had no other source of income. Still, she was a relative, after all, even if one didn't approve of the

life she led; and even if she was a light woman, one couldn't
very well refuse to let her sit down at the table with one.
Anyway, she didn't come very often. A man might have
made a row about it, for a man reads the newspaper or
belongs to some association with definite aims and is always
throwing his weight about, but Auntie merely made a few
cutting remarks after Julie had gone, and let it go at that.
So long as she was there, they couldn't help laughing at her
jokes, for she had a quick tongue and always knew more
about what was going on in town than anyone else. So, even
if they disapproved of her, there was no unbridgeable gap
between them; they had something in common.

The women from the jail were another example of the
same thing. Most of them were prostitutes too, and not long
afterwards the jail itself had to be moved to another district
because so many of them became pregnant while serving
their sentence, carrying mortar on the building sites where
male convicts worked as bricklayers. Now, these women were
also hired out to do housework. For instance, they were very
good at laundering, and they were very much sought after
by people in modest circumstances, because they were cheap.
Tonka's grandmother also had one in on washing-day; she
would be given a cup of coffee and a bun, and since one was
sharing the work with her it was all right to share breakfast
with her too—there was no harm in that. At midday someone had to see her back to the jail, that was the regulation,
and when Tonka was a little girl, she was generally the one
who had to do it. She would walk along with the woman,
chatting away happily, not in the least ashamed of being
seen in that company, although these women wore grey
prison uniform and white kerchiefs that made them easily
recognisable. Innocence one might call it: a young life in
all its innocence pathetically exposed to influences that were
bound to coarsen it. But later on, when the sixteen-year-old
Tonka was still unembarrassed, gossiping with Cousin Julie,

could one say that this was still all innocence, or was it that her sensibilities were blunted? Even if no blame attached to her, how revealing it was!

The house must also be mentioned. With its five windows looking on to the street, it was a survival between towering new buildings that had shot up around it. It was in the back premises that Tonka lived with her aunt, who was actually her much older cousin, and her aunt's little son, the illegitimate offspring of a relationship that she had regarded as permanent, and a grandmother who was not really the grandmother but the grandmother's sister. In earlier days there had also been a brother of her dead mother's living there, but he too had died young. All of them lived together in one room and a kitchen, while the genteel curtains of the five front windows concealed an establishment of ill repute where lower-middle-class housewives of easy morals, as well as professionals, were brought together with men. This was something that the family tacitly ignored, and since they wanted no trouble with the procuress they even passed the time of day with her. She was a fat woman, very set on respectability. She had a daughter of the same age as Tonka, whom she sent to a good school; she had her taught the piano and French, bought her pretty clothes, and took care to keep her well away from the business. She was a soft-hearted creature, which made it easier for her to follow the trade she did, for she knew it was shameful. In earlier times Tonka had now and then been allowed to play with this daughter, and so had found her way into the front part of the house, at hours when it was empty, and to her the rooms seemed enormous, leaving her with an impression of grandeur and refinement that was only reduced to proper proportions after he came on the scene.

Tonka was not her real name. At her baptism she had been given the German name Antonie, and Tonka was the abbreviated form of the Czech diminutive Toninka. The inhabitants of those back streets talked a queer mixture of the two languages.

But where do such thoughts lead? There it was, she had been standing by a hedge that time, in front of the dark open doorway of a cottage, the first in the village as one came out from town. She was wearing laced boots, red stockings, and a gaily-coloured, stiff, full skirt, and as she talked she seemed to be gazing at the moon, which hung pale over the corn stooks. She was at once pert and shy, and laughed a lot, as though she felt protected by the moon. And the wind blew across the stubble fields as if it were cooling a plate of soup. Riding home, he had said laughingly to his comrade-in-arms, young Baron Mordansky: "You know, I shouldn't at all mind having an affair with a girl like that, only it's too dangerous for my liking. You'd have to promise to make up a threesome, to keep me from going sentimental." And Mordansky, who had done a spell as a trainee in his uncle's sugar-mill, had thereupon told him about how, when the time came round for digging the beets, hundreds of such peasant girls laboured in the fields belonging to the mill, and it was said they were as submissive as black slaves to the supervisors and their assistants. And once, he remembered quite distinctly, he had cut short a similar conversation with Mordansky because it was an affront to his feelings. Yet it had not been at that time, he knew—what was now trying to impose itself on him as a memory was really something else, the tangle of thorns that had later grown inside his head.

In reality it was in the Ring that he had first seen her, in that main street with the stone arcades where the officers and the gentlemen who worked in the government offices stood chatting at corners, the students and young business men strolled up and down, and the girls wandered along in twos and threes, arm in arm, after the shops closed, or the more curious of them even during the lunch-hour. Sometimes a

well-known local lawyer would make his way slowly through
the crowd, lifting his hat to acquaintances, or a local deputy,
or, say, a respected industrialist; and there were even ladies
to be seen, on their way home after shopping. There her
glance had suddenly crossed with his, a merry glance, lasting
only for the briefest moment—like a ball accidentally landing
in a passer-by's face. The next instant she had looked away,
with a feigned air of innocence. He had turned round
quickly, supposing that now the usual giggling would follow,
but Tonka was walking on, looking straight ahead of her,
rather tensely. She was with two other girls, and taller than
either of them. She was not beautiful, but her face had a
clear-cut, definite quality. There was nothing in it of that
petty, cunningly feminine look which seems to result from
the face as a whole; in this face mouth, nose, and eyes were
each something clearly in their own right and could stand
up to being contemplated separately, delighting the be-
holder simply by their candour and the freshness irradiating
the whole face. It was odd that so gay a glance should stick
fast like a barbed arrow, and she herself seemed to have hurt
herself with it.

So much was now clear. Well, then, at that time she had
been working in the draper's shop. It was a large shop,
employing a great many girls to handle the stock. Her job
was to look after the rolls of material and get the right one
down when it was asked for, and the palms of her hands were
always slightly moist because of the irritation from the fine
hairs of the cloth. There was nothing dream-like about that,
and her face was guileless. But then there were the draper's
sons, and one of them had a moustache like a squirrel's,
turned up at the ends, and always wore patent-leather shoes.
Tonka was full of stories about how smart he was, how many
pairs of shoes he had, and how his trousers were every night
laid between two boards and weighed down with heavy
stones to keep them well pressed.

And now, as he got a clear glimpse of something real through the mist, that other smile emerged, the incredulous smile his mother wore—essentially an onlooker's smile, full of pity and disdain for him. That smile was real. What it said was: 'Heavens, not *that* shop, surely?' And although Tonka had still been a virgin when he came to know her, that smile, treacherously furtive or masked, had also turned up in many a tormenting dream he had. Perhaps it had never existed as a single smile; even now he could not be sure of that. And then too there are nuptial nights when one cannot be entirely sure; there are, so to speak, physiological ambiguities, times when even Nature does not give an unequivocal answer. And in the very moment when he remembered that, he knew that Heaven itself was against Tonka.

II

It had been rash of him to bring Tonka to act as nurse and companion to his grandmother. He was still very young then. He had worked out a little stratagem: Tonka's aunt, who went out doing sewing for 'the gentry', sometimes worked for an aunt of his, and he had contrived that she should be asked if she happened to know of a young girl, who . . . and so on. The idea was to get a girl to look after his grandmother, whose merciful release was to be expected in a couple of years. Apart from her wages, the girl would be remembered in the old lady's will.

But meanwhile there had been a number of little episodes. Once, for instance, he was going on an errand with her; there were some children playing in the street, and suddenly they both found themselves gazing at the face of a little girl who was howling—a face that wriggled and writhed like a worm, in the full blast of sunlight. The pitiless clarity of it there in the light seemed to him a symbol of life, over against the orbit of death that they had both just left. But Tonka was 'fond of children'. She bent down to the child, cheerfully and consolingly, perhaps even slightly amused by it—and that was all, however much he tried to make her see that behind the appearance there was something else. From however many sides he approached it, in the end he always found himself confronted with the same opacity in her mind. Tonka was not stupid, but something seemed to prevent her from being intelligent; and for the first time he felt this wide expanse of pity for her, this pity that was so difficult to account for.

Another time he said to her: "Tell me, how long is it now you've been with Grandmamma, Fräulein Tonka?" And when she had told him, he said: "Oh, really? It's a long time to have spent with an old woman like that."

"Oh," Tonka exclaimed, "I like being here."

"Well, you needn't be afraid to tell me if you don't. I can't imagine how a young girl can manage to put up with it."

"It's a job," Tonka answered, and blushed.

"All right, it's a job. But that isn't all one wants from life. Isn't that true?"

"Yes."

"And have you got that?"

"No."

"Yes, no. Yes, no." He grew impatient. "What's the sense of talking like that? Can't you even grumble about us?" But he saw that she was struggling to find an answer, that she kept on discarding possible answers just when they were on the tip of her tongue. And suddenly he felt sorry for her. "I dare say you'll hardly know what I mean. It's not that I think badly of my grandmother, poor woman. No, it isn't that. I'm not looking at it from that point of view at the moment. I can't help thinking of it from your point of view, and from your point of view she's a perfect old horror. Now do you see what I mean?"

"Yes," she said in a low voice, blushing more than ever. "I understood all right before. But I can't say it."

At that he laughed. "That's something that's never happened to me! But now I'm more curious than ever to know what you really think. I'll help you." He looked at her so intently that she became more embarrassed than ever. "All right, then. Here goes: do you like just having regular duties, a quiet, steady routine? Is that it?"

"Well, I don't know quite how you mean. I like my work all right."

"You 'like it all right'. But you're not exactly mad about it, I suppose? I mean, there are people who don't want anything but a steady job."

"What are you getting at?"

"Desires, dreams, ambition—that's what I'm getting at. Doesn't a fine day like this start something up in you?"

Between the stone walls of the streets the day was full of a quivering light and the honey of springtime.

Now it was she who laughed. "It isn't that either."

"It isn't that? Well, then, perhaps you have a special liking for darkened rooms, for talking in a whisper, for the smell of medicines, and all that? There are such people too, you know. But I can tell from your face that I haven't hit it this time either."

She shook her head and faintly turned her mouth down at the corners—perhaps in shy mockery, perhaps only out of embarrassment.

But he gave her no peace. "You see how wrong I go, how ridiculous I'm making myself in your eyes by keeping on guessing wrong like this! Doesn't that help you to come out with it? Come on now!"

And now at least she came out with it. Slowly. Hesitantly. As if choosing her words carefully, in order to make intelligible something that was very difficult to understand:

"You see, I have to earn my living."

Ah, how simple it all was!

What an ass he had been, and what a stony eternity lay in that so ordinary answer!

And another such time was once when he had secretly gone for a walk with Tonka. They used to go for long walks in the country whenever she had her day off, which was twice a month. It was summer. When evening came, the warmth of the air was exactly the same as that of one's face and hands, and, walking for a moment with closed eyes, one felt as though one were dissolving, expanding, floating. . . . He described this to Tonka and, when she laughed, asked her if she knew what he meant.

Oh, yes!

But he was still not sure that she did and so he tried to get her to describe it to him in her own words. And this she could not do.

So then, he said, she *didn't* know what he meant.

Oh, but she did! And suddenly she said: it made you want to sing.

For heaven's sake!

But yes—that *was* it, she protested.

They went on wrangling like this for a while. And then after all they both began to sing, rather in the spirit of someone firmly placing the *corpus delicti* on the table or inspecting the scene of the crime. They sang pretty badly, and something from a musical comedy, at that, but fortunately Tonka sang softly, and he was glad of that little sign of consideration for his feelings. He was positive she had not been to the theatre more than once in her life and that ever since then these trashy tunes summed up her notions of culture and elegance. However, it turned out that she had merely picked them up from the other girls at the shop where she had worked.

He asked her if she really liked these tunes. It always annoyed him to come across anything still linking her with that shop.

She did not know what it was, whether this music was beautiful or silly, merely that it made her want to be on the stage herself and put her whole heart into making the people in the audience happy or sorrowful. This was perfectly ridiculous, of course, in the light of what poor dear Tonka looked like while she was singing. It depressed him, and his own singing faded out on a sort of growl. Then Tonka suddenly broke off too, as if she felt the same thing, and for a while the two of them walked along in silence.

Then Tonka stopped and said: "That's not what I meant at all, about singing."

And since she saw in his eyes a little glint of responsive kindness, she began to sing again, still softly, but this time folk-songs from her own part of the country. So they walked along, with these simple tunes making everything vaguely sad, like the fluttering of cabbage-whites in the sunshine. And so now all at once it turned out, of course, that Tonka was right.

Now it was he who could not express what was going on in him. Because Tonka did not talk the ordinary language that other people used, but some language of the totality of things, she had had to suffer being thought stupid and insensitive. He realised now what it meant if one said: Songs just come into her head. It seemed to him that she was very lonely. If it were not for him, who would understand her? So they both sang. Tonka recited the Slavonic words and translated them into German for him, and then they joined hands and sang together like children. Whenever they had to leave off to regain their breath, there would be a little moment of silence ahead of them too, where the twilight was creeping across the road—and even if the whole thing was foolishness, the dusk itself was at one with their feelings.

And yet another time they were sitting at the edge of a
wood, and he was simply gazing into space through half-
shut eyelids, not talking, letting his thoughts roam. Tonka
began to be afraid she had offended him again. Several
times she took a deep breath, as if about to speak, but then
shyness held her back. So for a long time there was no sound
but the woodland murmur that is so tormenting, rising and
sinking away in a different place at every instant. Once a
brown butterfly fluttered past them and settled on a long-
stemmed flower, which quivered under the touch, swaying
to and fro and then quite suddenly being quite still again,
like a conversation broken off. Tonka pressed her fingers
hard into the moss on which they were sitting, but after a
a while the tiny blades stood up again, one after the other,
row on row, until there was finally no more trace of the hand
that had lain there. It was enough to make one weep, without
knowing why. If she had been trained to think, like her companion, at that moment Tonka would have realised that
Nature consists of nothing but ugly little things that one
hardly notices and which live as sadly far apart from each
other as the stars in the night-sky. The beauties of Nature....
A wasp was crawling over his shoe. Its head was like a
lantern. He watched it, contemplating his shoe, which was
sticking up broad and black, oblique against the brown of the
earth.

Tonka had often thought with dread of the moment when
a man would stand before her and she would have no way of
escape. The stories that the older girls in the shop had told
her with such delight gave her a feeling only of a crude,
boring frivolity, something that was not love at all, and she
was indignant at the way men were always making amorous
advances to her after scarcely exchanging more than a
few words with her. As she looked at her companion now,
she felt a sudden pang. It was the first time since she had
been with him that she realised he was a man; for this was

something completely different. He was lying back, resting on his elbows, his chin on his chest. Timidly, she tried to see into his eyes.

What she saw was a peculiar smile. He had one eye shut, and with the other he was gazing along the length of his body, as though aiming at something. Doubtless he knew how ugly his shoe looked at that angle, and perhaps too how little it amounted to that he was lying at the edge of a wood with Tonka. But he did nothing to change anything about it. Each detail was ugly, and the whole thing was happiness.

Quietly, Tonka got up. She suddenly felt a burning inside her head, and her heart was thudding. She could not make out what he was thinking, but she read it all in his eye; and all at once she caught herself wanting to take his head in her arms and cover up his eyes.

"It's time to go," she said. "It'll be getting dark soon."

As they were walking along the road, he said: "I'm afraid you must have been bored. But you will have to get used to me." He took her arm, because it was becoming difficult to see the road distinctly, and he tried to excuse himself for his silence and then, almost against his will, for his thoughts too. She did not really know what he was talking about, but in her own way she sensed the meaning of his words, which came so gravely through the rising mist. And when now he went further, even apologising for talking in such a solemn way, she did not know what to do. Even her silent prayer to the Blessed Virgin was of no avail, and so she linked her arm more closely with his, although she felt dreadfully shy of doing so.

He stroked her hand. "I think we get on well together, Tonka. But do you really understand me?"

After a while Tonka answered: "It doesn't matter if I know what you mean, or not. I couldn't say anything anyway. But I like you to be so serious."

These were all very slight experiences, of course, but the remarkable thing was that they happened all over again, exactly the same. Actually they were always there. And, even more remarkably, later they meant the very opposite of what they had meant in the beginning. Tonka always remained so simply and transparently the same that it was almost like having an hallucination, seeing the most incredible things.

III

Then came an event: his grandmother died before the expected time. Events are, after all, only things that happen untimely and out of place; one is, as it were, mislaid or forgotten, and one is as helpless as an object that nobody bothers to pick up. And even the events that took place much later were only the things that happen thousands of times, all over the world, and the only incomprehensible thing about it was that it should have happened with Tonka.

Well, and so the doctor came, the undertaker's men came, the death certificate was signed, and Grandmamma was buried. One thing followed on the other quite smoothly, as is proper in a respectable family. The will was read. He was glad not to be in any way involved. There was only one item among the bequests that demanded attention: the provision made for Fräulein Tonka with that dreamlike surname, one of those Czech surnames that mean things like 'He sang', or 'He came across the meadow'. There was a contract. Under the terms of the will the Fräulein was to receive—apart from her wages, which were low—a certain fixed sum for every completed year of service, and since it had been assumed that Grandmamma would linger on for quite a while, and since the sum had been fixed in gradually increasing amounts in accordance with the expected increase in the strain of nursing her, it turned out to be a sum that was bound to seem outrageously small to a young man who weighed out in minutes the months of her youth that Tonka had sacrificed.

He was present when Hyacinth reckoned up with her. He was pretending to read—the book was Novalis' *Fragments*—but in reality he was attentively following what was going on. He was ashamed when his 'uncle' named the sum. Even his 'uncle' seemed to feel something similar, for he began to explain to the Fräulein, in detail, the terms of the contract that had been made when she entered their service. Tonka listened intently, her lips tightly closed. The solemnity with which she followed the calculations gave her young face a very appealing look.

"So then that's correct, isn't it?" his uncle said, laying the money on the table.

It was obvious that she had absolutely no idea what it was all about. She pulled out her little purse, folded the notes, and squashed them in; but though they were few, folding them so much made a thick wad of them, and when the little purse had been replaced under her skirt, it made a bulge on her thigh, like a swelling.

She had only one question to ask. "When do I have to leave?"

"Well," his uncle said, "I suppose it will be a few days before the house is shut up. You can certainly stay till then. But you can also go before that, if you like, as you won't be needed any more."

"Thank you," she said and went off to her little room.

Meanwhile the others had begun sharing out the old woman's things among themselves. They were like wolves devouring a dead member of the pack, and they were already in a state of general irritation when he asked whether the Fräulein, who had got so little money out of it all, should not at least be given something of some value in memory of Grandmamma.

"We've decided to give her Grandmamma's big prayer-book."

"Well, yes, but I'm sure something useful would please her more. What about this, for instance?" He picked up a brown fur tippet that was lying on the table.

"That's for Emmi"—a cousin of his—"and anyway you must be mad, it's *mink*!"

He laughed. "Is there any law that poor girls can only be given something for the good of their souls? You don't want to make a miserly impression, do you?"

"I'd thank you to leave that to us," his mother said, and because she did not think he was entirely wrong, she added: "These are things you know nothing about. She won't be treated unfairly." And, with a gesture at once lavish and irritable, she put aside for Tonka some of the old woman's handkerchiefs, chemises, and drawers, and then added a black woollen dress that had scarcely been worn. "There, I think that'll do. It's not as though the Fräulein had been such a treasure, and she can't exactly be called sentimental, either. She never shed so much as a single tear, either when Granny died or at the funeral. So please don't let us hear any more about it."

"Some people don't cry easily. I mean, that doesn't prove anything," he said, not because it seemed important to say it, but because he felt the urge to argue for the sake of arguing.

"That will do!" his mother said. "Don't you realise that your remarks are out of place?"

At this rebuke he fell silent, not because he was in awe of his mother, but because suddenly he felt vastly pleased at the thought that Tonka had shed no tears. His relatives were all talking eagerly, all talking at once, and he noticed how skilfully each of them turned the situation to his or her own advantage. They expressed themselves, if not clearly, at least to some purpose and with the courage of their convictions. In the end each of them got what he or she wanted.

For them the ability to talk was not a medium of thought, but a sort of capital, something they wore like jewellery to impress others. As he stood by the table with the heaps of things to be given away on it, he found himself recalling a line of verse, 'To him Apollo gave the gift of song, and music sweet to hear', and for the first time he realised that it really was a gift. How inarticulate Tonka was! She could neither talk nor weep. But how is one to define something that neither can speak nor is spoken of, something that dumbly merges with the anonymous mass of mankind, something that is like a little line scratched on the tablets of history? What is one to make of such a life, such a being, which is like a snowflake falling all alone in the midst of a summer's day? Is it real or imaginary? Is it good, or evil, or indifferent? One senses the fact that here the categories have reached a frontier beyond which they cease to be valid.

Without another word he left the room and went to tell Tonka that he would provide for her.

He found her packing up her things. There was a big cardboard box on a chair, and there were two others on the floor. One of them was already tied up with string. The two others were not big enough for the amount of stuff still scattered about the room, and she was trying to solve the problem by taking things out again and putting them in differently—stockings and handkerchiefs, laced boots and sewing things—laying them first this way and then that. However scanty her possessions were, she would never get everything stowed away, for her luggage was still scantier.

Since the door of her little room was ajar, he was able to watch her for some time without her knowing. When she did notice him, she blushed and quickly stepped in front of the open boxes.

"So you're leaving us?" he said, charmed with her embarrassment. "What are you going to do now?"

"I'm going home to Auntie."

"Do you mean to stay there?"

She shrugged her shoulders. "I shall look around for something."

"Won't your aunt be vexed?"

"I've got enough for my keep for a few months. In that time I'll find a situation."

"But that means using up your savings."

"Can't be helped, can it?"

"And what if you don't find it so easy to get a new job?"

"Then I shall just get it served up to me again at every meal."

"Get what served up? How do you mean?"

"Not bringing anything in. That's how it was when I was working at the shop. I wasn't bringing much home, but I couldn't help that, and she never said anything. Only if she was angry. Then she always did."

"And so then you took the job with us."

"Yes."

"Look," he said abruptly, "you mustn't go back to your aunt. You'll find something else. I'll—I'll see to that."

She did not say yes or no. She did not thank him. But as soon as he had gone she began slowly taking one thing after another out of the boxes and putting them back in their places. She had blushed deeply. Now she could not collect her thoughts, and every now and then stood still with something in her hand, gazing blankly ahead of her, simply realising: So this was love.

But when he had gone back to the room where Novalis' *Fragments* was still lying on the table, he was suddenly aghast at the responsibility he had taken on. Quite unexpectedly something had happened that would determine the course of his life, and it was something that did not really concern him intimately enough. At this moment he perhaps even felt slightly suspicious of Tonka because she had accepted his offer without more ado.

Then he began to wonder: What on earth made me propose such a thing? And he did not know the answer to that question any more than why she had accepted. Her face had revealed just the same helplessness and bewilderment that he had been feeling. The situation was painfully comical: he had gone rushing up somewhere as in a dream and now he did not know how to get down again.

He had another talk with Tonka. He did not want to be anything but completely honest with her. He talked of personal independence, of intellectual values, of having a purpose in life, ambition, his distaste for the proverbial idyllic love-nest, his expectation that he would later have affairs with women of higher social standing—talked, in fact, like a very young man who wants a great deal and has experienced very little. When he saw something flicker in Tonka's eyes, he was sorry, and, all at once overcome by quite a different feeling, the fear of hurting her, he pleaded: "Don't misunderstand what I've been saying!"

"I understand all right," was all the answer Tonka gave.

IV

"But she's only a common little thing who used to work in that draper's shop!" they had said. What was the point of that? There were plenty of other girls who were quite ignorant, who had never been educated. Talking like that was like pinning a label on to the back of the girl's dress, where she couldn't get at it and take it off. What they meant was that people had to have learned something, had to have principles, had to be conventional and have the right manners. Simply being a human being wouldn't do. And what of all of them, who had all that and who did 'do'? It seemed to him that his mother was afraid of seeing the emptiness of her own life repeating itself in his. Her own choice was not one that she was proud of: her husband, his father, had formerly been an officer of the line—an undistinguished, jolly man. She was bent on seeing her son have a better life. She fought for that. Fundamentally he approved of her pride. So, then, why did the thought of his mother leave him unmoved?

Duty was second nature to her, and her marriage had taken on meaning only when his father fell ill. Henceforth she assumed a soldierly aspect, standing on guard, defending her position against overwhelming odds, at the side of this man who was steadily declining into imbecility. Up to then she had not been able either to go ahead or to withdraw in her relations with Uncle Hyacinth. He was not a kinsman at all, but a friend of both parents, one of those 'uncles' with whom children have to put up with from the age when they begin to notice things. He was a senior civil servant and, besides, a popular writer whose books sold very well indeed. He brought Mother the breath of culture and worldly sophistication that consoled her in the intellectual desert she lived in. He was well read in history, with ideas that seemed all the more grandiose the emptier they were, extending, as they did, over the sweep of the centuries and the great problems of man's fate. For reasons that had never become clear to the boy, his mother had for many years been the object of this man's steadfast, admiring, selfless love. Perhaps it was because as an officer's daughter she had high standards of honour and duty, which were the source of the moral integrity that lent her glamour in his eyes and made her the model for the heroines in his novels. Perhaps too he was obscurely aware that both the fluency of his talk and his narrative gift derived from his own lack of such integrity. But since he naturally did not care to acknowledge this as a deficiency, he had to magnify it and transform it into something universal, full of the *lacrimae rerum*, seeing the need to be thus complemented by another's strength of spirit as the

inevitable destiny of one so rich in intellectual resources as
himself. Thus the situation had no lack of agonising exalta-
tion for the woman either. Even in their own eyes they were
at pains to disguise their liaison as a spiritual friendship, but
in this they were not always successful. At times they were
quite dismayed by Hyacinth's weakness of character, which
would land them in dangerous situations, and then they
would not know whether to let themselves fall or strong-
mindedly climb back again on to their wonted heights. It
was only when her husband became ill that their souls were
provided with the support they needed and, reaching out for
it, they gained that inch in spiritual stature which they had
sometimes felt lacking. From that time on she was armoured
in her duty as a wife and was able to make up by redoubled
dutifulness for whatever sins she still committed in spirit.
And, by a simple rule that settled everything for them, they
were now safe from that particularly distressful wavering
between the obligation to be greatly passionate and that to
be greatly loyal.

So that was what respectable people turned out to be like,
manifesting their respectability in terms of mind and
character. And however much love-at-first-sight there might
be in Hyacinth's novels, anyone who without more ado
simply went after another being—like an animal that knows
where it can drink and where not—would to them have
seemed like a wild primeval creature devoid of morality.
The son, who felt pity for that good-natured animal, his
father, in all the little matters of family life fought Hyacinth
and his mother as though they were a spiritual plague. Thus
he had let these two drive him into the diametrically
opposite corner of the field of contemporary attitudes.

This brilliant and versatile young man was studying
chemistry and turned a deaf ear to all questions that had no
clear-cut answer. He was, indeed, an embittered opponent
of all such considerations and was a fanatical disciple of the

cool, soberly fantastical, world-encompassing spirit of
modern technology. He was in favour of doing away with the
emotions. He was the antagonist of poetry, kindness, virtue,
simplicity. Song-birds need a branch to perch on, and the
branch a tree, and the tree the dumb brown earth to grow
in; but he flew, he was between the ages, he was somewhere
in mid-air. After this age, one that destroys just as much as
it constructs, there will come one that will inherit the new
premises we are so ascetically creating, and only then will
it be possible to say what we ought to have felt about
things. Such was more or less his train of thought. For the
time being the thing was to be as tough and austere as on an
expedition.

With such a strong intellectual drive he could not fail to
attract his teachers' attention, even as a schoolboy. He had
conceived ideas for new inventions and, after taking his
degree, was to spend one or two years devoting himself to
working them out—after which he hoped to rise, surely and
steadily, above that radiant horizon which is a young man's
image of his glamorous unknown future.

He loved Tonka because he did not love her, because she
did not stir his soul, but rinsed it clean and smooth, like fresh
water. He loved her more than he himself believed. And the
occasional tentative, needling enquiries made by his mother,
who sensed a danger that she could not come to grips with
because she had no certainty of it, impelled him to make all
speed. He sat for his examinations and left home.

V

His work took him to one of the big cities in Germany.
He had brought Tonka with him, for he felt he would have
been leaving her at the mercy of her enemies if he had left
her behind in the same town as her aunt and his mother.

Tonka bundled up her things and left home as callously, as inevitably, as the wind goes away with the sun or the rain with the wind.

In the city to which they had moved she got herself a job in a shop. She was quick to pick up the new work and earned much praise. But why then was she so badly paid? And why did she never ask for a rise, which she only did not get because she did not ask for it? Whenever she needed money, she had no qualms about accepting it from him. Not because he minded this, but simply because he was sometimes irritated by her humble ways and lack of worldliness, he would occasionally lecture her on the subject.

"Why don't you tell him he must pay you more?"

"I can't."

"You *can't*. But you keep on telling me you're always the one they call for when they want something special?"

"Yes."

"Well, then, why don't you speak up for yourself?"

Such talk always made Tonka's face take on a stubborn look. She did not argue, but she was impervious to his reasoning.

"Look," he would say, "that's a contradiction." Or: "Look, why don't you tell me——?" It was all no good. Then he would say: "Tonka, I shall be cross with you if you go on like this."

It was only when he cracked that whip that the little donkey-cart of humility and stubbornness would slowly get under way, and then she would come out with some such thing as, for instance, that she was not good at writing and was afraid, too, of making spelling mistakes, things that she had hitherto kept from him out of vanity. Then there would be a quiver of anxiety round her dear kind mouth, and it would curve into a rainbow of a smile only when she realised that she was not going to be found fault with for such blemishes.

On the contrary, he loved these defects as he loved her deformed finger-nail, the result of an injury at work. He sent her to evening classes and was amused by the absurd commercial copperplate that she learnt to write there. Even the wrong-headed notions that she came home with were something he found endearing. She would bring them home, as it were, in her mouth, without eating them. There was something nobly natural in her helplessness, her inability to reject whatever was vulgar and worthless, even while with an obscure sense of rightness she did not adopt it as her own. It was astonishing with what sureness she rejected everything crude, coarse, and uncivilised in whatever guise it came her way, although she could not have explained why she rejected it. And yet she lacked any urge to rise beyond her own orbit into a higher sphere. She remained pure and unspoilt, like Nature herself. But loving this simple creature was by no means so simple.

And at times she would startle him by knowing about things that must be almost outside her ken, such as chemistry. When, preoccupied with his work, he would talk of it, more to himself than to her, he would suddenly find that this or that was something she had heard of before. The first time this happened he had been amazed and had asked her about it. She told him that her mother's brother, who had lived with them in the little house where the brothel was, had been a student.

"And what's he doing now?"

"He died. Right after the exam."

"And how did you pick it up from him?"

"Well, I was quite small, of course," Tonka recounted, "but when he was studying he used to get me to hear his lessons for him. I didn't understand a word of it, but he used to write the questions out for me, on a piece of paper."

That was all. And for ten years all that had been hidden, like pretty stones whose names one does not know, kept in a box! That was the way it was now, too. Sitting quietly in the same room with him while he worked was all she needed to make her happy. She was Nature adjusting itself to Mind, not wanting to become Mind, but loving it and inscrutably attaching itself to it. She was like one of those animals that actually seek man's company.

His relationship to her was at that time in a queer state of tension, equally remote from infatuation and from any wish for a casual affair. Actually they had got on for a remarkably long time at home, without the temptations of sex entering into their relationship. They had been in the way of seeing each other in the evenings, going for walks together, telling each other of the day's little happenings and little annoyances, and it had all been as pleasant as eating bread and salt. True, after a time he had rented a room, but only because that was part of the whole thing and, anyway, one can't go walking about the streets for hours on end in the winter. There they had kissed for the first time—rather stiffly, more as though to set the seal on something than for the pleasure of it, and Tonka was very agitated and her lips were rough and hard. Even at that time they had talked of 'entirely belonging to each other'. That is to say, he had talked and Tonka had listened in silence. With that painful clarity in which one's bygone follies insist on recurring to one's memory, he recalled his very juvenile and didactic exposition of why it would have to come to that. It was only then, he had explained, that two people really opened up to each other. And so they had remained suspended between emotion and theory. Tonka merely begged a few times that it might be postponed for some days. Finally, he was rather affronted and asked if she thought it too great a sacrifice. So then a day was fixed.

And Tonka had come: in her little moss-green jacket, in the blue hat with the black bobbles, her cheeks pink from the brisk walk through the evening air. She laid the table, she made the tea. The only difference was that she bustled a little more than usual and kept her eyes fixed on the things she was handling. And he himself, although he had been waiting impatiently all day long, now sat on the sofa, watching her, immobilised by the icy stiffness of his youth. He realised that Tonka was trying not to think of the inevitable, and he was sorry he had insisted on fixing a day for it—it made him feel like a bailiff. But it only now occurred to him that he ought to have taken her by surprise, that he ought to have enticed her into it.

How remote he felt from any joy! On the contrary, he shrank from taking the bloom off that freshness which was wafted to him like a cool breeze every evening they spent together. But it had to be, sooner or later. He clutched at the necessity of it, and while he watched Tonka rather mechanically bustling about, it seemed to him that his intention was like a rope tied round her ankle, shortening at every turn.

After the meal, which they ate almost without speaking, they sat down side by side. He attempted a joke, and Tonka attempted a laugh. But her mouth twisted, her lips were tight, and the next instant she was grave again.

All at once he asked her: "Tonka, are you sure it's all right? Have we really made up our minds?"

Tonka lowered her head, and it seemed to him that her eyes were veiled for a moment. But she did not say yes, and she did not say that she loved him.

He bent down to her, speaking softly, trying to encourage her, though he himself was embarrassed. "You know, at first it's all rather strange, perhaps even rather unromantic. After all, you know, we have to be careful. I mean, it isn't just. . . . So you'd better shut your eyes. And so——?"

The bed was already turned down, and Tonka went over to it. But suddenly irresolute again, she sat down on the chair beside it.

"Tonka!" he called out to her.

She stood up again and, with averted face, began to unfasten her clothes.

An ungrateful thought remained associated with this sweet moment.

Was Tonka giving herself of her own free will? He had not promised her any love. Why did she not rebel against a situation that excluded the highest hopes? She acted in silence, as though she were subdued by the authority of 'the master'. Perhaps she would also obey another who was equally determined?

There she stood in all the awkwardness of her maiden nakedness. It was moving to see how the skin enclosed her body like too tight a garment.

His flesh was wiser and more humane than his youthfully pseudo-sophisticated thoughts, and he made a move towards her.

As though she were trying to escape from him, Tonka slipped into bed, with a movement that was oddly clumsy and unlike her.

All he remembered of what happened after that was that in passing the chair he had felt the thing he was most intimate and familiar with had been left behind on that chair, with the clothes he knew so well. When he came by, there rose from them the dear fresh smell that he was always first aware of whenever they met. What awaited him in the bed was something unknown and strange. He hesitated a moment longer.

Tonka lay there, with her eyes shut and her face turned to the wall, for an endless age, in terrible lonely fear. When at last she felt him beside her, her eyes were wet with warm tears. Then came a new wave of fear, dismay at her ingratitude, a senseless word uttered as though in search of help, as though stumbling out of some infinitely long, lonely corridor, to transform itself into his name—and then she was his. He hardly grasped how magically, and with how much childlike courage, she stole into his being, what simple-minded strategy she had worked out in order to take possession of all she admired in him: it was only necessary to belong to him entirely and then she would be part of it all.

Later, he could not in the least remember how it had all happened.

VI

And then in a single day, in a single morning, it was all transformed into a tangle of thorns.

They had been living together for some years when Tonka one day realised that she was pregnant. It was not just any ordinary day. Heaven had so ordained it that if one counted back from that day it appeared that the conception must have taken place during a period when he was away on a journey. Tonka, however, claimed to have noticed her condition only when it was no longer quite possible to establish the beginning of it with certainty.

In such a situation there are certain obvious ideas that will occur to anyone. On the other hand, there was no man far and wide whom one could reasonably suspect.

Some weeks later destiny manifested itself still more plainly: Tonka fell ill. It was a disease that the mother's blood had been infected with, either by the child she had conceived or directly by the child's father. It was a horrible, dangerous, insidious disease. But whatever way she had been infected, the curious thing was that in either case there was a discrepancy between the various dates. Apart from this, as far as could be medically established with certainty he was not suffering from the disease himself. So there was either some mystical bond linking him with Tonka or she was guilty on an ordinary human level. There were, of course, also other possible explanations—at least theoretically, ideally speaking—but practically speaking their probability was as good as nil. On the other hand, from the practical point of view the probability that he was neither the father of Tonka's child nor the cause of her illness amounted to a certainty.

If one considers the situation for a moment, one can see how difficult it was for him to grasp this. 'From the practical point of view. . . .' If you go to a business man, not with a commercial proposition that will appeal to his profit-making instincts, but to harangue him about the spirit of the times and the moral obligations of the rich, he will know you have come to get money out of him. On that point he will never be mistaken, although there is of course always the possibility that you might have come quite unselfishly, just to give him some good advice. Similarly, a judge will not have a moment's doubt when the accused tells him that the incriminating article found on his person was given to him by 'a man he had never seen before'. And yet there is no reason why this should not really happen once in a while. But the management of human affairs rests on the fact that there is no need to reckon with all the possibilities, because the most extreme cases practically never do occur. But theoretically? The old doctor to whom he had first taken Tonka, and whom he had seen alone afterwards, had shrugged his shoulders. Was it possible? Well, of course one couldn't say that it was entirely impossible. . . . There was a kindly, mournful look in his eyes, and what he evidently meant was: Don't let us waste time talking about that—it's much too improbable to be worthy of serious consideration. A doctor is, after all, a human being, and rather than assume that he is dealing with something that is medically quite improbable, he will assume the cause to be a human lapse. For freaks of Nature are rare.

So the next phase was that of a kind of medical litigiousness. He went to doctor after doctor. The second doctor came to the same conclusion as the first, and the third to the same conclusion as the second. He argued with them. He tried to play off against each other the views of various medical schools of thought. The physicians listened to him in silence, sometimes with a tolerant smile, as though he were a lunatic or a blockhead past praying for. And of course he himself knew, even while he was arguing, that he might just as well have asked: 'Is there such a thing as immaculate conception?' And they would only have been able to tell him: 'We have no medical evidence of it.' They would not even have been able to produce a law excluding the possibility. All they knew was: There was no evidence. And yet if he were to accept this, he would be a cuckold past praying for!

Perhaps, indeed, one of the doctors whom he had gone to see had told him so to his face. Or perhaps he himself had thought of it; after all, there was no reason why he should not have thought of it. But it was as if one were to exert oneself thinking out all the possible combinations and permutations of relevant finger-movements just because one could not fix a collar-stud—for all this time, while he was producing theory after theory, he was confronted by the irrefutable experience of Tonka's face. It was all a walking through cornfields, a sense of the air, the swallows dipping and darting, and in the distance the spires of the town, girls singing . . . remote from all truth, in a world that does not know the concept 'truth'. Tonka was now living in the deep world of fairy-tale. It was the world of the Anointed, of the Virgin, and of Pontius Pilate, and the doctors said that Tonka would need to be nursed and cared for if she was to survive.

VII

Still, he went on trying, of course, every now and again to wring a confession out of Tonka. After all, he was a man, and he was no fool. At this time she was working in a big, trashy shop in a working-class district. She had to be there at seven

in the morning and could not leave before half-past nine in
the evening—kept there often merely for the sake of some
belated customer's few pence. She never saw the sun. She
did not sleep at his place, and there was no time to thrash
out their emotional problems. They could not count on even
this scanty source of income for any length of time, for
sooner or later her pregnancy would be noticed. And they
were already in financial difficulties. He had used up the
money provided for his studies, and he was not capable of
earning anything; this is always particularly difficult at the
beginning of a scientific career, and besides, he had come so
near to solving the problem he had set himself—though the
solution still just escaped him—that he felt he had to
concentrate all his energies on this work.

Living like this, never seeing the daylight and perpetually
in anxiety, Tonka began to fade. Poor Tonka, of course she
did not fade beautifully, as some women do, radiating an
intoxicating splendour in decay; she wilted like some dim
little herb in a kitchen garden that turns an ugly yellow
and shrivels away as soon as it loses the freshness of its green.
Her cheeks grew pale and hollow, and this made her nose
look too big and prominent, her mouth seemed too wide, and
even her ears seemed to stick out. Her body grew gaunt, and
the full, curving flesh wasted away, letting the peasant
skeleton peer through the skin.

He, whose well-bred face wore better under hardship and
whose store of good clothes lasted longer, noticed, whenever
he went out with her, that passers-by would sometimes cast
an astonished glance at them. And because he was not
without vanity, he bore Tonka a grudge for not having the
pretty clothes that he could not buy her. He was angry with
her for being so shabby, although it was his own fault. But
actually, if he could have afforded it, he would have bought
her pretty, floating maternity-clothes and would only then
have charged her with her infidelity.

Every time he tried to extract a confession from her, Tonka would utter the same denial. She said she did not know how it had happened. When he implored her, in the name of their old affection, not to lie to him, an anguished look would come over her face. And when he stormed at her, she merely said she was not lying. And what was anyone to do then? Should he have beaten her and sworn at her? Should he have abandoned her in her dreadful plight? He no longer slept with her. But even on the rack she would not have confessed, if only because she could not talk to him since she had realised that he mistrusted her. And this dumb obstinacy was all the more frustrating for him because his loneliness was no longer alleviated by any element of grace. He had to be tenacious, to watch and wait.

He had made up his mind to ask his mother for financial help. But his father had for a long time been hovering on the brink of death, and this meant there was no money to spare. He had no means of checking this, though he did know his mother was frightened of the possibility that he might intend marrying Tonka some day. Indeed, she was worried by the thought that any other marriage would be made impossible because Tonka was in the way. And when it all dragged on for so long, his studies still unfinished, success not yet achieved, his father still lingering on his death-bed, and all the domestic cares she had to cope with into the bargain, it seemed in some way or another to be all Tonka's fault. Tonka seemed to be not merely the cause of all that was going wrong now, but positively something like an ill omen, a herald of misfortune, in that it was she who had first disturbed the normal tenor of their life. This obscure conviction of his mother's had become apparent to him, both from her letters and during his visits home. What it came to fundamentally was that she felt it was a blot on the family honour for her son to be more attached to a girl 'of that sort' than was generally the case with young men.

Hyacinth was made to give him a talking to on the subject. And when the young man, taken aback by the implicit superstitiousness of this attitude, which reminded him of his own painful, irrational experiences, put up vehement opposition Tonka was referred to as 'an ungrateful creature' who had had no consideration for a family's peace of mind. Awkward allusions were then made to 'amorous arts' by means of which she kept 'a hold on him'. In short, what came to light was every respectable mother's entire ignorance of real life. The same thing was manifest in the answer that he got now, as though every single coin that helped to keep him with Tonka could only contribute to his undoing.

At this point he decided to write again and acknowledge himself to be the father of Tonka's child.

By way of answer his mother came in person, 'to straighten the whole thing out'.

She did not come to his lodgings, as though she were afraid of encountering something intolerable there. She summoned him to her hotel. By taking refuge in her sense of duty she had rid herself of a certain amount of embarrassment, and she spoke of the great concern he was causing them all, of the added danger to his ailing father's life, and bonds that would last a lifetime. With clumsy cunning she pulled out all the stops of proper feeling. Yet a note of indulgence pervading all she said kept her listener, bored though he was by the maternal tactics he could so easily see through, in a state of mistrustful curiosity.

"You see," she said, "this misfortune might make everything turn out for the best, even now, and that would be a lucky escape for all concerned. The main thing is to prevent any recurrence of such incidents in future."

To this end she had managed to persuade Father to provide a certain sum of money. So—she explained, as though it were a great benefaction—all the girl's claims could be settled and the child provided for.

To her surprise her son, having calmly asked how much was being offered and having heard the answer, shook his head and merely said, in the same calm tone: "It can't be done."

Clinging to her hopes, she retorted: "It must be done! Don't go on deluding yourself. Many young men commit similar follies, but they let it be a lesson to them. This is really your chance to free yourself. Don't miss it out of a misguided sense of honour. You owe it to yourself and to us."

"How do you mean, it's my chance?"

"It's quite obvious. The girl will show more good sense than you are doing. She knows very well that such relationships always come to an end when a child arrives."

He asked for time to think about it—until the next day. Something had flashed upon him.

His mother, the doctors with all their smiling reasonableness, the smooth running of the underground train by which he made his way back to Tonka, the steady movements of the policeman's arms regulating the traffic, the city's roar like the thundering of a waterfall: it was all one and the same thing. He stood in the lonely hollow space under the cascade of it—untouched by even a splash, but utterly cut off.

He asked Tonka if she would agree.

Tonka said: "Yes." How terribly ambiguous this Yes of hers was! In it there lay all the good sense his mother had predicted, but round the mouth that uttered it there was the twitching of bewilderment.

The next day he told his mother point-blank, before she could ask him any questions, that he was perhaps not the father of Tonka's child, that Tonka was ill, and that for all this he would rather consider himself ill and himself the father of the child than abandon Tonka.

His mother smiled in defeat, confronted with such wilful self-deception, bestowed a last, fond glance on him, and left. He realised she would dedicate herself to saving her flesh and blood from shame, and he now had a powerful enemy in league with him.

VIII

Finally, Tonka lost her job. He had been growing almost uneasy over the fact that this misfortune was so long delayed. The shopkeeper for whom Tonka worked was a small, ugly man, but in their distress he had seemed to them like some superhuman power. For weeks they had been guessing: "He must know by now. . . . Well, obviously he's a decent sort and doesn't hit someone who's down. . . ." and then again: "He hasn't noticed, thank heaven he hasn't noticed anything yet!" And then one day Tonka was called into the office and asked, point-blank, about her condition. She could not get any answer out, her eyes merely filled with tears. And this practical man was quite unmoved by the fact that she was too upset to speak. He gave her a month's wages and dismissed her on the spot. He was so furious that he shouted at her, complaining that it was all her fault if he was now shorthanded and that it had been dishonest of her to conceal her condition when she took the job. He did not even send the typist out of the room before saying such things to her.

Afterwards, Tonka felt very wicked, and even he secretly admired that sordid nameless little tradesman, who had not hesitated for a minute but had sacrificed Tonka to his business sense, and with her her tears, a child, and heaven alone knew what inventions, what souls, what human destinies—things of which the man had no notion, things in which he had no interest.

Now they had to have their meals in small, working-class places, amid dirt and incivility, where for a few pence they got a kind of food that did not agree with him. He would call for Tonka punctually and fulfil his duty by taking her to

have these meals. He cut a strange figure, in his well-made
clothes, among the labourers and market-porters, grave,
taciturn, and constant at the side of his pregnant companion.
Many sneering glances were cast at him, and many respectful ones, which were no less painful. It was a strange life he
was leading, with his invention in his head, and with his
conviction of Tonka's infidelity, amid the flotsam and
jetsam of the great city. He had never before felt the common
beastliness of mankind so intensely: wherever he walked
through the streets, there it went, yapping and growling
like a pack of hounds, each person alone in his greed, but
all of them together one pack—and only he had no one to
whom he could turn for help or to whom he could even
have told his story.

He had never had time for friends, doubtless indeed had
taken little interest in them, nor had he himself been
attractive to others. He went though life burdened with his
ideas, and that is a burden dangerous to the very life of him
who bears it, so long as people have not realised there is
something in it that they can turn to their own advantage.
He did not even know in what direction he might have
searched for help. He was a stranger in the world. And what
was Tonka? Spirit of his spirit? No—perhaps a symbol, some
cryptic correspondence to himself, an alien creature who had
attached herself to him, with her secret locked within her.

There was a little chink, a far-off gleam towards which his
thoughts were beginning to move. The invention he was
working at would in the end turn out to be of great importance for others as well as himself, and it was clear that
something else was involved besides the intellectual pro-
cesses—a courage, a confidence, an intuitive sense of the
future, that never deceived him, a healthy urge to live, like
a star that he followed. And in all this he too was only
pursuing the greater probabilities, and always in one of
them he would find what he wanted. What he relied on was

that everything would turn out to be the way it always was, so that he could hit upon the one thing in which he could discover the desired otherness. If he had set out to test every possible doubt, as he was doing with Tonka, he would never have come to the end of it. Thinking means not thinking too much, and no invention can be made without sacrificing something of the boundlessness of the inventive talent. This half of his life seemed to be under the influence of the star of a happiness or a mystery beyond proving. And the other half lay in darkness.

Now he and Tonka bought sweepstake tickets. On the day of the draw he met Tonka and they went and bought the list of results. It was a miserable little sweepstake with a first prize of only a few thousand marks; but that did not matter, it would have tided them over the immediate future. Even if it had been only a few hundred marks, he could have bought Tonka what she most needed in the way of clothes and underclothes, or have moved her out of the unhealthy garret where she lived. And if it had been only twenty marks, it would have been some encouragement, and he would have bought more sweepstake tickets. Indeed, even if they had won no more than five marks, it would have been a sign that the attempt to restore contact with life was regarded with favour in unknown regions.

But with all their three tickets they drew blanks. Then, of course, he had to pretend he had only bought them for fun. Even while he had been waiting for Tonka there had been an emptiness in him that heralded failure. The truth probably was that he had been wavering between hope and despair all the time. In his circumstances even a few pennies wasted on a newspaper meant a real loss. He suddenly felt there was an invisible power that wished him ill, and he felt himself to be surrounded by hostility.

After that he became downright superstitious. The man who became so was the one who called for Tonka in the evenings, while the other man he was went on working like a scientist.

He had two rings, which he wore alternately. Both were valuable, but one was a piece of fine old workmanship, and the other was only a present from his parents, which he had never particularly cherished. Then he noticed that on days he was wearing the newer one—which was only an ordinary expensive ring—he seemed to be spared further deterioration of his situation rather more than on days when he was wearing the good, old one; and from that time on he could not bring himself to put it on again, but wore the other, like a yoke laid upon him.

Again, one day when he happened not to have shaved, he had good luck. The next day, when he did shave in spite of having observed the omen, he was punished for his transgression by another of those trivial sordid misfortunes that would not have amounted to anything more than absurdity in a situation less desperate than his. From then on he could not bring himself to shave any more. He grew a beard, doing no more than carefully trimming it to a point, and he continued to wear it through all the sad weeks that followed.

This beard disfigured him, but it was like Tonka: the uglier it looked, the more anxiously it was tended. Perhaps his feeling for her became all the more affectionate the more profoundly it was disappointed; for like the beard it was inwardly so good because of the outward ugliness. Tonka did not like the beard and did not know what it meant to him. And without her he would never have known how ugly this beard was, for one knows little of oneself unless one has someone else in whom one is reflected. And since what one knows is really nothing, might it not be that at times he wished Tonka dead so that this intolerable existence might be over and done with? And perhaps he liked the beard simply because it was like a mask, concealing everything.

IX

There were still times when he would, as it were, try to
ambush her: he would ask what seemed to be a perfectly
harmless question, hoping that the smooth sound of the
words would take her off her guard. But more often it was
he who was taken unawares and defeated.

"Look, it's absolutely senseless going on denying it," he
would say coaxingly. "Come on now, tell me. Then everything'll be just the way it used to be. How on earth did it
happen?"

But her answer was always the same: "Send me away if
you won't believe me."

That was, of course, her way of making the most of her own
helplessness, but it was also the most genuine answer she
could give. For she had no medical or philosophical argu-
ments to defend herself with: all she could do was to vouch
for the truth of her words with the truth of her whole being.

Then he would go with her whenever she went out, because
he did not dare to leave her alone. There was nothing definite
that he feared, but it made him uneasy to think of her alone
in the great alien streets of the city. And when he would meet
her somewhere in the evenings, and they walked along, and
in the dusk they would pass some man who gave no sign of
knowing them, he would sometimes have the feeling that the
man's face was familiar, and it seemed to him that Tonka
blushed; and all at once he would remember that there had
been an occasion when they had been together with this
man. Instantly, then, and with a certainty equal to the
certainty he felt when gazing into Tonka's innocent face, he
would have the conviction: This is the one! Once it seemed
to be a well-to-do young man who was learning the business
in an export firm and whom they had met a few times. Once
it was a tenor who had worked in a *café chantant* until he lost

his voice and who had a room in the same lodging-house as Tonka. They were always such ludicrously marginal figures; they were like dirty parcels thrown into his memory, tied up with string, each parcel containing the truth—but at the first attempt to undo it, the package would disintegrate, leaving him with nothing but an agonising sense of helplessness and a heap of dust.

These certainties of Tonka's infidelity had, indeed, something of the quality of dreams. Tonka endured them with all that touching, dumbly affectionate humility of hers. But how many different meanings that could have! And then, going through his memories, he began to see how ambiguous they all were. For instance, the very simplicity of the way she attached herself to him could equally well mean that she did not care one way or the other or that she was following her heart. The way she served him could indicate either apathy or a delight in doing it. Might that dog-like devotion of hers not mean that she would follow any master like a dog? This was something he had, after all, sensed in that first night. Had it in fact been her first night? He had only paid attention to her emotional reactions, and certainly there had been no very perceptible physical signs. Now it was too late. Her silence was now a blanket over everything, and might equally well indicate innocence or obduracy, it could equally well mean cunning or sorrow, remorse, or fear; but then too it might mean that she was ashamed on his behalf. Yet it would not have helped him even if he could have lived all of it all over again. Once a human being is mistrusted, the plainest signs of faithfulness will positively turn into signs of unfaithfulness. On the other hand, where there is trust, the most glaring evidence of unfaithfulness will seem to be signs of misunderstood faithfulness, crying like a child that the grown-ups have locked out. Nothing could be interpreted on its own merits alone, one thing depended on the other, one had to trust or mistrust the whole of it, love it or take it for deceit and delusion. If one was to understand Tonka, one had to respond to her in one definite way; one had, as it were, to call out to her, telling her who she was. What she was, depended almost entirely on him. And so Tonka would become a blur, mildly dazzling as a fairy-tale.

And he wrote to his mother: 'Her legs are as long from the foot to the knee as from the knee to the hip, long legs that walk like a pair of twins, without tiring. Her skin is not delicate, but it is white and without blemish. Her breasts are almost a little too heavy, and the hair in her armpits is dark and matted, which looks charmingly shameful on that slender white body. Her hair hangs down in loose strands over her ears, and at time she thinks she has to take the curling-tongs to it and do it up high, which makes her look like a servant-girl. And that, surely, is the only harm she has ever done in her life. . . .'

Or he would write in answer to his mother: 'Between Ancona and Fiume, or perhaps it is between Middelkerke and some town whose name I don't remember, there is a lighthouse, the light of it flashing out over the sea at night like the flick of a fan. One flick, and then there is nothing. And then another flick. And edelweiss grows in the meadows of the Venna valley.

'Is that geography or botany or nautical science? It is a face, it is something that is there, solitary, quite alone, eternally —and so in a way, too, it isn't there at all. Or what is it?'

Naturally he never posted these senseless answers to his mother's letters.

There was something impalpable missing, something that was needed to make his certainty complete.

Once he had been travelling by night with his mother and Hyacinth, and in the small hours, out of the depths of that inexorable fatigue which makes the bodies in a train sway to and fro in search of some support, it seemed to him that his mother was leaning against Hyacinth, and that she knew she was, and that Hyacinth was holding her hand. His eyes had widened with anger at the time, for he was sorry for his father. But when he leaned forward, Hyacinth was sitting at some distance and his mother's head was inclined to the other side, away from him. Then after a while, when he had settled back in his seat, the whole thing happened all over again. That seeing and not seeing something was torment, and the torment itself was a darkness through which it was hard to see. Finally he told himself that now he was really sure, and he resolved to challenge his mother about it in the morning. But in broad daylight the whole thing had vanished like the darkness itself.

And another time, again when they were on a journey, his mother fell ill. Hyacinth, who had to write to Father on her behalf, said irritably: "But I don't know what to say." This from Hyacinth, who wrote reams to Mother whenever he was away! Then there was a quarrel, for again the boy had grown angry, and his mother began to feel worse: she seemed to be seriously ill. Something had to be done for her, and Hyacinth's hands kept on getting in the way of his, and he kept on pushing them aside. At last Hyacinth asked rather mournfully: "Why do you keep on pushing me away?" The note of unhappiness in that voice quite shocked him. How little one knows what one knows, or wants what one wants.

That is not difficult to understand. Yet he was capable of sitting in his room, tortured by jealousy and telling himself that he was not jealous at all, that it was something quite different, something out of the ordinary, something oddly invented; and yet this was himself and his own feelings. When he raised his head and looked about him, everything seemed to be the same as usual. The wallpaper was green and grey. The doors were reddish brown, with faint gleams of light reflected on them. The hinges were dark, made of copper. There was a chair in the room, brown mahogany and wine-red plush. But all these things seemed to be somehow tilted, leaning to one side. There was a suggestion, in their very uprightness, that they were about to topple over. They seemed endless and meaningless.

He rubbed his eyes and then looked round again. But it was not his eyes. It was the things. The fact was that belief in them had to be there before they themselves could be there; if one did not look at the world with the world's eyes, the world already in one's own gaze, it fell apart into meaningless details that live as sadly far apart from each other as the stars in the night-sky. He only needed to look out of the window to see how the world of, say, a cab-driver waiting in the street below was suddenly intersected by the world of a clerk walking past. The result was something slashed open, a disgusting jumble, an inside-out and side-by-side of things in the street, a turmoil of focal points moving along their tracks, and around each of them there extended a radius of complacency and self-confidence, all aids to walking upright through a world in which there was no such thing as above and below. Volition, cognition, and perception were like a tangled skein. One noticed this only when one tried to find the end of the thread. But perhaps there was some other way of going through the world, other than following the thread of truth? At such moments, when a veneer of coldness separated him from everything, Tonka was more than a fairy-tale: she was almost a visitation.

'Either I must make Tonka my wife,' he told himself, 'or I must give her up and give up these thoughts.'

But no one will blame him for doing neither one nor the other, despite these reasonings of his. For although all such thoughts and feelings may well be justified, nobody nowadays doubts that they are very largely figments of the imagination. And so he went on reasoning, without taking his reasoning seriously. Sometimes it seemed to him that he was being sorely tried, but when he came to himself again

and spoke to himself again, as it were, man to man, he had
to tell himself that this ordeal consisted, after all, only of
the question whether he would force himself to believe in
Tonka against the ninety-nine per cent probability that she
had been unfaithful to him and that he was simply a fool.
Admittedly this humiliating possibility had by now lost much
of its importance.

X

It was, oddly enough, a period in which his scientific work
went remarkably well. He had solved the main problems
involved in his project, and it could not be long now before
he got results. There were already people coming to see him,
and even if it was chemistry that they talked about, they
brought him some emotional reassurance. They all believed
that he was going to succeed. The probability of it already
amounted to ninety-nine per cent! And he drugged himself
with work.

But even although his social existence was now taking on
firmer outlines and entering, so to speak, the state of worldly
maturity, the moment he stopped working his thoughts no
longer ran along in definite grooves. The faintest reminder
of Tonka's existence would start a drama going in his mind:
figures in a play, one taking over from the other, none of
them revealing its meaning, all of them like strangers daily
encountering each other in the same street. There was that
commercial traveller of a tenor whom he had once suspected
of being the man with whom Tonka had betrayed him. And
there were all the others to whom he had ever pinned his
certainty. It was not that they did anything. They were
merely there. Or even if they did do that frightful thing, it
no longer meant much. And since they were sometimes two
or even more persons rolled into one, it was no straightforward matter being jealous of them. The whole situation

became as transparent as the clearest air, and yet clearer still, until it reached that state of freedom and emptiness which was void of all egoism, and under this immovable dome the accidents of terrestrial life pursued their microscopic course.

And sometimes all this turned into dreams. Or perhaps it had all begun in dreams, in a pallid shadowy realm from which he emerged the instant he shed the weight of his working hours, as though it were all meant as a warning to him that this work was not his true life.

These real dreams were on a deeper level than his waking existence; they were warm as low-ceilinged, bright-coloured rooms. In these dream-rooms Tonka would be harshly scolded by her aunt for not having shed any tears at Grandmamma's funeral; or an ugly man acknowledged himself to be the father of Tonka's child, and she, when he looked at her queryingly, for the first time did not deny it, but stood there, motionless, with an infinite smile. This had happened in a room with green plants in it, with red rugs on the floor and blue stars on the walls. But when he turned his eyes away from that infinity the rugs were green, the plants had big ruby-red leaves, the walls had a yellow glimmer as of soft human skin, and Tonka, still standing there, was transparently blue, like moonlight.

He almost fled into these dreams as into some simple-hearted happiness. Perhaps it was all mere cowardice. Perhaps all they meant was that if only Tonka would confess, all would be well. He was much confused by their frequency, and yet they had not the intolerable tension of the half-waking state, which was gradually bearing him higher and higher, away out of it all.

In these dreams Tonka was always as great as love itself, and no longer the care-worn little shop-girl she was in real life. And she looked different every time. Sometimes she was her own younger sister (not that she had ever had a sister) and often she was merely the rustling of skirts, the ring and cadence of another voice, the most unfamiliar and surprising of movements, all the intoxicating charm of unknown adventures, which came to him, the way such things come only in dreams, out of the warm familiarity of her name— and they gave him the floating sense of joy that lies in anti- cipation, even though still tense with unfulfilment. These ambiguous images made him feel a seemingly undefined, disembodied affection and more than human intensity of emotion, and it was hard to say whether these feelings were gradually detaching themselves from Tonka or only now really beginning to be associated with her. When he reflected on this he guessed that this enigmatic capacity for trans- ference and independence that love had must also manifest itself in waking life. It is not that the woman loved is the origin of the emotions apparently aroused by her; they are merely set behind her like a light. But whereas in dreams there is still a hair's-breadth margin, a crack, separating the love from the beloved, in waking life this split is not apparent; one is merely the victim of *doppelgänger*-trickery and cannot help seeing a human being as wonderful who is not so at all. He could not bring himself to set the light behind Tonka.

The fact that he so often thought of horses at this time must have been somehow connected with this, and obviously was a sign of something significant. Perhaps it was Tonka and the sweepstake in which they drew blanks. Or perhaps it was his childhood—those beautiful brown and dappled horses, their heavy harness decorated with brass and fur. And then sometimes there would be a sudden glowing of the child's heart in him, the heart for which magnanimity, kindness, and faith were not yet obligations that one dis- regarded, but knights in an enchanted garden of adventures and liberations. Yet perhaps too this was merely the last flaring up of a flame about to die, the itching of a scar that was beginning to form. For it was like this. The horses were always hauling timber, and the bridge was always echoing under their hooves, a muffled wooden sound, and the timbermen wore their short, checkered jackets, purple and brown. They all doffed their hats as they passed the tall cross, with the tin Christ on it, halfway across the bridge. Only a little boy who stood there by the bridge, looking on, in the winter, refused to doff his hat, for he was a clever little boy and didn't believe in such things any more. And then he suddenly couldn't button up his coat. He couldn't do it. The frost had numbed his little fingers, they grasped a button and tugged at it, hard, but just as they were pushing it into the button-hole, it jumped out again, and his fingers were left helpless and amazed. However hard they tried, they always ended up in paralysed bewilderment.

And it was this memory that came back to him so often.

XI

Amid all these uncertainties Tonka's pregnancy took its course, revealing the harshness of reality.

There was the shambling gait, with Tonka seeming in need of a supporting arm, the heavy body that was mysteriously warm, the manner of sitting down, with legs apart, unwieldy and touchingly ugly: all the changing aspects of the miraculous process, steadily transforming the girlish body into a seed-pod, altering all its proportions, broadening the hips and pressing them down, taking the sharpness from the knees, thickening the neck, making the breasts into udders, streaking the skin of the belly with fine red and blue veins, so that it was startling to see how close to the outer world the blood circulated—as though that were a sign of death. All this unshapeliness was in fact a new shape, moulded as much by passivity as by main force; and the same distortion of human normality was reflected in her eyes:

they now had a blank look, and her gaze would linger on things for a long time, shifting only with an effort. It would often rest for a long time on him. She was now keeping house for him again, waiting on him laboriously, as though she wanted to prove to him in these last days that she lived only for him. She showed no trace of shame for her ugliness and deformation, only the desire to do as much as she could for him in spite of her awkwardness.

They were now spending nearly as much time together as in earlier days. They did not talk much, but they liked to be near each other, for her pregnancy was advancing like the hand of a clock, and they were helpless in the face of it. They ought to have talked the whole thing out together, but they did nothing about it, and time moved on. The shadowy being, the unreal element on him, sometimes struggled for words, and the realisation that everything ought to be measured by quite different standards almost broke surface —but, like all understanding, even this was ambiguous and without certainty. And time was running on, time was running away, time was running out. The clock on the wall had more to do with reality than their thoughts had.

It was a suburban room where nothing of importance could happen. There they sat, and the clock on the wall was a round kitchen clock, telling kitchen time. And his mother bombarded him with letters proving everything up to the hilt. Instead of sending money to him, she spent it on getting opinions from doctors, in the hope of making him see reason. He quite understood this and no longer resented it. Once she sent him a medical statement that made it really clear to him that Tonka *must* have been unfaithful to him at that time. But far from upsetting him, it was almost a pleasant surprise. As though it had nothing to do with him, he wondered how it had happened, and all he felt was: Poor Tonka, she has had to pay so dearly for a single passing aberration! Yes, sometimes he had to pull himself up short, on the point of saying quite cheerfully: 'Listen, Tonka—I've only just realised what we've been forgetting about—who it was you were unfaithful to me with, that time!' So everything petered out. Nothing new happened. There was only the clock. And the old familiar bond between them.

And even although they had not talked about it, this brought back the moments when the bodies desired each other. They came like old friends who, returning after long absence, will simply walk into the room. The windows on the far side of the narrow courtyard were eyeless in the shadow, the people were all out at work; down below the yard was dark as a well; and the sun shone into the room as though through frosted glass, making each object stand out sharply, in a dead gleam. And there, for instance, lay a little old calendar, open as though Tonka had just been going through it, and on the wide expanse of one leaf, like a memorial erected to that one day, there was a small red exclamation-mark. All the other leaves were covered with everyday domestic entries, shopping-lists, sums, and the like, and only this one was empty except for the one sign. Not for an instant did he doubt that this betokened the memory of the incident that Tonka denied. The time just about fitted. His certainty was like a rush of blood to the head. Yet certainty itself merely lay in this vehemence, and in the next instant it had again dwindled into nothingness. If one was going to believe in what this exclamation-mark might signify, then one might just as well believe in the miraculous. What was so appalling was, after all, the very fact of believing in neither.

There was a startled glance exchanged between them. Tonka had obviously seen him looking at that page in the calendar.

In the queer indoor light all the things in the room now looked like mummies of their former selves. The bodies grew cold, the fingertips became icy, the intestines were hot coils of tubing in which all vital warmth was contained.

True, the doctor had said that Tonka must be spared any sort of stress if complications were to be avoided. But at this moment doctors were the very people whom he must not trust. And yet all his efforts to trust in something else were also futile. Perhaps Tonka was not strong enough? She remained a half-born myth.

"Come here," Tonka said gently.

And they shared their anguish and their warmth, in mournful resignation.

XII

Tonka had gone into hospital. The turn for the worse had come. He was allowed to see her at visiting-hours. So the time had slipped away, irrevocably.

On the day she left the house he had his beard shaved off. Now he was more like himself again.

Later on he discovered that that very day she had lost patience, lost her head, in fact, and had gone and done something she had been putting off all this time for the sake of saving money: as though making a last gesture of independence before going into hospital, she went and had a decayed molar extracted. Her cheek must now be sadly sunken, and all because she would never let herself be properly looked after.

Now his dreams began to intensify again.

One dream recurred in many forms. A fair, plain girl with a pale complexion was telling him that his new girl—some invented figure in the dream—had left him, at which he became curious to hear more and exclaimed: "And do you think Tonka was any better?" He shook his head, with an expression of doubt on his face, to provoke the girl into making some equally vehement protestation of Tonka's virtues, and he already had a foretaste of the relief he would get from her decisive answer. But then he saw a frightful slow smirk gradually spreading over the girl's face. And she said: "Oh, her! But she was a dreadful liar! She was quite nice, of course, but you couldn't believe a word she said. She always wanted to be a smart woman of the world." What caused him most anguish in this dream was not that dreadful smile, which was like a knife cutting into his flesh, but the fact that he could never ward off the eager platitudes at the end of it: powerless in his sleep, he heard them being uttered as though out of the depths of his own mind.

And so when he went to visit Tonka, he would often sit at her bedside with nothing to say. He would gladly have been as magnanimous as in certain dreams he had had earlier, and he might actually have brought himself to be so if he had devoted to Tonka some of the energy with which he was working on his invention.

Although the doctors had never been able to find any trace of the disease in him, he was linked with Tonka by the possibility of some mysterious connection: he only had to believe her, and instantly he would be diseased. And perhaps (he told himself) that would have been possible in some other age. He was beginning to enjoy letting his imagination rove back into the past, telling himself such things as that in some other age Tonka's fame might have spread far and wide and that princes would not have disdained to woo her. But nowadays? This was something he really ought to think about at length some day.

So he would sit at her bedside, being kind and affectionate to her, but never uttering the words: 'I believe you.' And this although he had long believed in her. For he believed her only in such a way that he was no longer able to be unbelieving and angry, and not in such a way that he could face the rational consequences of it. This not believing kept him immune and safely anchored to the earth.

The things that went on in the hospital tormented his

imagination: it was all doctors, examinations, routine. The world had snatched Tonka away and strapped her to the table. Yet he was almost beginning to regard this as her own fault; if she was indeed something of deeper significance, under the surface of what the world was doing to her, then everything in the world ought to be different too, so that one would want to fight for it. And he was already beginning to surrender. Only a few days after their separation she was already a little remote from him, for he was no longer able to make daily amends for the strangeness of her all too simple life, that strangeness which he had always felt, in however slight degree.

And because he usually had so little to say when he visited Tonka in hospital, he wrote letters to her, saying a great deal that he otherwise kept to himself. He wrote to her almost as seriously as to some great love. Yet even these letters stopped short of ever declaring: 'I believe in you.' He was quite disconcerted to receive no answers from Tonka, until he realised that he had never posted these letters. The fact was, he could not be sure that he meant what he wrote; it was simply a state of mind that he could do nothing about except write it out of his system. That made him realise how lucky he was, despite everything—he could express himself. Tonka could not do that. And the moment he saw that, he saw Tonka for just what she was; a snowflake falling all alone in the midst of a summer's day. But the very next moment this no longer explained anything. Perhaps it all amounted to no more than that she was a dear, good girl. And time was passing too quickly. One day he was horribly overtaken by the news that she would not last much longer. He reproached himself bitterly for having been so careless, for not having looked after her properly, and he did not attempt to hide this from her.

Then she told him of a dream she had had a few nights earlier. For Tonka also had dreams.

"In my dream I knew I was going to die soon," she said. "And it's a funny thing, you know, but I was very glad. I had a bag of cherries, and I said to myself: 'Never mind, you just gobble them up quick before you go.'"

The next day they would not let him in to see her.

XIII

Then he said to himself: 'Perhaps Tonka wasn't really so good as I imagined.' But that again only went to prove how mysterious her goodness was. It was the kind of goodness that a dog might have had.

He was overwhelmed by a dry, raging grief that swept through him like a storm. It went howling round the solid walls of his existence, crying: 'I can't write to you any more, I can't see you any more.' 'But I shall be with you like God Himself,' he consoled himself, without even knowing what this was supposed to mean. And sometimes he could simply have cried out: 'Help me, help me! Here I am kneeling before you!' Sadly he said to himself: 'Think of it, a man walking all alone with a dog in the mountains of the stars, in the sea of the stars!' And he was agonised with tears that became as big as the globe of the sky and would not come out of his eyes.

Wide awake, he now dreamt Tonka's dreams for her.

Once, he dreamed to himself, when all Tonka's hope had gone he would suddenly come into the room again and be there with her. He would be wearing his large-checked, brown tweed travelling-coat. And when he opened it, underneath it he would be quite naked, nothing on his slender white body but a thin gold chain, with tinkling pendants on it. And everything would be like one single day, she would be quite sure of that.

This was how he longed for Tonka, as she had longed for

him. Oh, she was never a loose woman! No man tempted her. If someone pays court to her, she will rather give him to understand, with slightly awkward mournfulness, that such affairs are likely to come to a bad end. And when she leaves the shop in the evening, she is quite full of all the noisy, jolly, annoying events of her day, her ears are full of it all, inwardly she goes on talking of it all, and there is no scrap of room for any stranger. But she knows too that there is a part of her that remains untouched by all this: there is a realm where she is grand, noble, and good, where she is not a little shop-girl, but his equal, deserving of a great destiny. And this was why, in spite of all the difference between them, she always believed she had a right to him. What he was concerned with achieving was something of which she understood nothing at all; it did not affect her. But he belonged to her because at bottom he was good; for she too was good, and somewhere, after all, there must be the palace of goodness where they would live united and never part again.

What then was this goodness? It did not lie in action, nor yet in being. It was a gleam when the travelling-coat opened. And time was moving much too fast. He was still clinging to the earth, he had not yet uttered the thought 'I believe in you!' with conviction, he was still saying: 'And even supposing everything were like that, who could be sure of it?' He was still saying that when Tonka died.

XIV

He gave one of the nurses a tip, and she told him of Tonka's last hours and that she had sent her love to him.

Then it crossed his mind, casually, as one remembers a poem and wags one's head to the rhythm of it, that it was not really Tonka at all he had been living with: it was something that had called to him.

He said these words to himself over and over again; he stood in the street with these words in his mind. The world lay around him. He realised, indeed, that he had been changed in some way and that in time he would be yet again another man, but this was, after all, his own doing and not really any merit of Tonka's. The strain of these last weeks —the strain, that is, of course, of working on his invention— was over. He had finished. He stood in the light and she lay under the ground, but all in all what he felt was the cheer and comfort of the light.

Only, as he stood there looking about him, suddenly he found himself gazing into the face of one of the many children round about—a child that happened to be crying. There in the full blast of sunlight the face wriggled and writhed like a ghastly worm. Then memory cried out in him: 'Tonka! Tonka!' He felt her, from the ground under his feet to the crown of his head, and the whole of her life. All that he had never understood was there before him in this instant, the bandage that had blindfolded him seemed to have dropped from his eyes—yet only for an instant, and the next instant it was merely as though something had flashed through his mind.

From that time on much came to his mind that made him a little better than other people, because there was a small warm shadow that had fallen across his brilliant life.

That was no help to Tonka now. But it was a help to him. And this even though human life flows too fast for anyone to hear each of its voices clearly and find the answer to each of them.

PICADOR *Classics*

Robert Musil
Young Törless £3.95

Written while Musil was still a student, *The Confusions of Young Törless* survives as the only completed novel by the author of *The Man Without Qualities*. In a military academy on the eastern borders of the Austro-Hungarian Empire, Törless is drawn into the vicious brutalities of his fellow cadets in the secret attic that provides a torture chamber for sadistic homosexual ritual. Musil's parable of power corrupted chillingly evokes the tides of thought and action that were to plunge Europe into disastrous conflict twice in less than half a century.

Translated by Eithne Wilkins and Ernst Kaiser

Frederick Rolfe
Hadrian the Seventh £3.95

A novel of singular fascination, this best-known of Rolfe's writings under his real name is the key to the enigma of the man who called himself Baron Corvo. Reflecting the life and fantasies of its strange, doomed creator, it is the bizarre chronicle of a shabby outcast, a rejected priest and impoverished writer living in a London slum, who is raised by the Byzantine intricacies of Vatican politics to the Papal throne. His reforming Papacy shrouds the machinations of an intellect tinged with degeneracy and in pursuit of a personal revenge.

'One of the most extraordinary achievements in English literature'
A. J. A. SYMONS

'An unusually successful fantasy, an odd, unique piece of fantasy'
IRIS MURDOCH

Jules Laforgue
Moral Tales £3.50

First published just a few months after their author's untimely death at the age of only twenty-seven, Laforgue's *Moralités légendaires* were acclaimed as a masterpiece and are still today his most celebrated work. The six poetic prose parodies of classic legends – *Hamlet, The Miracle of the Roses, Lohengrin, Son of Parsifal, Salome, Perseus and Andromeda*, and *Pan and the Syrinx*, – have been enormously influential, most prominently on French poets from Apollinaire to Prévert, but also on such major figures in modern literature as James Joyce and T. S. Eliot.

Translated by William Jay Smith

All these books are available at your local bookshop or newsagent, or can be ordered direct from the publisher. Indicate the number of copies required and fill in the form below.

Send to: **CS Department, Pan Books Ltd., P.O. Box 40, Basingstoke, Hants. RG21 2YT.**

or phone: 0256 469551 (Ansaphone), quoting title, author and Credit Card number.

Please enclose a remittance* to the value of the cover price plus: 60p for the first book plus 30p per copy for each additional book ordered to a maximum charge of £2.40 to cover postage and packing.

*Payment may be made in sterling by UK personal cheque, postal order, sterling draft or international money order, made payable to Pan Books Ltd.

Alternatively by Barclaycard/Access:

Card No.

Signature: _____

Applicable only in the UK and Republic of Ireland.

While every effort is made to keep prices low, it is sometimes necessary to increase prices at short notice. Pan Books reserve the right to show on covers and charge new retail prices which may differ from those advertised in the text or elsewhere.

NAME AND ADDRESS IN BLOCK LETTERS PLEASE:

....

Name————————————————————————————

Address————————————————————————————

————————————————————————————

————————————————————————————

————————————————————————————

3/87